Lauren
Laurens, Stephanie
Lady Osbaldestone and the
  missing Christmas carols

$13.99
on1057726534

LADY OSI
THE MIS

CAROLS

LADY OSBALDESTONE'S CHRISTMAS CHRONICLES
VOLUME 2

STEPHANIE LAURENS

DISCARD

ABOUT LADY OSBALDESTONE AND THE MISSING CHRISTMAS CAROLS

#1 NYT-bestselling author Stephanie Laurens brings you a heartwarming tale of a long-ago country-village Christmas, a grandmother, three eager grandchildren, one moody teenage granddaughter, an earnest young lady, a gentleman in hiding, and an elusive book of Christmas carols.

Therese, Lady Osbaldestone, and her household are quietly delighted when her younger daughter's three children, Jamie, George, and Lottie, insist on returning to Therese's house, Hartington Manor in the village Little Moseley, to spend the three weeks leading up to Christmas participating in the village's traditional events.

Then out of the blue, one of Therese's older granddaughters, Melissa, arrives on the doorstep. Her mother, Therese's older daughter, begs Therese to take Melissa in until the family gathering at Christmas—otherwise, Melissa has nowhere else to go.

Despite having no experience dealing with moody, reticent teenagers like Melissa, Therese welcomes Melissa warmly. The younger children are happy to include their cousin in their plans—and despite her initial aloofness, Melissa discovers she's not too old to enjoy the simple delights of a village Christmas.

The previous year, Therese learned the trick to keeping her unexpected guests out of mischief. She casts around and discovers that the new organist, who plays superbly, has a strange failing. He requires the written music in front of him before he can play a piece, and the church's book of Christmas carols has gone missing.

Therese immediately volunteers the services of her grandchildren, who are only too happy to fling themselves into the search to find the missing book of carols. Its disappearance threatens one of the village's most-valued Christmas traditions—the Carol Service—yet as the book has always been freely loaned within the village, no one imagines that it won't be found with a little application.

But as Therese's intrepid four follow the trail of the book from house to house, the mystery of where the book has vanished to only deepens. Then the organist hears the children singing and invites them to form a special guest choir. The children love singing, and provided they find the book in time, they'll be able to put on an extra-special service for the village.

While the urgency and their desire to find the missing book escalates, the children—being Therese's grandchildren—get distracted by the potential for romance that buds, burgeons, and blooms before them.

Yet as Christmas nears, the questions remain: Will the four unravel the twisted trail of the missing book in time to save the village's Carol Service? And will they succeed in nudging the organist and the harpist they've found to play alongside him into seizing the happy-ever-after that hovers before the pair's noses?

Second in series. A novel of 62,000 words. A Christmas tale full of music and romance.

Praise for the works of Stephanie Laurens

"Stephanie Laurens' heroines are marvelous tributes to Georgette Heyer: feisty and strong." *Cathy Kelly*

"Stephanie Laurens never fails to entertain and charm her readers with vibrant plots, snappy dialogue, and unforgettable characters." *Historical Romance Reviews*

"Stephanie Laurens plays into readers' fantasies like a master and claims their hearts time and again." *Romantic Times Magazine*

Praise for Lady Osbaldestone And The Missing Christmas Carols

"Lady Osbaldestone's rambunctious grandchildren are back and hoping for a repeat of the previous year's Christmas capers. Brimming with the sweet sights and sounds of the season, this book hits all the right notes in a most charming and nostalgic holiday tale."
Angela M., Line Editor, Red Adept Editing

"Recalling their sleuthing triumph of the previous year, Lady Osbaldestone's grandchildren have returned to Little Moseley in hopes of finding another Christmas adventure. They haven't long to wait: a music book has gone missing, without which the church organist will not be able to play the village's traditional carol service. They undertake the search, eager to produce a Christmas miracle—one that includes nurturing new love along the way."
Kim H., Proofreader, Red Adept Editing

"Lady Osbaldestone's Christmas Chronicles has just what Stephanie Laurens's readers enjoy about her stories—engaging characters, a mystery or two, and budding romances, all in an authentic Regency setting. It's enjoyable to read about the competent matchmaker and grande dame of the ton attempting to play the role of grandmother. Laurens has created a new favorite Christmas tradition—seeing what Christmas has in store for Therese and her grandchildren."
Laura B., Proofreader, Red Adept Editing

OTHER TITLES BY STEPHANIE LAURENS

The Promise in a Kiss

By Winter's Light

Cynster Next Generation Novels

The Tempting of Thomas Carrick

A Match for Marcus Cynster

The Lady By His Side

An Irresistible Alliance

The Greatest Challenge of Them All

A Conquest Impossible to Resist (March 14, 2019)

Lady Osbaldestone's Christmas Chronicles

Lady Osbaldestone's Christmas Goose

Lady Osbaldestone and the Missing Christmas Carols

The Casebook of Barnaby Adair Novels

Where the Heart Leads

The Peculiar Case of Lord Finsbury's Diamonds

The Masterful Mr. Montague

The Curious Case of Lady Latimer's Shoes

Loving Rose: The Redemption of Malcolm Sinclair

The Confounding Case of the Carisbrook Emeralds

The Murder at Mandeville Hall

Bastion Club Novels

Captain Jack's Woman (Prequel)

The Lady Chosen

A Gentleman's Honor

A Lady of His Own

A Fine Passion

To Distraction

Beyond Seduction

The Edge of Desire

Mastered by Love

LADY OSBALDESTONE AND THE MISSING CHRISTMAS CAROLS

This is a work of fiction. Names, characters, places, and incidents are either products of the writer's imagination or are used fictitiously and are not to be construed as real. Any resemblance to actual events, locales, organizations, or persons, living or dead, is entirely coincidental.

LADY OSBALDESTONE AND THE MISSING CHRISTMAS CAROLS

Copyright © 2018 by Savdek Management Proprietary Limited

ISBN: 978-1-925559-15-6

Cover design by Savdek Management Pty. Ltd.

ALL RIGHTS RESERVED.

No part of this work may be used, reproduced, or transmitted in any form or by any means, electronic or mechanical, without prior permission in writing from the publisher, except in the case of brief quotations embodied in critical articles or reviews.

Savdek Management Proprietary Limited, Melbourne, Australia.

www.stephanielaurens.com

Email: admin@stephanielaurens.com

The name Stephanie Laurens is a registered trademark of Savdek Management Proprietary Ltd.

❀ Created with Vellum

Little Moseley, Hampshire

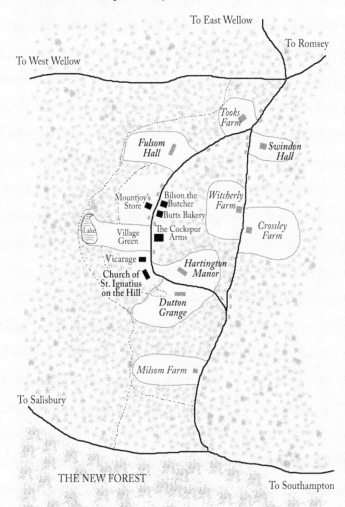

To East Wellow

To Romsey

To West Wellow

Tooks Farm

Fulsom Hall

Swindon Hall

Mountjoy's Store

Bilson the Butcher

Witcherly Farm

Butts Bakery

Lake

Village Green

The Cockspur Arms

Crossley Farm

Vicarage

Hartington Manor

Church of St. Ignatius on the Hill

Dutton Grange

Milsom Farm

To Salisbury

THE NEW FOREST

To Southampton

THE INHABITANTS OF LITTLE MOSELEY

At Hartington Manor:
Osbaldestone, Therese, Lady Osbaldestone – *mother, grandmother, matriarch of the Osbaldestones and arch-grande dame of the ton*
Skelton, Lord James, Viscount Skelton (Jamie) – *grandson of Therese, eldest son of Lord Rupert Skelton, Earl of Winslow, and Celia, née Osbaldestone*
Skelton, George – *grandson of Therese, second son of Lord Rupert Skelton, Earl of Winslow, and Celia, née Osbaldestone*
Skelton, Lady Charlotte (Lottie) – *granddaughter of Therese, eldest daughter of Lord Rupert Skelton, Earl of Winslow, and Celia, née Osbaldestone*
North, Melissa Abigail – *granddaughter of Therese, second daughter of Reginald North, Lord North, and Henrietta, née Osbaldestone*
Live-in staff:
Crimmins, Mr. George – *butler*
Crimmins, Mrs. Edwina – *housekeeper, wife of Mr. Crimmins*
Haggerty, Mrs. Rose – *cook, widow*
Orneby, Miss Harriet – *Lady Osbaldestone's very superior dresser*
Simms, Mr. John – *groom-cum-coachman*
Daily staff:
Foley, Mr. Ned – *gardener, younger brother of John Foley, owner of Crossley Farm*

Johnson, Miss Tilly – *kitchen maid, assistant to Mrs. Haggerty, daughter of the Johnsons of Witcherly Farm*

Wiggins, Miss Dulcie – *housemaid under Mrs. Crimmins, orphaned niece of Martha Tooks, wife of Tooks of Tooks Farm*

At Dutton Grange:

Longfellow, Christian, Lord Longfellow – *owner, ex-major in the Queen's Own Dragoons*

Longfellow, Eugenia, Lady Longfellow – *née Fitzgibbon, older half sister of Henry Fitzgibbon*

Longfellow, Cedric Christopher – *baby son of Christian and Eugenia*

Hendricks, Mr. – *majordomo, ex-sergeant who served alongside Major Longfellow*

Jiggs, Mr. – *groom-cum-stable hand, ex-batman to Major Longfellow*

Wright, Mrs. – *housekeeper, widow*

Cook – *cook*

Jeffers, Mr. – *footman*

Johnson, Mr. – *stableman, cousin of Thad Johnson of Witcherly Farm*

At Fulsom Hall:

Fitzgibbon, Sir Henry – *owner, still a minor attending Oxford*

Woolsey, Mrs. Ermintrude – *cousin of Henry and Eugenia's late father, widow*

Mountjoy, Mr. – *butler, cousin of Cyril Mountjoy of Mountjoy's Stores*

Fitts, Mrs. – *housekeeper*

Phipps – *Henry's valet*

Billings, Mr. – *Henry's groom*

Hillgate, Mr. – *stableman*

Terry – *stable lad*

James – *footman*

Visitors:

Dagenham, Viscount, Julian (Dags) – *eldest son of the Earl of Carsely, friend of Henry from Oxford*

Kilburn, Mr. Thomas – *friend of Henry from Oxford*

Wiley, the Honorable Mr. George – *heir to Viscount Worth, friend of Henry from Oxford*

At Swindon Hall:

Swindon, Mr. Horace (Major) – *owner, ex-army major, married to Sarah*
Swindon, Mrs. Sarah (Sally) – *wife of Horace*
Collison, Faith - *niece of Horace*
Colton, Mr. – *butler*
Colton, Mrs. – *housekeeper*
Higgins, Mrs. – *the cook*
Various other staff

At the Vicarage of the Church of St. Ignatius on the Hill:
Colebatch, Reverend Jeremy – *minister*
Colebatch, Mrs. Henrietta – *the reverend's wife*
Hatchett, Mrs. – *housekeeper and cook*

In church cottages along the village lane:
Filbert, Mr. Alfred – *deacon and chief bell-ringer*
Mortimer, Mr. Richard – *organist and choirmaster*
{Goodes, Mr. Philip and Mrs. Goodes – *previous choirmaster and wife - moved to Hove*}

At Butts's Bakery on the High Street:
Butts, Mrs. Peggy – *the baker, wife of Fred*
Butts, Mr. Fred – *Peggy's husband, village handyman*
Butts, Fiona – *Peggy and Fred's daughter*
Butts, Ben – *Peggy and Fred's son*

At Bilson's Butchers on the High Street:
Bilson, Mr. Donald – *the butcher*
Bilson, Mrs. Freda – *Donald's wife*
Bilson, Mr. Daniel – *Donald and Freda's eldest son*
Bilson, Mrs. Greta – *Daniel's wife*
Bilson, William (Billy) – *Daniel and Greta's son, Annie's twin*
Bilson, Annie – *Daniel and Greta's daughter, Billy's twin*

At the Post Office and Mountjoy's General Store in the High Street:
Mountjoy, Mr. Cyril – *proprietor*
Mountjoy, Mrs. Gloria – *Cyril's wife*
Mountjoy, Mr. Richard (Dick) – *Cyril and Gloria's eldest son*
Mountjoy, Mrs. Cynthia – *Dick's wife*

Mountjoy, Gordon – *Dick and Cynthia's son*
Mountjoy, Martin – *Dick and Cynthia's second son, recently arrived in December 1811*

At the Cockspur Arms Public House in the High Street:
Whitesheaf, Mr. Gordon – *proprietor*
Whitesheaf, Mrs. Gladys – *Gordon's wife*
Whitesheaf, Mr. Rory – *Gordon and Gladys's eldest son*
Whitesheaf, Cameron (Cam) – *Gordon and Gladys's second son*
Whitesheaf, Enid (Ginger) – *Gordon and Gladys's daughter*

At Tooks Farm:
Tooks, Edward – *farmer*
Tooks, Martha – *Edward's wife, aunt of Dulcie, Lady Osbaldestone's housemaid*
Tooks, Mirabelle – *eldest daughter of Edward and Martha*
Tooks, Johnny – *eldest son of Edward and Martha*
Tooks, Georgina – *younger daughter of Edward and Martha*
Tooks, Cameron (Ron) – *younger son of Edward and Martha*

At Milsom Farm:
Milsom, Mr. George – *farmer*
Milsom, Mrs. Flora – *wife of George, works part time in the bakery with her sister Peggy Butts*
Milsom, Robert – *eldest son of George and Flora*
Milsom, William (Willie) – *younger son of George and Flora*

At Crossley Farm:
Foley, Mr. John – *farmer, brother of Ned, Lady Osbaldestone's gardener*
Foley, Mrs. Sissy – *wife of John*
Foley, William (Willie) – *son of John and Sissy*
Various other Foley children, nephews, and nieces

At Witcherly Farm:
Johnson, Mr. Thaddeus (Thad) – *farmer, father of Tilly, Lady Osbaldestone's kitchen maid, and cousin of Mrs. Haggerty, Lady Osbaldestone's cook, cousin of Johnson, stableman at Dutton Grange*
Johnson, Mrs. Millicent (Millie) – *wife of Thad, mother of Tilly*

Johnson, Jessie – *daughter of Thad and Millie, Tilly's younger sister*
Various other Johnson children

Others from farther afield:
The Rector of East Wellow

CHAPTER 1

DECEMBER 9, 1811. HARTINGTON MANOR,
LITTLE MOSELEY, HAMPSHIRE

I truly am happy to have them with me again.

Smiling fondly upon the three children playing before the hearth in her private parlor, Therese, Lady Osbaldestone, admitted to being a touch relieved. Although she and her household had thoroughly enjoyed the weeks the three had spent with them the previous Christmas, children grew up so rapidly that she hadn't counted on Fate being kind a second time. Indeed, it hadn't been she or even the children's parents who had suggested a repeat visit but the children themselves.

This year, with the entire clan in good health and no illness threatening, Therese had assumed she would next see Jamie, George, and Lottie when she traveled to join all her children and their families for their customary joint Christmas celebration at Winslow Abbey, the trio's home. Instead, the previous evening, the three had turned up on her doorstep, their faces alight with innocent confidence in their welcome. Jamie had proffered a letter from their mother—Therese's younger daughter, Celia, Countess of Winslow—explaining that the three had insisted that they *needed* to spend the two weeks preceding Christmas with their grandmother in Little Moseley and that they'd assured Celia that Therese wouldn't mind. Celia's missive had concluded with a recommendation that if the children's expectation of welcome was unfounded, Therese should pack them back into the carriage and send them home, thus teaching them a lesson in making unwise assumptions as to other people's wishes.

The three had rushed into her quiet household on a wave of laughter, shrill voices, and bubbling joy, leaving all her staff smiling—and her, too. The effect of young children and their antics and pronouncements was nothing short of remarkable; in their presence, her lips were constantly curved upward.

That morning, she'd sent the Winslow Abbey coach on its way home, empty. When it came time to travel to the abbey later in the month, the children would accompany Therese in her traveling coach.

Over breakfast, she'd endeavored to learn how they'd been faring—how they'd spent the months since last they'd been there, what new accomplishments they'd mastered, all else about their lives that had changed, and their expectations for the coming year. Somewhat to her surprise, the three had been happy to volunteer answers to all her questions, while their counter-inquisition centered on the village.

George's first question had been whether Farmer Tooks's geese had wandered off again. The easiest way to answer—and to keep them amused—had been to show them; once their breakfasts had been consumed and their faces washed again, they'd donned coats, scarves, gloves, and mufflers and scrambled into her gig, and she'd driven down the drive, into the lane, and up the track that led past the Dutton Grange stables to the small holding at the rear of the property.

A corner of the dilapidated cottage had been made habitable again, and Johnny Tooks had come out to greet them. Therese had watched the reunion between Johnny, Jamie, George, and even Lottie with an indulgently approving smile.

After securing her permission, Johnny had taken the three Skeltons around the cottage and into the ancient orchard, where the once-wayward flock were now contentedly fattening themselves on the fallen fruit.

"It's my job to watch over them, you see," Johnny had proudly proclaimed. "Da and Lord Longfellow decided that if, come December, this is where the flock wants to be, then it'd be a waste of time trying to stop them, and they clean up the orchard, too."

Therese had stood to one side and listened as the youngsters had shared their news. Johnny's information that the word in the village was that the ice on the lake wouldn't be thick enough for the village skating party to be held before Christmas—that, in fact, Dick Mountjoy, who was the authority on the matter, had given it as his opinion that, this year, it would be well into January before the lake was safe to skate—resulted in glum faces and cast a temporary pall, but then Lottie asked, and Johnny assured them that the other village Christmas events—the carol service in the church and the pageant including the re-enactment of the Nativity— were definitely on the calendar.

"Wouldn't be Christmas without them," Johnny said.

Although they'd spent only one Christmas in Little Moseley, Therese and her three grandchildren had agreed wholeheartedly with that sentiment. Indeed, listening to the three chatter as, after parting from Johnny, they'd clambered back into the gig, Therese had deduced that a large part of the attraction of spending the weeks prior to Christmas at Hartington Manor was the chance to immerse themselves in the communal spirit that surrounded such village events.

She'd flicked the reins, and they'd headed down the track, only to find Christian Longfellow—Lord Longfellow of Dutton Grange— loitering in his stable yard, waiting to waylay them with an invitation to join him and his wife and their new baby for morning tea.

Therese and the children had accepted with alacrity. As Jamie, George, and Lottie had ably assisted Therese in nudging the prickly Eugenia Fitzgibbon, as she'd then been, and the deeply reluctant ex-guardsman Christian, with his scarred face and stiff leg, into each other's arms, it was a happy reunion; Therese and the children felt a certain sense of accomplishment at seeing Eugenia so transparently happy and Christian so very proud of his two-month-old heir.

Therese had noted with approval that the children had played gently with young Cedric, named for Christian's deceased older brother; as she'd assured Eugenia, "They're accustomed to babies—their younger sister is just two years old."

The four of them had spent an enjoyable hour at Dutton Grange, then returned to the manor for luncheon, after which the children had asked for and been granted permission to join the village youngsters on the green. Given they were each a year older—with Lottie, the youngest, a sturdy six years old, George, at eight, apparently growing ever more serious, and Jamie a staunchly responsible nine—Therese had felt comfortable allowing them to roam while she dealt with her holiday correspondence.

They'd proven her assessment correct and had returned in good time to wash and change for dinner.

Now, looking like nothing so much as tousled angels, the three sat before the cheery fire, sipping from mugs of the rich cocoa Mrs. Haggerty, the cook, had prepared especially for them and idly poking through the box of games they'd brought.

All in all, Therese's first day with them had passed very pleasantly, and there was no doubt whatever that the presence of the children injected an expectant energy into the household, which otherwise had been rolling into the festive season in rather boring style.

That said...

From the expressions on their faces, Therese seriously doubted the box of games was going to provide sufficient distraction for a twelve-day stay. They would commence the two-day journey to Winslow Abbey on the twenty-first; between then and now...she knew the children were hoping for an engrossing and exciting time similar to their sojourn last year, when they'd embarked on the hunt for Tooks's missing geese.

The three might look like angels, but they were her grandchildren; occupation—intellectual and physical—was as essential as air to breathe.

Indeed, if Therese was any judge, it was the trio's innate quest for such occupation that had prompted their return to Little Moseley.

She wondered if there was any mystery lurking about the village, waiting to be solved.

Their ponderings—hers on possible mysteries and theirs on which game to play—were interrupted by the rumbling crunch of carriage wheels rolling slowly up the drive.

The children sat up and looked toward the curtained window. Then they looked at her.

Therese arched her brows. "I'm not expecting anyone."

"I'll look." Jamie set aside his mug of cocoa and scrambled to his feet. He rushed to the window, closely followed by his siblings. Jamie hauled back the heavy curtains, and all three crowded before the sill, peering out at the forecourt.

The weather had been unseasonably mild—hence the lack of ice on the lake—but a cold east wind had gusted in late that afternoon and sent the children scurrying home. As Therese looked over the children's heads into the night, the light from the porch lamps glinted on snowflakes and sleet, swirling and dancing on the wind.

"The ground's white," Lottie reported.

"It's a traveling carriage," George said. "A large, heavy one."

The carriage wheels halted, and the thudding stamps of horses' heavy hooves on the gravel reached them, then Jamie, heightened interest coloring his tone, said, "That's Uncle North's coachman on the box."

"It is?" Therese blinked and sat up. "Good heavens." *What on earth...?*

The doorbell rang.

The three swung to the door, poised to race out into the front hall. "No." Therese held up an imperious hand. "You are not heathens." The trio flashed identical grins her way, but obediently fell in with her subsequent directives to close the curtains and return to the sofa opposite her chair.

Crimmins's footsteps crossed the hall. A second later, the rumble of male voices could be heard. There was a pause as if someone else had spoken, but not even straining six-year-old ears could make out who spoke or what was said.

Then Crimmins opened the parlor door and solicitously ushered in a tall, willowy figure bundled up in a thick winter coat of dull deep red. A black woolen scarf was wound over and about her head, largely concealing her face, and her gloved hands were buried in a small black muff.

Therese couldn't have said why, but the figure struck her as forlorn.

Crimmins half bowed to Therese and informed her, "Miss Melissa, my lady."

The figure stared across the room at Therese, then, as if only just remembering, dutifully bobbed a curtsy. She raised a gloved hand and pushed aside the folds of the scarf veiling her face. The dark blue eyes of Melissa, Therese's elder daughter Henrietta's second daughter, peered out from under a fall of dark hair. "Hello, Grandmama."

Registering how husky—how adult—Melissa's voice sounded and the uncertainty in the faintly wavering words, Therese, her imagination running wild, pushed to her feet.

She was about to ask Melissa why she was there when the girl drew a folded note from her muff and held it out.

"Mama said to give you this."

That brought some relief; presumably, Henrietta was alive. As far as Therese could tell, Melissa hadn't even noticed her cousins, and for their part, they were wisely keeping mum and as still as statues. The child— well, girl; Melissa was fourteen, after all—was holding herself rigidly, every muscle tensed and taut.

Therese had no idea what was going on, but instinct prodded sharply, and she surrendered to it. She walked forward and, ignoring the note, embraced Melissa, enfolding her granddaughter in a gentle yet definite and warm embrace. "Welcome to Hartington Manor, my dear."

For an instant, Melissa remained frozen and stiff, but then her unnatural rigidity melted; she softened and, for several seconds, leaned into Therese.

As Therese eased her hold, Melissa sighed softly and drew back.

Therese took the note from Melissa's slack grasp, but instead of immediately opening the missive, she patted Melissa's shoulder—the girl looked set to be as tall as Therese—and bracingly said, "Give your wraps to Crimmins, my dear, then…" Therese looked at Celia's three, who had picked up their mugs and were sipping, interested eyes peering over the rims. "Perhaps Crimmins might bring you a mug of cocoa to chase away the chill."

Melissa finally saw her cousins. She took in the mugs in their hands and hesitated; in the evening, cocoa was a drink for children, and she was fourteen…

Jamie grinned at her and raised his mug. "It's really good."

Melissa glanced at Therese, who arched her brows, then Melissa looked at Crimmins. "Thank you. A mug of cocoa would be welcome."

"Good." Therese directed Melissa to the sofa. The other three shuffled up, leaving the end closer to the fire free.

Therese returned to her armchair, sank down, and watched as Melissa, her expression still serious and closed, quietly greeted her cousins, and they grinned and cheerfully welcomed her. Therese glanced at Henrietta's note, then broke the seal and unfolded it.

"Have you come to stay, too?" Lottie asked.

Melissa flicked a glance at Therese, who pretended not to notice it. Melissa looked back at Lottie. "That's up to Grandmama."

Indeed? Therese fumbled for her pince-nez. They had to be in her pockets somewhere; these days, she rarely went anywhere without them.

"When did you three arrive?" Melissa asked Lottie, Jamie, and George.

While hunting through her numerous pockets, Therese inwardly narrowed her eyes as, by dint of a series of never-ending questions, Melissa encouraged the other three to tell her about themselves, the manor, and the village, simultaneously avoiding the questions Jamie and George tried to ask her.

Therese finally located her pince-nez tucked into her cleavage. She drew the spectacles out, settled them on the bridge of her nose, and focused on Henrietta's perfect copperplate.

Crimmins arrived with a mug of cocoa for Melissa and a jug to top up Jamie's, George's, and Lottie's mugs; courtesy of Mrs. Haggerty's wonderful cocoa, by the time Crimmins withdrew, a comfortable silence had descended.

Therese grasped the moment to first scan, then more thoroughly peruse Henrietta's letter, in which Henrietta figuratively threw herself—and Melissa—on Therese's mercy.

The letter read:

Dearest Mama,

I hope you are well. I am appealing to you for help in a most unexpected situation.

Although she is only fifteen, Amanda has been invited to attend a pre-Christmas house party at the Trevallayans' estate, and despite it being early days yet, we all know how critical youthful friendships can be in paving the way in one's first Season.

Naturally, I would have taken Melissa, too—she and Amanda are only a year apart, after all—but she has grown so moody of late, her responses so uncertain, that I simply cannot risk her in such company. I pray you will take pity on her, me, and Amanda, too, and allow Melissa to join you at Hartington Manor for these next few weeks. If that is impossible, then Celia has said she will take her, but of course, with Celia's older three with you at this time, then Melissa would be rattling around the abbey on her own—and that might be the worst thing possible.

I do not know what it is that afflicts Melissa. I know she is a clever girl—arguably cleverer than me or Amanda—but it seems more a case of lack of direction. Or do I mean motivation? Regardless, I vow she hasn't smiled in months and has taken to insisting on wearing black whenever she can—black, for heaven's sake! Quite aside from the inappropriateness, the color makes her look horridly sallow.

I am hoping that you might have some insights that I have not, or that your quiet village might provide the sort of distraction that will draw Melissa past this bothersome stage.

With my love, however distracted, Henrietta.

Although Therese kept her gaze on the letter, she was conscious of Melissa surreptitiously watching her, waiting to gauge her reaction. The seal on the note had been unbroken, and Therese felt certain her elder daughter would not have told Melissa what she'd written; Henrietta might not think of herself as clever, but she was innately shrewd.

Therese would be the first to admit that she knew very little about schoolgirls going through their tiresome phase. She did recall that girls went through such stages, but for herself, she'd simply handed her daughters into the care of their excellently well-qualified governesses, and when next she'd seen Henrietta and Celia, they'd been well-behaved and perfectly groomed for their debuts into society.

Being a highly regarded diplomat's wife who had spent most of her children's formative years posted out of the country had, for Therese, meant that she'd avoided many of the parental ruts in life's road.

So she'd never faced the challenge of guiding a young girl past the difficult stage—when, as far as she'd seen, they jibbed like unbroken fillies at every constraint society imposed upon them. That much, she understood; she could even sympathize. Indeed, her own solution, now she thought back over the years, had been to find ways around the constraints—or at least around the constraints that had mattered to her. The others, she'd accepted without a qualm, which was how, in her view, one successfully carved one's own path through life.

Sadly, she doubted lecturing Melissa on her own long-ago approach would help; the young were so resistant to believing their elders had ever suffered through the same experiences. Nevertheless, not for a moment did Therese consider sending Melissa on to Celia; the poor girl would be bored witless, and her unfortunate ways of dealing with her present challenges might only grow more entrenched.

Perhaps the same sort of distraction Therese was hoping to find for Jamie, George, and Lottie might also serve to give Melissa a purpose—one beyond worrying about how others saw her. Therese knew of no current issue in Little Moseley that required sleuthing or manipulation, but surely something would turn up; minor village incidents were, after all, the norm rather than rarities.

After an instant's further debate, she glanced at Jamie. "Ring for Crimmins, if you would, dear boy."

Jamie leapt to his feet and tugged the bellpull hanging by the mantelpiece while Therese returned her gaze to Henrietta's letter.

Crimmins walked in a minute later. "Yes, my lady?"

Therese finally looked up, met Melissa's uncertain gaze, and smiled. "Please ask Mrs. Crimmins to make up the room next to mine and tell her and the rest of the staff that Miss Melissa will be spending the next few weeks at the manor—she'll travel on to Winslow Abbey with the rest of us."

The announcement was greeted with cheers from Celia's three and insufficiently disguised relief from Melissa. Had the poor girl really thought Therese would deny her and send her on? Therese felt her heart constrict a little at the thought.

"Indeed, ma'am." Crimmins smiled. "At once." He bowed and withdrew.

Directing her words at Melissa, Therese went on, "That room is one of the smaller bedchambers, but as Jamie, George, and Lottie have laid claim to the nursery, I thought you might prefer a more private space."

Melissa nodded; Therese could almost see her tension easing—like a tightly furled flower oh-so-tentatively opening.

Therese smiled. "Once again, my dear, welcome to Hartington Manor and Little Moseley."

Melissa hadn't yet relaxed enough to smile, but she inclined her head and gravely said, "Thank you, Grandmama."

Therese tipped her head in gracious acknowledgment and inwardly vowed that before she and her tribe of four left the manor for Winslow Abbey, Melissa would be smiling again.

CHAPTER 2

*A*t eleven o'clock the following morning, Therese led her grandchildren—all four of them—down the manor's drive. Melissa had been somewhat reluctant to leave the house and meet others —whoever was lurking in the village—but the enthusiasm of her cousins had left her with no real choice.

Therese had simply smiled and behaved as if Melissa accompanying them was a foregone conclusion.

The day was once again mild, and melted by the rays of the December sun, weak though it was, the fallen snow had retreated to pockets along the verges and the shady spots under trees. The air felt cold and damp rather than crisp, but at least it wasn't raining, and the wind was no more than a breeze.

A pleasant enough day to go hunting for a mystery. Therese had evaluated her options and decided that if anyone would know of a suitable quest to engage her youthful visitors, it would be the Colebatches. More likely Henrietta Colebatch, who heard of all the problems in the village, not just the spiritual ones.

On reaching the end of the drive, their small company turned right. Therese had intended to follow the lane to the vicarage's gate, located a little farther around the bend, but the music issuing from the church halted them all in their tracks.

St. Ignatius on the Hill sat perched on what might once have been a hill, but was now part of a ridge that rose above the opposite side of the lane. The rapturous chords of what sounded like a professional organ recital poured like a river from the open church door and engulfed them. The music was powerful and stirring.

Along with her grandchildren, Therese stared up at the church. "I had heard that the new organist has a remarkable touch."

"It's wonderful," Melissa breathed.

Therese glanced at Melissa. Her gaze was fixed on the church, and her face was alight. Therese recalled Melissa was partial to music and had an excellent voice. Therese turned and looked at Celia's three, lined up on her other side; even they were caught by the surging peals of the organ, although they weren't as blinded to all else as Melissa.

Jamie shifted, glanced at George, then looked up at Therese. "Can we go and play in the churchyard?"

"You mean," Therese translated, "can you play tag among the gravestones."

Jamie's grin was unrepentant. "Can we?"

Therese studied the three, all now sporting butter-wouldn't-melt-in-their-mouth expressions; taking them with her to the vicarage and having them fidgeting constantly while they tried hard to be seen and not heard loomed as an exercise in irritation all around. "Very well, but remember not to squeal so loudly you alert Reverend Colebatch. While I might see no harm in you running about the graveyard, the good reverend has views on the decorum to be maintained around the church, and we do not wish to cause him the slightest anxiety." She arched her brows. "Do you understand?"

All three grinned cheekily and chorused, "Yes, Grandmama."

George confirmed, "We can play, but we mustn't be seen or heard—at least not by Reverend Colebatch."

"Come on!" Jamie led the way across the lane, through the lychgate, and up the rising path to the church.

Meanwhile, the unseen organist—a Mr. Richard Mortimer—had smoothly segued from the previous rousing anthem to a quieter air.

Beside Therese, Melissa stirred. "I'll go up to the church, too, and keep an eye on them." She glanced briefly at Therese. "If that's all right?"

Therese wondered what view of the three Melissa would have from inside the church; that she would go within in search of the source of the muted yet still glorious music seemed certain. But... "Yes, if you wish." Therese was seeking a distraction, and even if only temporary, the music would serve. "I have quite a few things to discuss with the Colebatches—you would likely be bored."

Melissa nodded, and together, they crossed the lane. While Melissa slipped through the lychgate and started up the church path, Therese continued on along the lane to the vicarage.

Mrs. Colebatch welcomed Therese warmly, and they settled to have tea in the vicarage's sitting room. Over the year or so since making Henrietta Colebatch's closer acquaintance, Therese had grown quite fond of the reverend's wife; she was a practical sort who was deeply attuned to all that went on in the village and surrounding farms that made up the parish to which her husband ministered.

"I saw you have your three grandchildren to stay again." Henrietta poured their tea. "I trust their parents are not again indisposed?"

"No, no—no mumps this time. Or anything else, thankfully." Therese accepted her cup and saucer. "The children themselves begged for a return visit." Raising the cup, she sipped, then added, "It seems our small village offers them opportunities and adventures of a sort not available to them at their home."

And that, she reflected, was no more than the truth. In Little Moseley, Jamie, George, and Lottie were, in the main, treated as merely another three children. At home, Jamie was the heir to the earldom, and George and Lottie likewise occupied an elevated station that largely precluded them from freely associating with any village or farm children.

Here, they were free to rub shoulders—indeed, were encouraged to rub shoulders within the obvious limits—with all and sundry. Therese was a firm believer in understanding society from the ground up.

"We've had an unexpected addition to our company this year." She rested her cup on her saucer. "My elder daughter—she's Henrietta, too—has sent her younger daughter, her second child, to join us for the next few weeks. It seems Melissa is going through one of those difficult patches young girls are prone to mire themselves in."

Mrs. Colebatch made sympathetic noises; although she and the reverend hadn't been blessed with children, aiding him as she did with the care of his flock, she understood the issue perfectly. "It can be such a... well, *fragile* time for all concerned."

Therese tipped her head. "Just so. I'm hoping the village will work its magic and help her find her balance."

From there, Therese steered the conversation into the wider sphere of village life; she had returned to the manor only three weeks previously after her customary visits to her close friends elsewhere in the country. As she had expected, Henrietta Colebatch knew chapter and verse of all that was going on; however, no problem or issue presented itself as a possible quest for Therese's grandchildren to undertake. She doubted they could help with the problem of the worms that had infested fully half of George Milsom's winter cabbages, nor were the trio qualified to assist with tracking the poachers who had been taking game from the Fulsom Hall preserves.

Suddenly, the organ music, which had been continuing in the background, swelled in another anthem. Glancing at the window, Therese saw that, despite the cold, it was open several inches.

Mrs. Colebatch saw her noticing. "I keep it open so I can hear the music. So wonderful—quite uplifting in its way, don't you think?"

Therese recognized the piece. "Unless my ears deceive me, that's one of Beethoven's more stirring works." She arched her brows at Mrs. Colebatch. "Not precisely church music."

Mrs. Colebatch lightly grimaced. "Mr. Mortimer maintains he practices more thoroughly when employing a wider repertoire."

Therese's brows arched again, but then she lowered them and inclined her head. "I suppose there's some sense in that."

"Indeed. And one can't help but acknowledge that securing Mr. Mortimer as our new organist has proved something of a coup. His playing is truly sublime."

"How long has he been in the position?" Although Therese had returned to the village three weeks ago, a lingering cold had kept her from church for the first two Sundays. The previous Sunday had been the first time this season that she'd attended service at St. Ignatius on the Hill, and she'd been as pleasantly surprised by the organist's ability as anyone, but of course, by then, to all others in the village, Mr. Mortimer and his talents had been old news.

After the service, Mortimer had remained at the organ, playing a medley of spiritual pieces while the congregation milled on the lawn. As far as Therese had seen, he hadn't joined the villagers but had remained inside the church, at least while she had lingered.

"Mr. Mortimer arrived just over three weeks ago—he's played at three Sundays and three Wednesdays thus far." Mrs. Colebatch leaned closer and lowered her voice. "Jeremy says the congregation is swelling with quite a few of the farmhands and workers who don't normally join us coming in simply to indulge in the music. Jeremy's torn over that, of course, but I told him that anything that gets men into God's house should be welcomed and made the most of."

Therese smiled. "And how are the Goodeses? Has anyone had word of them?" Mrs. Goodes had been the previous organist, while her husband had been the choirmaster. Both had been sufficiently talented, but at journeyman level, not that of a master.

"Yes, indeed—Jeremy had a letter last week. They've settled in well at Hove, and their new congregation has been welcoming. Goodes's lungs have improved, and he's much recovered, and of course, Mrs. Goodes is grateful to be closer to her mother now that the old lady is ailing."

They moved on to discuss the unexpected visits of several young ladies and their mamas to the village. "Thinking to stumble on young Henry, it seems." Mrs. Colebatch's eyes gleamed with mischief. "Apparently, they hadn't heard that he was still up at Oxford, and none of the villagers they asked gave the poor boy away."

"Good heavens." "Young Henry" was Sir Henry Fitzgibbon, owner of Fulsom Hall—a good-hearted young gentleman of whom Therese had grown mildly fond. After a moment, she said, "I must remember to drop a word of warning in Eugenia's ear." Eugenia, now the lady of Dutton Grange, was Henry's sister. "I spoke with her yesterday," Therese went on, "but I didn't, then, know of these visits. The very last thing Henry needs is to find himself painted as a recluse—to some young ladies and even some mamas, that's the equivalent of a red rag to a bull. Hinting that he's traveling somewhere might serve everyone—village and Hall—better."

"Ah." Mrs. Colebatch nodded. "I take your point." She glanced at Therese's cup. "More tea?"

"Thank you." Therese held out her cup and saucer.

After replenishing both their cups, Mrs. Colebatch sat back. She raised her cup and sipped, then, a slight frown on her face, said, "Actually, my lady, there's one issue with which you, more than anyone else, might be able to help."

Recalling her purpose in visiting, Therese opened her eyes wide. "Oh?"

Once again, Mrs. Colebatch leaned closer and lowered her voice. "It's Mr. Mortimer and his reclusive—well, more like hermit—ways. He's... well, I can't say *refused*, but he's sidestepped every invitation, and in a village this size, as you know, that can and eventually will lead to all manner of speculation."

Therese blinked. "Perhaps he's shy."

"I suppose that might be so, yet I have to say I've seen nothing of shyness in his manner."

Therese reflected that someone should have warned Mortimer that refusing Henrietta Colebatch's overtures to join the village community was another red rag waved before a very determined lady. No matter Mortimer's reasons for wishing to keep his own company, he should have simply stiffened his spine and accepted the first invitation to a small dinner and that would have been that, at least for several months.

Mrs. Colebatch fixed Therese with a hopeful look. "But if you were to invite him to dine...you will know how to make such an invitation impossible to refuse."

Therese failed to keep a smile from her lips. "That, my dear Henrietta, is true." Therese set down her cup. "For the sake of the village, I'll see what I can do. With the pageant and the carol service coming up, I can think of several pretexts for hosting a dinner party."

Mrs. Colebatch sat back. "Excellent!"

"No, no, my dear—I fear it's not excellent at all." Reverend Colebatch came bumbling through the door, his manner distracted well beyond his customary vagueness. His clerical collar was askew, his dark coat seemed positively dusty, and his hair looked as if he'd run his hands through it several times, clutching at the sides enough to make tufts stand up. Indeed, his hands were rising as if to clutch at his hair again, but then his eyes lit on Therese, and he lowered his arms and beamed. "Lady Osbaldestone! I didn't see you there." He half bowed, and murmuring a greeting, Therese gave him her hand. He barely clasped it before releasing it and turning again to his wife. "Henrietta, my dear, have you seen it?"

Inured to her husband's ways, Mrs. Colebatch calmly asked, "Have I seen what, Jeremy?"

"Why, the church's book of carols, of course. The one with all the music for the carols. I've been searching high and low, but I can't seem to put my hand on it. You really don't know where it might be?"

"I'm sure I don't know, and I certainly haven't seen it." Mrs. Colebatch studied her spouse's expression. "But why this panic? It must be somewhere."

"So one would think," Reverend Colebatch returned. "But now that Mortimer needs it, it's vanished."

"Mr. Mortimer, the new organist, needs the book of carols?" Therese clarified.

Reverend Colebatch nodded emphatically. "It seems he can't play without written music." He waved toward the window. "As you can hear —brilliant player, utterly superb—but he has to have the music in front of him."

Therese rose and, turning, followed the reverend's gaze to the church. "All that, and he's playing from music sheets?"

"Yes. Apparently, he plays strictly from the sheets, so if we're to have our carol service, we need to find the book."

Therese blinked. She'd come there looking for an innocent mystery to absorb her grandchildren. What could be more appropriate than a quest to find a missing book of carols? But was the book truly missing? "Where does this book of carols normally reside?"

"In the vestry with all the other church music," Reverend Colebatch replied. "But that was the first place we searched—Mortimer and I—and it's simply not there." The reverend frowned. "No one asked me if they could borrow it—they usually ask either me or Deacon Filbert." His expression eased as hope crept in. "Perhaps Filbert knows who has it."

Therese held up a hand. "You may leave the matter with me—that is, myself and my four grandchildren. James, George, and Charlotte are visiting with me again, and last night, another granddaughter, Melissa, joined us. I was hoping to find some matter with which to distract them, and hunting down the book of carols will do excellently well, at least to begin with. We'll ask Filbert and proceed from there, and once we have the book in our hands, we'll deliver it to you..." Therese glanced at Mrs. Colebatch. "Or perhaps place it directly in Mr. Mortimer's hands."

Mrs. Colebatch smiled with conspiratorial approval.

"Oh." Reverend Colebatch paused, then nodded. "Good-oh!" He clapped his hands together. "Truth to tell, your ladyship, leaving the search in your capable hands would suit me very well—I have three Christmas sermons to write, and I've wasted all morning hunting through my study."

Therese touched his arm. "Leave the matter with me—we all want the village to have the best carol service possible."

Reverend Colebatch blinked. "I mustn't have been clear—it's not just the composition of the service that's at stake, it's having a service at all."

Therese regarded him for a moment, not entirely sure she'd understood him. "Do you mean to tell me that Mr. Mortimer cannot play *at all* without written music?"

Reverend Colebatch nodded. Once, emphatically. "That's it—so, you see, without the book, we will have no carol service to speak of. We found music for only three of the less-popular and rather dreary carols, and really, they simply won't do. And regardless, we need more than three."

"Indeed." The carol service lasted for a full hour, and most of that was filled with carols. But Therese couldn't imagine... "Perhaps I had better go over to the church and meet our Mr. Mortimer." A player of such skill who couldn't play without sheet music? She had trouble comprehending that, and it was entirely possible Jeremy Colebatch had misinterpreted and twisted the organist's meaning.

"Indeed, indeed!" The prospect of delegating the search to Therese had significantly brightened Reverend Colebatch's mood. "Come—I'll introduce you. Least I can do given you and your youngsters are to take on the task of finding the wretched book." He frowned as he turned and waved Therese to the door. "Although I suppose one shouldn't call Christmas carols wretched, but I'm sure you and the good Lord know what I mean."

Therese exchanged a faintly amused and equally long-suffering look with Henrietta Colebatch, then allowed the good reverend to usher her out of the house, across the lawn, and through the hedge into the churchyard. As Therese walked briskly beside Jeremy Colebatch toward the church's open main door, she swiftly scanned the graveyard, but saw no sign of children darting amongst the gravestones. Given Reverend Colebatch paced beside her, that was a good thing, although she did wonder where the children were—or more to the point, what they were up to.

Listening to the music proved to be the somewhat surprising answer.

On entering the church, Therese and Jeremy Colebatch halted in the small foyer at the end of the nave—rocked to a standstill by the power of the music that issued forth from the organ, which sat at an angle in a buttressed alcove in the left wall, across from the pulpit. The impact of the music was almost that of being assaulted by a physical force; it surged and swept around them and held them transfixed.

As transfixed as Melissa, who was seated in the rear left-hand pew with Lottie, George, and Jamie beside her, all held captive by the soaring, dipping, then lightly cavorting magic of the music.

Therese had heard Mortimer play on the previous Sunday during the service, but he'd obviously been constrained by the occasion. Now, he'd let his talent loose, and it was pouring out of him through his fingers on the organ's keys.

Any suspicion that Henrietta Colebatch had overstated Mortimer's skill died a swift death. As an organist, the man was undeniably brilliant.

Yet Therese could see the music sheets propped on the organ's stand before him; as she watched, he raised a hand and swiftly turned a page. The piece he was playing was, she thought, by a Russian composer and was, again, not music normally heard in a church.

As if sharing her thoughts, Reverend Colebatch bent nearer and murmured, "Mr. Mortimer is particularly strong on foreign works." He paused, then, in more distracted vein, added, "Sadly, he's not so well versed in our hymns, but he can play them beautifully from the sheets."

Therese merely nodded. The sheer quality of the music continued to hold her silent—in thrall, virtually in homage—until Mortimer reached the end of the piece and, in a series of crashing chords, brought his performance to a rousing end.

As the last echoes thrown back by the stones of the church faded, Lottie, Jamie, and George burst into spontaneous applause.

Freed at last, Therese moved forward—enough to see that their faces were alight, their eyes shining with real pleasure.

As rapt as her younger cousins—and no doubt as tempted to applaud —Melissa had hesitated, but now hissed a faintly scandalized "Not in church!" to the exuberant trio.

Then all four heard Therese's and Reverend Colebatch's footsteps and turned as Therese appeared in the aisle beside them.

Far from depressing the children's youthful fervor—even Melissa looked uplifted, her face aglow—Therese smiled approvingly and, with a reassuring nod, stated, "It was, indeed, a superb performance."

She looked down the nave to the organist's bench. Mortimer had finally realized he'd had an audience; his music, the generation of it, had plainly engrossed him to the point he'd been unaware of his surroundings, but his head had whipped around at the clapping.

Now, seeing Therese and Reverend Colebatch approaching, Mortimer rose and hesitated—as if contemplating bolting—but then his shoulders straightened, and he stepped around the bench to face them.

Alerted by that fractional hesitation, Therese kept a gentle smile on her lips while she scrutinized all she could see of Richard Mortimer. He was tall—

long and lean—and his face was as well, the lines of his clean-shaven cheeks falling from a wide forehead and high cheekbones to a decidedly squared chin. His eyes, a strong mid-blue, were well set beneath straight brown brows; his gaze was steady, yet to Therese appeared uncertain, even wary. His hair was an unremarkable brown, but fashionably cut in the latest style, and an aquiline nose blended well with the aristocratic cast of his features.

Hard on the heels of those observations came the realization that Mortimer was a gentleman. He was of that social class over which Therese—along with the other grandes dames—ruled supreme.

I should know him. Although she was certain she'd never met Richard Mortimer before, Therese felt oddly annoyed—definitely challenged—that she couldn't immediately place him. Recognizing familial connections was her stock-in-trade, yet Richard Mortimer's antecedents eluded her.

More, as he stared back at her, she sensed he would have much preferred to have slipped away... Had he been avoiding her? Little Moseley was a small village, and they'd both been in residence for the past three weeks; regardless of her temporary indisposition, it seemed absurd that this was the first time they had come face-to-face.

As she halted before the railing of the organ corral and Reverend Colebatch made the introductions, Therese continued to study Mortimer closely.

His expression shuttered, he half bowed. "Lady Osbaldestone." His tone was noncommittal, neither encouraging nor overtly discouraging, but his stance remained stiff and guarded.

Ensuring her expression remained pleasantly mild, Therese inclined her head in response. "Mr. Mortimer. I'm delighted to make your acquaintance." She waved at the organ. "Your talents are prodigious. Little Moseley is lucky to have you as our organist."

Despite being, she judged, in his mid-thirties, Mortimer managed to look boyishly bashful as he mumbled a polite disclaimer.

"You are entirely too modest, sir." She tipped her head, her gaze still locked on his face. "Are you, by any chance, related to the Mortimers of Gloucestershire?"

Mortimer ducked his head. "No, ma'am."

She widened her eyes. "Perhaps the Shropshire branch?"

He denied it.

Therese wasn't surprised; as a rule, the Mortimers were stocky, with nothing like this Mortimer's elongated frame. But although she waited, he didn't counter by offering any details of his family.

Instead, he transferred his gaze to Reverend Colebatch. "Did you manage to locate the book of carols, sir?"

Recalled from what were almost certainly thoughts on his sermons, the good reverend shook his head. "I hunted high and low in my study, but the book isn't there. However, dear boy"—Reverend Colebatch's expression lightened—"Lady Osbaldestone herself has taken on the task. She and"—he turned and waved up the nave at the four children, who had crept closer to listen to the exchange—"her grandchildren will scour the village and surrounds for the book."

Reverend Colebatch beamed at the children—who, unsurprisingly, looked taken aback—then Reverend Colebatch turned his smile on Mortimer. "I can assure you the hunt for the book is now in excellent hands. Why, just last year, her ladyship and the youngsters found the village's wayward flock of geese—it was quite a triumph."

Mortimer didn't look convinced.

"If you don't mind," Reverend Colebatch said, "I'll leave you to continue your discussion. I've just thought of the right theme for next week's sermon, and I really must get it down."

"Of course, Jeremy." Therese released him with a gracious nod.

Mortimer murmured his thanks for the reverend's efforts in searching for the carol book and watched as Reverend Colebatch strode back up the aisle.

Therese seized the moment to further examine Mortimer. When he returned his gaze to her, she said, "Reverend Colebatch explained that you need the written music in order to play—is that correct?" Therese found it difficult to credit that a player of Mortimer's caliber truly needed sheet music.

Yet Mortimer's grimace was entirely genuine. "Sadly, it is. It's not that I can't remember the music without the sheets, but when it comes to playing, if I attempt even the easiest ballad without the music in front of me, I invariably stumble and, eventually, will halt altogether." He shrugged lightly in transparent self-disparagement. "That just seems to be the way my mind works."

"Hmm." Therese had heard of highly strung virtuosos who had certain foibles—things that must be just so for them to perform at their best or even at all. Perhaps having the written music in front of him was Mortimer's foible. Therese noticed the children had drawn closer still, until they were in the pew just behind her. Recalling the rapt expressions on their faces earlier, she asked, "Do you practice often?"

"Yes." Mortimer clearly was wondering why she asked, but reluctantly conceded, "You'll find me here every morning. Well, other than Sunday...although, of course, I'm here then, too, just not for practice."

From the corner of her eye, Therese saw the four children exchange what she mentally termed a plotting look. To Mortimer, she said, "Excellent. Once we locate the book, we'll know where to find you."

He shifted under her gaze. "We did find the music for three carols in the vestry. Sadly, they're not carols either Reverend Colebatch or I would choose to use for the carol service, and from what I understand of the village's traditional service, three carols will be nowhere near enough."

"No, indeed." Therese remembered the previous year's service very well. She caught Mortimer's gaze and inclined her head. "You may rest assured that I and my helpers"—with a wave, she included the four children—"will leave no stone unturned in our quest to locate the book of carols. I believe we all agree that the village deserves the very best carol service it can have." She allowed her expression to soften. "And not being able to make the most of a talent as sublime as yours would be a travesty."

Mortimer actually blushed. He ducked his head, then murmured, "If you'll excuse me, I must get on."

"Yes, indeed—as must we. Farewell, Mr. Mortimer." Therese acknowledged his bow with a nod, then turned and surveyed her troops. "Come, children. We have work to do."

She noted that all four directed polite nods Mortimer's way before following her up the aisle and into the soft gray light of the winter's day.

Jamie, George, and Lottie immediately clustered around her, eager to hear of their new quest. Melissa, of course, hung back, yet she trailed close enough to listen to the ensuing discussion.

"Is it true, Grandmama? That we're to hunt for some missing book?" Jamie asked.

"A book of carols," Lottie said.

"Is it big?" George asked. "Do you know?"

Therese blinked. "As it happens, I have no idea what the book looks like, but I understand it contains the music for many carols, so it must be of reasonable size."

"So where will we start?" Jamie asked.

"It seems that various people are in the habit of borrowing music from the vestry. Apparently, the procedure is to ask permission from either Reverend Colebatch or Deacon Filbert. Reverend Colebatch can't recall anyone asking him about borrowing the carol book. However, as it isn't in the vestry, then it's possible—even likely—that someone asked Deacon Filbert's permission and borrowed the book. So I propose we start our search by questioning the good deacon."

"Now?" Jamie asked, eyes alight.

Therese considered, then shook her head. "It's too close to lunchtime, and you know you'll want your lunch." That was an understatement; she and her household continued to be amazed at the quantities of food the boys especially required on a regular basis. "After lunch, I'll send to Deacon Filbert's cottage and see if he's available to speak with us."

Melissa had drawn closer and was now walking just behind Therese's left shoulder. After a moment, Melissa said, "You should ask the deacon to describe the book. The larger something is, the harder it is to mislay it..." She glanced up to find four pairs of eyes on her face and ducked her head and mumbled, "Or at least, that's what I would think."

Therese nodded encouragingly. "That's a valid point. We must remember to ask Filbert for a detailed description of the book."

As she led her small tribe through the lychgate and across the lane, she congratulated herself on a morning well spent. She'd found an excellent distraction, moreover one that held some hope of engaging Melissa as well as the younger three. Indeed, as the weak sun shone between the gray clouds and fell warmly on their backs, Therese mentally crossed her fingers that, even with Melissa, Little Moseley would work its magic.

CHAPTER 3

*A*s it transpired, when appealed to, Crimmins reported that Deacon Filbert always spent his Tuesdays visiting his mother in a nearby village and wouldn't return to his cottage until late. Consequently, it was the following morning before Therese, with her grandchildren in tow, could call on the deacon.

His cottage was one of several the church owned along the village lane. Filbert's home sat opposite the vicarage and the village green and was located between the Cockspur Arms and the manor's drive, so the cottage was only a few minutes' walk from Therese's door.

She stepped onto the stone stoop of Filbert's cottage at precisely ten-thirty, the earliest hour at which she would consent to call on any man—gentleman or otherwise, in town or country. Had the timing been left to Jamie, George, or Lottie to dictate, Filbert would have been disturbed over breakfast; now that the trio had a quest before them, they were eager to get on.

They crowded behind Therese as she raised the small brass knocker and beat a sharp tattoo.

As they waited for Filbert to answer, Therese glanced back at Melissa; Therese had wondered if Melissa would allow her curiosity to get the better of her and come—and she had. Therese had made no comment either way, judging that if she tried to push, Melissa would dig in her heels and resist. However, from all Therese had thus far observed, her older granddaughter possessed just as much native curiosity as her younger cousins; now that Melissa had learned of the need for the book to be found, participating in the search and helping to solve the riddle of where the book had gone was too tempting to step back from.

There was also precious little else she might do to entertain herself.

Regardless, she was there, and Therese was pleased. She suspected that with girls of Melissa's age, change was a matter of one hurdle at a time.

Footsteps neared, then the door opened, and Filbert looked out. He was a neat, somewhat retiring individual, a confirmed bachelor in his forties, very precise in both movement and attire; according to Mrs. Colebatch, he had served the parish for more than a decade and lived alone. He blinked when he saw the small delegation about his front step. "Good morning, Lady Osbaldestone. What can I do for you, my lady?"

"We're on another quest, Filbert—similar to our last year's hunt for the geese."

"Oh?"

"Indeed. If we might come in, we would like to pick your brains over the missing book of carols."

Filbert frowned. "Is it missing? I hadn't heard."

"Reverend Colebatch and Mr. Mortimer have searched the vestry, and the reverend has also searched his study, all to no avail. Reverend Colebatch can't recall anyone mentioning borrowing the book to him, but thought whoever has it might have spoken about borrowing it to you."

"Ah." For a moment, Filbert's expression grew distant, then he nodded and stepped back. "Please come in, and I'll endeavor to remember those who mentioned needing to borrow it."

He ushered them into a scrupulously neat, yet still cozy parlor. Therese paused and, once Filbert shut the door, waved at her grandchildren. "Mr. Filbert, I believe you are acquainted with Viscount Skelton, the Honorable George Skelton, and Lady Charlotte." She paused while the boys made their bows and Lottie bobbed a wide-eyed curtsy. "And the last member of our group is another granddaughter, Miss North."

Melissa inclined her head. "Mr. Filbert."

Filbert gravely bowed in reply, then waved Therese to an armchair, the best one beside the hearth. She moved to claim it. There was only one other armchair, somewhat smaller, and a small, two-person sofa; without waiting for direction, Melissa moved to the sofa, drawing Lottie with her, and George followed. Jamie smiled sweetly and propped on the sofa's padded arm.

Filbert inclined his head to the children in approval, then sat in the second armchair, facing them all. He looked at Therese. "Forgive me, your ladyship, but are you wanting to borrow the book of carols?"

"No, no—it's for Mr. Mortimer."

"Oh." Filbert's expression cleared. "Yes, of course. I hadn't thought... Well, Mrs. Goodes knew every carol ever written by heart. But playing only from sheet music as he does, I expect Mortimer will need the book in order to play at the carol service."

"According to Reverend Colebatch and Mr. Mortimer, in order to put on the carol service at all."

Any suspicion Therese may have harbored that Filbert, who had been a close friend of the Goodeses, didn't approve of Mortimer and wouldn't care if he failed was slain by the horrified understanding that filled Filbert's face.

"Great heavens!" the deacon said. After a second, he went on, "I hadn't realized...but of course, you're quite right. Well, now—let me see." He frowned, then cast her an apologetic look. "I have to admit to not paying strict attention to who borrows what music. Given Mrs. Goodes rarely if ever used any of the sheets, not once she'd memorized them, I long ago took the stance that people borrowing the sheets meant that at least the hymns were being played in various houses, and that was all to God's good."

"Indeed." Therese inclined her head. "But do you recall anyone asking to borrow the book of carols recently?"

Jamie leaned forward and confided, "We need somewhere to begin our search."

Filbert nodded. "I believe I can list for you all those who asked after the book over the last few months. That said, I can't say when they actually took it, nor if they returned it, much less when. Our loaning of the music sheets has always operated on an honor system."

"Naturally," Therese responded. "So who do you recall asking after the book?"

"Mrs. Swindon—she often borrows sheets from the church. She likes to play. I know she mentioned borrowing the book of carols—I believe it was sometime last month." Filbert paused, then went on, "Mrs. Woolsey also expressed an interest, although I'm not sure she ever actually borrowed the book. I gather she felt that with Eugenia now at Dutton Grange and Henry up at Oxford, she—Mrs. Woolsey—had time to polish her lapsed skill on the pianoforte. Many borrow the book of carols especially for that purpose, or when they're learning, as the pieces are familiar and so easier to pick up. But speaking of Dutton Grange, the Longfellows asked to borrow the book, but not for the Christmas carols—they were interested in the other special hymns included in the back of the book. In their case, they were deciding on the hymns for young Cedric's christening service."

Filbert frowned, clearly racking his memory. "The only other person I recall asking specifically for the book of carols was the Rector of East Wellow. Their parish wished to copy several of the more unusual carols. At the time he approached me, as far as I knew, the Longfellows had the book. I don't know if he spoke with them or waited and later borrowed it from the vestry…or indeed, if he has as yet borrowed the book at all."

When Filbert lifted his gaze to her face, Therese said, "So you recall four people specifically asking after the book of carols. Did anyone else ask for music sheets in general?"

"Not to my knowledge—not over recent months." Filbert paused, then grimaced and said, "Prior to that, the Goodes were still here. Any number of people might have spoken with Goodes, or Mrs. Goodes, or the reverend, or even Mrs. Colebatch about borrowing the book, but not acted on their intention until later—meaning more recently."

George shifted on the sofa. "Reverend Colebatch said that all the music sheets and the book of carols are kept in the vestry. Are they in some cupboard? Is it locked?"

Filbert shook his head. "No, young sir. All the church's music sheets, including the book of carols, are kept stacked on a shelf in the vestry. Anyone—well, any adult—could reach them."

Therese was aware of Melissa trying to catch her eye, but avoided looking in her granddaughter's direction.

Defeated, Melissa spoke up. "Mr. Filbert, if I could ask… The book of carols—can you tell us what it looks like?"

Filbert's brows rose, and he paused, plainly consulting his memory. Then he offered, "It's quite a collection, so the spine is more than one inch wide, and the sheets are the same size as the usual music sheets, so the book's dimensions are the same as the sheets."

"I assume the music is in the form of a piano-vocal score?" Melissa asked.

Filbert colored. "I really couldn't say, miss. I'm not musically trained."

Melissa smiled faintly. "I don't suppose it matters, really—we just need to find the book. What is the title?"

"The Universal Book of Christmas Carols." Filbert frowned. "I believe it was compiled by Holdsworth and Sons."

"What color is the book?" Jamie asked.

"Red," Filbert replied. "A dull red with black lettering and a black design on the cover."

Therese regarded her brood and arched her brows, but that seemed to be the extent of their questions. She looked at Filbert and asked, "Is there anything more you can tell us, Mr. Filbert, that might assist us in locating the book?"

Filbert thought, but eventually shook his head. "Sadly, no—I have no further clues as to its whereabouts." He said the last with a faintly smiling glance at the children.

"In that case, we'll take our leave of you." Therese used her cane to lever herself to her feet. "Thank you for your time, Mr. Filbert."

Filbert saw them out, at the last wishing them luck with their search. "By God's grace, you'll find the book quickly. I'm sure the Almighty wouldn't deny the villagers their traditional service in honor of His son's birth."

"So we shall hope, Filbert—so we shall hope." Therese raised a hand in farewell, then started down the lane.

After hearing Filbert's door close behind them, she slowed and eyed her four helpers as they kept pace, two on either side. "Well, then. It's too close to lunchtime to call on anyone immediately. I suggest that, after luncheon, we should call at Swindon Hall and see what Mrs. Swindon can tell us."

"Yes!" Lottie gave a little skip. "I like Mrs. Swindon."

"And," George, ever practical, added, "she's the one most likely to be able to tell us something useful. Mrs. Woolsey will be vague and uncertain, and the Longfellows have a young baby—they probably won't remember even borrowing the book."

Apparently, George's memories of his parents coping with his younger sisters' births remained strong and clear.

Jamie nodded. "Swindon Hall feels like the right place to start."

Therese slanted a glance at Melissa, but she was looking at the ground and evincing no overt interest in the hunt that had fired her cousins' enthusiasm.

Yet Melissa had felt compelled to ask several critical questions of Filbert.

Suppressing a smile, Therese said, "It's settled then. We'll call at Swindon Hall this afternoon and see what we can learn." Jamie, George, and Lottie cheered. Therese turned her head and regarded Melissa. "You should come along, too, Melissa—at the very least, I should introduce you to the other local landowners."

Without raising her gaze, Melissa lifted a shoulder in a vague shrug. "If you wish, Grandmama."

Therese managed not to narrow her eyes—or allow the smile that threatened to curve her lips. Melissa might not want to admit that she'd been infected with the same questing fervor as her cousins, but Therese felt confident that the essential seed of curiosity that would drive any of her descendants to pursue the lost book of carols had been successfully planted.

From her point of view, all she needed to do now was sit back and watch it bloom.

～

As if to prove Therese's point, as they walked toward the manor and drew level with the church and, again, heard the most wonderful music—this time, a Haydn concerto—pouring forth through the open doors and they all halted to listen, after no more than a minute, Melissa turned to Therese and said, "There's nearly an hour before luncheon—I thought I might go and check in the vestry, on the shelf, just to see if anyone has returned the book since Mr. Mortimer and the reverend looked. At least a day must have passed since they searched there."

Jamie nodded. "And who knows? The book might have been there all along, jumbled in with all the other music sheets, and they just missed seeing it."

George agreed. "We should check before searching further."

Therese looked at the four—*four*—eager faces turned her way. Three were openly enthusiastic, while Melissa was still attempting to appear merely interested. "Very well," Therese said. "By all means, go and confirm that the book isn't in the church. Just be sure to return to the manor before the church clock tolls for twelve-thirty. Don't be late, or Mrs. Haggerty will be cross."

"And," Jamie and George chorused, repeating a favorite saying of their father's, "it's never wise to make a cook cross."

Therese tried to keep her lips straight. "Precisely." She waved them across the lane. "Now go and be back in good time."

They went, the three younger children all but scampering up the church path, while Melissa walked with a purposeful stride in their wake.

Watching her fourteen-year-old granddaughter climb the rise, Therese was visited by a sudden qualm. What was drawing Melissa to the church —the quest for the book of carols, the remarkable music, or was it infatuation of a different sort?

There was no doubt that Richard Mortimer was quietly handsome; he was, quite possibly, just the sort of reserved musical genius who might appeal to a girl of Melissa's character and inclinations.

Therese narrowed her eyes on Melissa's back. "Hmm."

After a long moment, Therese turned and headed for the entrance to the manor's drive. "I'll have to keep an eye on that."

Melissa slipped into the church behind her cousins. To give them their due, the three weren't silly; they quietly crept along the narrow aisle that ran down the opposite side of the church from where Mr. Mortimer sat before the organ. His attention was wholly focused on the music propped on the organ shelf before him. His fingers flowed smoothly over the keys, his touch confident and sure.

He didn't see or sense the three children slipping past. They reached the door to the vestry and carefully pushed it open. It didn't creak, and the three vanished into the vestry, carefully closing the door behind them.

Melissa didn't immediately follow. Her feet had slowed, and she halted in the shadows, just inside the main doors.

The music swelled and surged like a tamed but powerful sea. She closed her eyes and could almost feel the waves reaching her, beckoning and engaging her senses.

She had always loved music, and as it was one of those skills suitable for a young lady of her station to excel in, her parents had indulged her with a succession of music tutors. She was more than competent on any keyboard instrument, and her voice had been trained to a degree that, her tutor had quietly informed her, would be more than sufficient for entry into the chorus of any of the great opera companies.

Not that she, Miss Melissa North, daughter of Lord North of North Oaks, Buckinghamshire, would ever be permitted to audition, not even for a highly regarded company. Still, it was comforting to know that she could do something right. And when she was, eventually, allowed to venture into the ton, she would have one accomplishment at which she would shine.

For now...she let the music wrap about her and draw her into its embrace. In music, she felt safe; she knew how to respond, how to *feel* within it.

She'd been so...not angry but upset and mortified over needing to be shuffled off to stay with her rather scarifying grandmama. But she hadn't actually wanted to go with her mother and Mandy; it was Mandy who had been invited, not her, and tall and lanky as she was, she wasn't yet ready to face the narrow-eyed assessing glances she knew would be leveled at all the girls who attended the Trevallayans' house party.

She wasn't ready yet. She'd known that deep inside, and she hadn't wanted to go, but she couldn't admit that she was *afraid* of showing her face—also too long and lanky in her opinion—at a social gathering, not to her mother and not even to Mandy. With no better option in sight, she'd supposed that spending a few weeks in Hampshire was better than staying at home with just the servants or going weeks early to her aunt at Winslow Abbey and rattling around there.

Now...as the most glorious music she'd ever heard wove about her soul, she felt her heart lift—just a little. Thus far, coming to stay with her grandmama had been nothing like the trial she'd feared. All those she'd met in Little Moseley—well, other than her grandmama—were unthreatening and undemanding; they didn't care what she looked like, and on closer acquaintance, even her grandmama had been less scarifying than she'd imagined. In fact, the village was proving to be an inspired choice as a place to catch her breath before being plunged into the whirl of the family Christmas gathering.

Stealthy footsteps approached, and she felt a sharp tug on her sleeve. Melissa opened her eyes to see George peering up at her.

"You need to come and help," he whispered, nevertheless managing to make the words insistent. "None of us are tall enough to reach the shelf where the music's kept."

Melissa blinked. It wasn't often that her height was seen as an advantage. "All right," she whispered back. After one last glance at Mortimer, still entirely engrossed at the organ, she followed George down the side aisle and through the vestry door.

The shelf in question was level with her chin. It was over ten feet long and littered with an untidy conglomeration of loose music sheets. "Multiple books could be hidden beneath this," she murmured. Then she gathered a stack of sheets and handed them to Jamie.

He took them to a nearby sideboard. "We may as well sort these while we're at it."

As George followed him with the next stack Melissa had handed down, he muttered, "Or at least tidy them."

By the time Melissa gathered the last of the loose sheets and carried them to the sideboard, Jamie, George, and Lottie were busy going through the sheets and setting them in neat piles.

"We're sorting by hymn number," George explained.

"Even I know my numbers," Lottie said, putting another sheet on a pile.

Melissa sighed, set her stack down, and started shuffling through it. "But there's no book of carols."

"No," Jamie said. "But I suppose we should look on the bright side. If the book had been here, we wouldn't have anything to keep searching for."

"At least this way, we still have a quest." George neatened one of the larger piles.

They worked steadily through the mass of sheets, sorting, then dividing them into neat piles and ferrying them back for Melissa to arrange on the shelf.

When the task was complete, they all stood back and surveyed the now well-organized shelf.

"That's better!" Lottie grinned up at Melissa. "Grandmama says we should always try to leave things better than we found them."

Melissa arched her brows and found herself smiling.

She led the way back into the nave.

Mortimer was still playing; he'd moved on to some quite complicated piece and was concentrating ferociously on the sheets propped on the organ's music shelf. Melissa wondered where the sheets had come from; such pieces wouldn't have been in the vestry hoard—those had all been hymns, processionals, and the like. Mortimer must have brought the music sheets himself—all the sheets for all the pieces she'd heard him play.

Music sheets were expensive, yet clearly Mortimer had an extensive collection.

The music swirled and tugged at her; she was sure the clock hadn't yet tolled the half hour. She was aware the other three had, like her, lingered, listening; they were all well educated, and music was an important part of their curricula. Without glancing their way, she silently walked to the nearest pew and sank onto the seat.

After a moment, the trio joined her, and in silence, they listened to Mortimer play.

Eventually, in a series of rippling chords, he reached the end of the piece, and his hands came to rest on the keys.

Melissa glanced swiftly at Lottie, George, and Jamie and was relieved to see that, this time, they weren't about to burst into spontaneous applause. Not that the performance didn't deserve it, but as Mortimer returned the sheets he'd been following to a stack on a chair beside the organ, it was obvious that he hadn't yet realized he had an audience, and Melissa hoped that, if they remained as quiet as the proverbial mice, he might play more pieces.

Presumably, the other three were thinking along similar lines, for they barely breathed as they all watched Mortimer flick through the stack of sheets. He selected several more from the pile, arranged them on the music shelf, then set his fingers to the keys and played.

He'd chosen a light country air, one with words they all knew. Melissa felt the ephemeral tug as the introduction drew to a close, leading into the first phrase—

Unable to resist, Lottie started singing, her pure and delicate soprano rising to float like a silk thread weaving its way into the tapestry of sound the organ laid on the air.

Mortimer heard; his shoulders tensed.

Lottie realized what she'd done and wildly looked up at Melissa.

Melissa met her young cousin's eyes, read the wordless plea therein—and smiled reassuringly and joined in, her much stronger alto lifting and supporting Lottie's young voice.

Mortimer's fingers didn't falter, but he shot a glance over his shoulder. He saw them—then had to turn back to his music.

On the next phrase, Jamie and George raised their voices and seamlessly joined the swelling chorus.

Melissa filled her lungs and sang more strongly, instinctively balancing the three sopranos.

The next time Mortimer glanced at them, he stared for a second, then smiled and nodded encouragingly before his need of the music sheets forced him to look away.

They reached the end of the piece. Mortimer played the final chords, reached out and flicked to another sheet of music, and the introduction to "Greensleeves" rang out.

He glanced swiftly their way. "Do you know the parts?"

Melissa looked at her cousins; all three nodded, and she called back, "Yes."

Mortimer nodded and played on, allowing the organ to swell more powerfully, then fade as the choral section approached.

Melissa rose to her feet and filled her lungs; beside her, the others did the same.

Then they sang, well-nigh flawlessly fitting their voices to the interweaving harmonies.

All four had been trained to sing; it was a talent deemed necessary to the social positions they would one day fill.

And Mortimer joined them, his voice a pleasing baritone, lending depth and weight to the rendering.

It was a delight—a joy—to sing in such company, with a virtuoso accompaniment evoking their very best efforts. They stood in a line, let their voices free, and sang and rejoiced in their creation.

They reached the end of the song. Drawing deep, satisfied breaths, they listened to the closing chords from the organ, then Mortimer's fingers stilled, and silence—a profound and peaceful silence in the wake of glorious sound—fell.

Richard lifted his hands from the keys and turned on the bench to face his unexpected choristers. For a moment, he regarded them, then asked, "How long will you be staying in the village?"

The older girl blinked and didn't immediately answer.

The older boy shot her a glance, then replied, "We'll be here until the twenty-second. Then we leave for our home—well, mine, George's, and Lottie's—but Melissa and Grandmama will be going there, too."

"I see." A novel idea was taking shape in Richard's brain. "So you'll be here for the carol service."

"Yes." The younger boy—George—nodded emphatically. "We're helping to search for the book of carols."

"Ah." Richard hesitated, yet their voices were among the best he'd heard in a very long while—and as their grandmother had intimated, letting such talent go to waste, especially when he had a carol service to perform, might not be just a travesty but possibly an idiocy. He surveyed them, then said, "In that case, assuming the book of carols is found in time...and possibly even if it isn't, I wonder if you four would be interested in forming a special guest choir for the occasion?"

The younger three would have leapt at the chance—their eagerness shone in their faces—but the older girl, Melissa, asked, "Isn't there a village choir?"

"There used to be, but Mr. Goodes—the previous choirmaster—had been ill for some time, and the choir disbanded. I haven't yet had time to reform it." And he doubted he would remain in the village long enough to make a go of it. That was, in part, one of the spurs pricking him to make the carol service and the church's Christmas celebrations the very best he could—the most joyous and uplifting—to repay the village and the congregation that had, however unwittingly, provided him safe harbor, safe refuge in his time of need.

Of course, when he'd answered the advertisement for an organist in a country village, he hadn't imagined that one of the arch-grandes dames of the ton would have her dower property there. He'd done his best to avoid her, afraid she would take one look at him and know who he was, but apparently, he'd been spared that fate; she'd been puzzled, but she hadn't made the connection—she'd thought he was a Mortimer. Given that, presumably spending time with her grandchildren wouldn't expose him to any further threat.

"So we won't put anyone's nose out of joint by forming a special guest choir for the carol service," Melissa said.

He had to give her credit for thinking of that. "No. You won't be usurping anyone."

She thought for a moment more, her dark gaze weighing him and his proposition, then she glanced at her three...cousins, was it?

Regardless, the younger three, siblings on appearance alone, nodded enthusiastically.

Melissa looked at him. "What would forming a special guest choir entail? What would we need to do?"

Despite her youth, she was definitely not just a pretty face atop a willowy figure.

Richard arched his brows in thought, then offered, "You've all been trained, haven't you?"

Melissa and her cousins nodded.

"I thought as much," he said. "You all have strong, clear voices. If we work together, we could lead the congregation and provide the solos no one else in the village can perform. But of course, that will mean practice. From the sound of things, none of you have sung in a choir before. You'll need to get your ears in, and that means practicing scales and harmonies." He paused, steadily regarding them, then said, "Given the carol service is scheduled for Friday week, I believe daily practice is called for. For one hour every day except Sunday—ten until eleven." He arched his brows at them. "Can you commit to that?"

Melissa looked at her cousins, meeting their eyes one after another. Unstated between them hung the words: *It's only for one hour a day.* They would have plenty of time left to hunt for the book of carols.

And there was precious little else to do—at least for Melissa—in such a small village.

Added to such considerations was the lure of actually *doing* something—accomplishing something. Something that, of all in the village, they with their vocal training were especially qualified to do. Melissa hadn't met that many of the villagers, but she sensed the other three would be glad of the chance to do something special for the community they'd insisted on returning to in this Christmas season.

As things were, she stood in lieu of the adult in charge of their band of four; she tried to catalog the drawbacks to Mortimer's suggestion, but could see nothing beyond the loss of their time.

She raised her gaze and, across the intervening space, met his eyes. "Yes. We can do that—one hour of practice every day except Sunday." Then she bethought herself of their situation and added the caveat, "If Grandmama permits, of course."

CHAPTER 4

$\mathcal{T}$he four cousins reached the door of the manor just as the church bell tolled for twelve-thirty.

Therese met them in the front hall and took in their smiles; before they could launch into a recitation of whatever had caused those smiles, she recommended they wash and tidy themselves before joining her in the dining room.

The boys groaned, but scampered up the stairs in the girls' wake.

Three minutes later, hair brushed, coats and dresses straightened, the four slipped into their now-customary seats about the table.

At Therese's upraised finger, they waited until they were served—all but jigging on their chairs with impatience.

Once the first sups of soup had been consumed, she finally asked, "Well, then—did you find anything in the vestry?"

"No," Jamie said, "but it was a terrible mess."

Out poured an accounting of all they had done. Therese listened and approved their reorganization of the music sheets, then Lottie, who had been all but swelling with the need to unburden herself, burst out with, "And we're going to make a special choir to sing at the carol service!"

Surprised, Therese arched her brows—and Jamie and George leapt to fill in the gap between, describing how, impromptu, they had sung the country song, then "Greensleeves" in parts when Mortimer had asked if they could.

Melissa recounted Mortimer's subsequent suggestion of them forming a special guest choir to lead the congregation for the carol service. "I thought it seemed a reasonable thing to do," she said more quietly. "But we will have to practice for an hour every morning—except Sunday, of course."

"We agreed to do that," Jamie said, quite proudly.

Therese took in their eager faces; they really wanted to do this—even Melissa, although she was cloaking her enthusiasm behind a rather thin veil of indifference. Therese smiled upon them all. "I think that's an excellent idea. Kudos to Mr. Mortimer for thinking of it."

She paused, realizing what that said of Mortimer—that he'd known that children of her grandchildren's station would be voice-trained, more or less as a matter of course. *Hmm.*

"So," Melissa said, "do we have your permission to work with Mr. Mortimer and sing as his special guest choir?"

The unstated yearning in Melissa's question reminded Therese that of all her grandchildren, Melissa was the most drawn to music. "Yes, indeed. It will be an excellent way to repay the village as a whole for all the little kindnesses bestowed upon you."

And to Therese's mind, Mortimer's suggestion was another instance of Little Moseley working its magic upon those who sought refuge there.

All four children—even Melissa—beamed, then fell to demolishing Mrs. Haggerty's latest jelly.

For herself, as she took in their happy faces, Therese was duly grateful; she really had had no idea how to reach past Melissa's self-imposed shell, but music and the prospect of singing in a choir for the village had done the trick.

Melissa was, once again, smiling freely.

When the last smidgen of jelly had vanished and their spoons clattered in their empty bowls, Jamie looked around the table, determination in his face. "Now all we have to do is find *The Universal Book of Christmas Carols.*"

They set off for Swindon Hall in the carriage; with Melissa joining them —as a matter of course, Therese had noted with silent satisfaction—there were too many of them to manage in the gig, and the day had turned drizzly. Calling for the carriage had delayed them, and what with stopping to chat with Peggy Butts, who had been returning from visiting her sister

Flora at Milsom Farm, and pausing to exchange tidings with Mrs. Johnson, encountered at the gate of Witcherly Farm, it was nearly three o'clock by the time they drew up in the forecourt before the Hall's door.

They descended from the carriage, marshaled on the porch, then Jamie rang the bell.

Colton, the Swindons' butler, opened the door to them. He beamed and welcomed them inside, then went to inform his mistress before returning to usher them into the long, airy drawing room.

Sally Swindon rose to greet them, along with a fair-haired young lady who had been sharing the sofa with their hostess. Judging by the hoops in their hands, both ladies had been embroidering.

Smiling, Therese walked forward and greeted Sally, who welcomed her warmly.

"Lady Osbaldestone—Therese. Well met." After squeezing fingers and touching cheeks, Sally drew back and turned to the younger lady. "Therese—you must allow me to present Horace's niece, Miss Faith Collison. Faith, this is Lady Osbaldestone, who I've told you so much about."

Miss Collison was of average height, with a nicely rounded figure and soft blond hair. Her most outstanding feature was her face—even features and clear, light-green eyes set in a flawless complexion with the coloring of a Dresden shepherdess—but her prettiness was somewhat dimmed by gold-rimmed spectacles.

Miss Collison smiled with a perfectly judged curving of rose-colored lips and curtsied to just the right degree. "It's an honor to meet you, ma'am. My aunt mentioned you live in the village."

"Indeed." Therese nodded graciously; Miss Collison appeared to be a polite, well-brought-up young lady with unexceptionable manners. Then Therese waved at her followers. "In turn, allow me to present my grandchildren. Miss Melissa North is my older daughter Henrietta, Lady North's, daughter."

Melissa curtsied to Mrs. Swindon, then exchanged bobs and hellos with Miss Collison.

"And," Therese went on, "Sally, you will remember these three imps. Miss Collison, allow me to introduce Lord James, Viscount Skelton, his brother, George, and sister, Lady Charlotte, known to all as Lottie."

Celia's three children, long inured to the process of polite introductions, bowed and bobbed, first to Mrs. Swindon, then to Miss Collison.

"Now we have the introductions out of the way"—Sally Swindon waved to the numerous chairs facing the sofa—"let's make ourselves comfortable, and I'll ring for tea and..." She paused to glance out of the window at the now-gray and increasingly chilly day. "Perhaps crumpets wouldn't go amiss."

The children smiled hugely, wordlessly assuring Mrs. Swindon that her supposition was correct.

Therese claimed the armchair closest to the fire, opposite Sally Swindon's position on the sofa. Melissa duly sank into the chair opposite Miss Collison, while after a momentary hesitation, Celia's brood wriggled themselves onto the small love seat between the armchairs.

As she resumed her seat on the sofa, Sally went on, "When we last corresponded, I believe I mentioned that we were intending to visit Faith's parents—Horace's sister and her husband—in London."

Therese inclined her head. "You did. I trust your sojourn in the capital passed without mishap?"

"Indeed—it was quite pleasant. I hadn't been to town in an age, and it being so late in the year, the absence of crowds made getting about much easier." Mrs. Swindon regaled them with a brief list of the sights she'd made a point of seeing, then said, "But the primary reason we visited was to farewell Margo and Vincent—Faith's parents. Vincent is with the Foreign Office and has been posted to Constantinople." Mrs. Swindon glanced fondly at Faith. "Lady Osbaldestone knows all about such postings—her husband was also in the Foreign Office."

Therese smiled reminiscently. "I saw much of the world by dear Gerald's side."

Lottie was quiet, big ears flapping, but both Jamie and George were starting to fidget. Therese glanced at them, then arched a brow at Sally. "I wonder if Mrs. Higgins might need some help preparing those crumpets."

Sally smiled at the three younger children. "I'm sure if you go through to the kitchen, Mrs. Higgins would be glad of some help."

The mention of food had instantly captured Jamie's and George's interest, and even Lottie was willing to be diverted.

Therese nodded to the three. "You may go and tell Colton you've been sent to assist Mrs. Higgins." She was sure Colton would understand.

The children leapt up, bowed to Mrs. Swindon and Faith, then hurried to the door.

As it closed behind them, Therese looked at Faith Collison. "Am I to take it, Miss Collison, that you elected to remain in England?"

Mrs. Swindon put in, "We all felt that Constantinople was perhaps not the best place for a young lady of Faith's station, whether on the marriage mart or not."

Therese arched her brows. "In this case, I would certainly agree— being so fair, Miss Collison, you would unquestionably have attracted far more attention than you would have been at all comfortable with."

Faith nodded. "Papa feared so, and when he explained…well, I was happy enough to stay behind." She glanced at Mrs. Swindon and returned her smile, equally fondly. "And Aunt Sally and Uncle Horace invited me to stay for the year or so that my parents will be away."

Sally's mention of the marriage mart had piqued Therese's curiosity, and being a grande dame gave her the social license to baldly ask, "Am I correct in thinking, Miss Collison, that you count yourself finished with the marriage mart?"

Miss Collison's green eyes met Therese's, and the young woman lightly shrugged. "As I understand we're to be neighbors, ma'am, please call me Faith. And whether I'm finished with the marriage mart or it with me is, I suspect, a moot point. But this year's Season was my third, and I confess that I've yet to meet any gentleman able to fix my interest for longer than a few hours."

"You have had three offers, Faith, and from three perfectly eligible gentlemen." Mrs. Swindon's tone suggested this was an ongoing argument.

"Be that as it may, Aunt Sally, I could not see myself married to any of the three." Faith met Therese's gaze. "I am in the lucky position of not having to marry unless I so choose. Mama and Aunt Sally say I'm too picky, but I would rather live my life comfortably alone than married to a gentleman I did not love."

Mrs. Swindon made a frustrated sound. "Love will come if you give it a chance."

Faith's lips fractionally curved. "My point precisely, Aunt Sally. However, I see no reason to imagine that continuing to dance attendance in London's ballrooms is likely to yield a better result than it has to this time. Three years is enough."

Therese considered Faith and what she could see in that slight smile. Unless she missed her guess, Faith Collison's apparent softness and the undramatic nature of her beauty concealed a spine of tempered steel. One needed strength to turn one's back on the ton. "Tell me, Faith, what was it that you found so lacking in your gentlemen suitors?"

Again meeting Therese's gaze, Faith succinctly replied, "Trustworthiness."

Therese was impressed; she inclined her head in acknowledgment. "I would definitely recommend that quality in a future husband." Therese noticed Melissa was paying close attention. "I know many gentlemen who possess that trait. You must have had reasons for believing your three suitors lacked it."

The expression on Faith's lovely face suggested that, when it came to gentlemen, she had lost faith. "Odd though it may seem, my spectacles"—she raised a hand and tapped the gold rim of one lens—"allow me to see through the blandishments of ambitious suitors. And once those blandishments were stripped away, all that remained of those three gentlemen's motivations to marry me was, indeed, ambition."

Mrs. Swindon heaved a sigh, but offered no rebuttal.

Therese found herself respecting Faith Collison more than she'd anticipated. "I take your point."

In other circumstances, Therese might have seen Miss Collison's situation as a challenge, but in Little Moseley, there were precious few gentlemen of suitable caliber to put forward as potential candidates for any young lady's hand, much less that of a jaded lady who knew her own mind.

Turning to Sally Swindon, Therese inquired after her husband, and from there, she and their hostess settled to trade information on village events. Although Therese had returned only three weeks ago, Sally, Horace, and Faith had been back for a mere two days.

"I feel I've so much to catch up on," Sally said.

Melissa had little interest in local affairs and doubted Faith Collison had, either. She caught the young lady's eye and ventured a smile.

Faith immediately smiled back. After glancing at her aunt—in close converse with Melissa's grandmother—Faith rose from the sofa and came to sit on another chair closer to Melissa's.

"Tell me," Faith said, "do you know Little Moseley well?"

Melissa shook her head. "Hardly at all." If Faith had had three seasons already, she had to be at least twenty-one. But Melissa knew that because of her height, most people thought her older; Faith probably took her for sixteen or seventeen—close enough in age to be friends. Melissa saw no reason to correct any misapprehension; she could do with a friend herself. "I only arrived on Monday night."

"Oh—that's when we reached the village, too," Faith said. "Just ahead of the worst of the sleet." She shivered dramatically. "My parents live in London, and we'd been there until then, so that was my first real taste of winter. I have to say I'm quite looking forward to a country Christmas with white fields under snow."

"I came from our house in Buckinghamshire, so it wasn't such a shock." Melissa paused, then said, "I heard that your father is with the Foreign Office. Mine is, too."

"I did wonder," Faith admitted. "Papa has often spoken of Lord North. Your father's one of the senior men there, isn't he?"

Melissa nodded. "He's based in London and has been for years. He and Mama entertain constantly."

Faith nodded sagely. "When I was young, I never thought I would ever say this, but dinners and balls every night can get to be quite boring."

Melissa grinned. "Indeed." She studied Faith's face, then said, "I'm only here until Christmas, but it seems you have a whole year of Little Moseley ahead of you. How do you think to fill your time?"

Faith widened her eyes. "I really don't know." She glanced at her aunt, then lowered her voice. "As you've probably gathered, I have, more or less, given up on the notion of marriage." She paused, then said, "Three Seasons of being a wallflower, followed by three offers, each of which was prompted more by my father's talents than mine…" Her chin firmed. "I believe I know where I stand with gentlemen—eligible ones, anyway—and as I don't need to marry for money, I've decided to do something else with my life."

Melissa didn't miss the bitterness that rode beneath Faith's words, no matter how resigned she otherwise seemed.

Faith met Melissa's eyes. "My problem is that, having been reared, as we all are, to imagine no other life but marriage, I have no idea what alternatives exist. I view this coming year as a time to cast around and see what other avenues I find appealing."

Slowly, Melissa nodded. "You asked about the village. Like you, I haven't seen much of it yet. Hartington Manor, Grandmama's house, lies opposite the church, and I've only just started going out and about. In fact, the only public building I've been to is the church. If you're partial to music, the organist is quite amazingly talented."

Faith wrinkled her nose. "Church music."

"But no." Melissa leaned closer. "Mr. Mortimer practices every day, and he plays mostly secular pieces by the great composers. For anyone who loves music, it's worthwhile stopping by and just standing at the back of the nave and letting his music wash over you."

Faith stared at her. "Just from your voice, I can tell you truly love music—and I do, too. I play the harp."

"Pianoforte, clavichord, and harpsichord," Melissa returned with a smile. "I also play the violin and cello, but didn't think to bring either with me."

Faith sighed. "Aunt Sally and Uncle Horace have a lovely music room, but no harp. I wish I'd thought to get our staff in London to pack up my harp and send it here, but it's a large one and so unwieldy. And now I don't dare send home and ask for someone to find where it's been stored and send it on—if they don't pack it properly, it'll end in bits."

Melissa frowned. "Sadly, Grandmama doesn't have a music room, but from what she's said, I gather there are several large houses around the village. Perhaps one might have a harp you can borrow."

"I love to sing, too," Faith confided, "but I prefer to play the harp while doing so."

Melissa was about to mention the special choir, but the door opened at that moment, and all four ladies turned to behold a procession. Lottie was in the lead with a small tray on which four different jams were displayed in cut-glass dishes. She was followed by George, who carried a bowl of freshly churned butter, and behind him paced Jamie, bearing a large platter piled with golden crumpets, which were still steaming.

The scent of freshly toasted crumpet teased everyone's senses.

Faith grinned and whispered to Melissa, "I did wonder if those three would remember that there are others here who might enjoy a crumpet, too."

Melissa chuckled. "I thought Grandmama was being rather reckless sending the boys to help—they eat all the time. There might well have been none left by the time the platter reached us."

The next fifteen minutes were spent in devouring Mrs. Higgins's delicious crumpets, slathered with her prize-winning jams. Tea was poured and sipped in between bites.

When all present were satisfactorily replete and sat back, wiping their lips and sighing contentedly, Therese decided it was finally time to broach the purpose of their visit. "While it's been delightful to chat and catch up, Sally, we had another reason to call."

"Oh?" Relaxed against the sofa cushions, Mrs. Swindon arched her brows.

"As you know, the village carol service is approaching—apparently, it's scheduled for Friday next week. However, the village's wonderful new organist, Mr. Mortimer, who in all other respects is a superlative musician, can only play from music sheets. He needs the written music."

Sally Swindon frowned. "But the church owns a book of carols. I borrowed it not long ago—a little before we left for London."

Therese nodded. "So we learned. However, at some point in time, the book of carols has been misplaced. To say it's vanished is probably over-stating things—mislaid, I suspect, is nearer the mark." She looked at Sally. "Do you remember what you did with the book?"

Sally nodded. "Quite clearly. I had it…" Her eyes narrowed. "It must have been sometime in November. I wanted to copy some of the hymns—sadly, not the carols but the others included in the back of the book. I heard about them from Eugenia when she had the book to look for hymns for little Cedric's christening. It only took me two days to copy what I wanted, then Reverend Colebatch called to wish us Godspeed for our journey, and I put the book of carols into his hands." Sally met Therese's eyes. "I remember doing so quite clearly, just before he left, so he must have taken the book back to the church."

Therese well knew Jeremy Colebatch's propensity for becoming distracted. "Where were you when you handed him the book? Was it in the front hall? If so, I agree—he must have left with the book."

Sally grimaced. "No—I had the book in the music room, and I went there to fetch it, and he followed. As I said, I put the book into his hands, but then Mrs. Colton needed me to look at some stain, and I left Jeremy in the music room…" Sally Swindon knew Jeremy Colebatch even better than Therese. Eyes widening, Sally stared at Therese. "Oh dear. Perhaps he left the book in the music room. We departed for London the next morning, and I haven't been in there since I left him standing in the middle of the room, book in hand."

George hopped to his feet. "We could search the music room—if you would like?"

Jamie and Lottie both bobbed up, too, hope lighting their expressions.

Smiling, Sally Swindon eyed the children's eager faces. "Do you know where it is?"

"I'll take them." Faith rose.

"I'll go, too." Melissa got to her feet. "Just in case the book's been put on some shelf out of sight."

Sally Swindon waved them to the door. "By all means—I hope you find it. Clearly, if the village is to enjoy a carol service, we need to find that book."

Melissa followed Faith into the front hall.

Faith directed the children, who were ahead of them, down one of the corridors. "The door to the music room is the last one on the right."

With Faith, Melissa strolled in the children's wake. When she entered the music room, George and Lottie had the piano stool open and were poring over the contents.

Lottie looked up. "There's lots of music in here."

"But no red book of carols," George reported.

Between them, Jamie, Faith, and Melissa found several other piles of music sheets. They also found several books of music, two of which were red. Sadly, neither was the book of carols.

Disappointed, they tidied all the music away again, then at Jamie's suggestion—reasoning that Reverend Colebatch might have left the book on a table or sideboard, but it had subsequently fallen and been accidentally kicked out of sight—they did a full circuit of the room, looking behind curtains and even under the sideboards.

Finally, Melissa straightened and sighed. "No book. It looks like Reverend Colebatch did, indeed, take it back to the church."

Dejected, the three Skeltons trailed Faith and Melissa back to the drawing room.

Under their grandmother's interested gaze, they slumped into the seats they'd recently vacated.

"I take it," Therese said, "that the book is not in the music room here."

"No," Jamie said. "We searched everywhere, too. It's definitely not there."

Faith had returned to the chair beside Melissa; she looked from Therese to Melissa. "You said the organist is very talented. Surely he must be able to play at least a handful of carols—enough for a carol service."

All three children shook their heads.

"It's not the usual sort of carol service," George explained. "We were here for it last year, and it lasted for a whole hour."

"At least eight carols, dear," Sally Swindon confirmed. "And we rarely have the same carols—maybe three of the most popular—but the tradition is that we have a full choral service with the carols standing in for the narrative of the Nativity, as it were."

"Oh." Faith blinked, clearly trying to envision it. "So this service is a major event for the village."

"Indeed," Therese rather grimly said. "And for a concatenation of reasons, we absolutely must find that book."

"By Friday next," Jamie put in.

"Well, it's Wednesday," Sally said, "so you still have time, and it is a small village."

"Actually"—Melissa caught Therese's eye, then turned to address Faith—"quite aside from the hunt for the book, we—my cousins and I—have agreed to help Mr. Mortimer to make the carol service an extra-special event by forming a special guest choir to lead the congregation and sing solos and harmonies." Melissa paused, then said to Faith, "You mentioned that you love music, too, and you love to sing. Would you consider joining our choir? There are only the four of us at present—we could do with more trained voices." Melissa glanced at Therese. "I'm sure Mr. Mortimer would agree."

Clever girl. Whether Melissa had intended to inveigle Faith Collison—a young lady in need of the right husband—into the orbit of Richard Mortimer, he who was the only potentially suitable bachelor in the area, Therese didn't know; regardless, the result was exactly what she—arch-grande dame that she was—wished to see. She nodded encouragingly. "That is, indeed, an excellent idea—as things stand, Mortimer's special guest choir is rather small. What part do you sing, Faith?"

Behind her lenses, Faith's eyes had widened. "Er...soprano. I'm a run-of-the-mill soprano."

"That should work well," Melissa hurried to assure her. "I sing alto, and as you would expect, the children's voices are light and high. Having you to anchor the soprano part against my alto and Mortimer's baritone will greatly help."

Faith didn't need much persuading. It was soon agreed that she would come to Hartington Manor the following morning and walk to the church with the other four would-be choristers to practice with Mortimer.

"Perhaps," Faith said, looking first at Mrs. Swindon and then at Therese, "if we could find a harp somewhere, I could play as well—I'm accustomed to singing and playing simultaneously, and the harp will blend well with the organ."

Therese inclined her head. "We can certainly ask at the other houses when we visit in pursuit of the book of carols. Someone must have a harp tucked away, and I'm sure they'll be happy to see it put to use in such a good cause."

Lottie, Jamie, and George had waited patiently for all to be settled.

Now, Lottie stirred and piped, "But first, we have to find the book."

Everyone looked at her, then Therese replied for all. "Indeed, my dear, we need to hunt down *The Universal Book of Christmas Carols* forthwith."

∾

The following morning, as arranged, Faith arrived on the manor doorstep at ten minutes to ten o'clock.

In a flurry of coats, scarves, and mittens, the other four rushed to get themselves suitably accoutered, then the five set out to walk the short distance down the drive, across the lane, through the lychgate, and up the path to the church.

Therese watched them go with approval and a touch of pride. She'd wondered if Melissa's liking for the church and her attraction to the special choir had been driven by infatuation, there being little doubt that Richard Mortimer was just the sort of gentleman to inspire such fancies in an inexperienced girl. However, Melissa's readiness to introduce Faith to Mortimer argued firmly against any tendre on Melissa's part—for which Therese was duly thankful. Coping with unsuitable infatuations was a tricky business she'd hoped she'd left far in her past.

The small group vanished around the curve in the drive. Smiling, Therese turned away from the window. It seemed it was merely Mortimer's music that drew Melissa his way.

∾

Melissa led the way into the church, her heart lifting—she truly felt as if it lightened and rose in her chest—at the prospect of hearing more of Mr. Mortimer's playing. She knew music well enough to recognize a rare gift when it fell at her feet, and being able to enjoy what amounted to all-but-private performances from a player of Mortimer's caliber was a gift she was determined to savor for as long as she possibly could.

With Faith beside her, Melissa walked boldly up the nave to where Mortimer was—as usual—playing the organ. She halted before the low wooden railing at the front of the organ corral; as, oblivious, Mortimer continued playing, she glanced at Faith and smiled when she saw an expression of stunned wonderment on her new friend's face.

The other three joined them, and they waited in silence, simply enjoying the music, until Mortimer reached the end of the piece.

As the last chord faded, he seemed to return to himself. He glanced over his shoulder and saw Jamie, George, and Lottie lined up to Melissa's left. "Ah—you're here."

Mortimer rose and stepped around the organ bench, then his gaze fell on Faith, standing on Melissa's other side, and he checked his stride.

"Good morning, Mr. Mortimer." With one hand, Melissa indicated Faith. "We found another visitor to the village who loves to sing and would like to join the special guest choir. Allow me to introduce Miss Collison, who has come to stay with her uncle and aunt, Major and Mrs. Swindon of Swindon Hall."

Mortimer stared, then appeared to recollect himself. His gaze locked on Faith, he stepped down to the floor so that only the low railing separated them. Then he held out his hand.

Melissa watched, intrigued, as Faith, seemingly dazed, placed her gloved hand in his palm.

Mortimer closed his fingers about hers and bowed. "Miss Collison. It's a pleasure to make your acquaintance."

Faith blushed and dropped into a curtsy. "The pleasure is all mine, sir." They both straightened. She stared into Mortimer's face for a second more, then stuttered, "I hope... That is..." She paused and drew breath and, raising her head, started again. "Miss North told me of the special choir, and I would very much like to join." Especially after hearing him play; his truly was a superb talent.

Mortimer was still staring at her in an intent, concerted way. Faith couldn't recall any gentleman looking at her in such a fashion, as if his focus had drawn in and he literally saw only her. Surely he could see her spectacles—well, he could hardly miss them. Most gentlemen—in her experience, all gentlemen—saw the gold-rimmed lenses, and it was as if their gazes were instantly deflected. But not Mortimer; he seemed to actually see *her*, even with lithe and dramatically attractive Melissa standing right beside her.

Faith would have wagered that the younger girl was far more the sort to fix the attention of a brilliant-but-eccentric musician.

She blinked. Had she—Faith Collison—somehow managed to fix the brilliant Mr. Mortimer's attention?

That was such a novel thought, she wasn't sure what to make of it.

"I...ah." She had to say something to break the spell. She swallowed and offered, "I'm a soprano, and I play the harp as well."

Finally, Mortimer blinked and, as if having to force himself to do so, released her hand. "You will be a very welcome addition to our small band."

Faith realized she hadn't been breathing properly and rectified the omission.

Melissa had been following the interplay between Mortimer and Faith with utter fascination. She noticed that, beside her, Lottie, wide-eyed, had been doing the same. To Melissa, it seemed that Faith and Mortimer needed a little help to get on. "Sadly," Melissa said, "Miss Collison didn't bring her harp with her, and the Swindons don't have one."

"But while we're searching for the book of carols," Jamie put in, "we're going to search for a harp to borrow as well."

"That is," Faith said, "if you feel having a harp to add to the accompaniment would be beneficial."

Now it was Mortimer who looked fascinated. "I've never played beside a harp before—I would think it will add depth and harmonic complexity." He smiled at Faith. "I look forward to hearing the combination." Finally, he looked at the others. "I certainly hope you manage to locate a suitable instrument."

One part of Richard's brain was attempting to remind him that the other four were there to practice—and so was he. He wasn't there to moon over a pretty face, which was all the larger part of his mind wanted to do. But he also wanted to learn more of the riveting Miss Collison— why she had so riveted his attention he had no clue; all he knew was that she had claimed his focus in a way no other young lady ever had—and the fastest way to do that was to carry on.

Forcing his eyes from Miss Collison's angelic countenance, he ran his gaze over the others. "First names are best for choir work, or so I think. My name is Richard. And you are?" He pointed to the last boy in line, the older one.

"Jamie." The lad grinned.

"I'm George," the younger lad volunteered.

"And I'm Charlotte, but everyone calls me Lottie," the little girl piped.

"Melissa," Miss North said.

"And I'm Faith," Miss Collison revealed.

Richard found his gaze had snagged on her again. He forced himself to nod and wave all five to the entrance of the organ corral. "Let's try this with the sopranos to my left and the alto—Melissa—on my right." He resumed his seat before the organ and waited while the others filed in and arranged themselves. He looked at his four sopranos; Faith Collison had led the others in and was standing farthest from the organ. "Hmm. I think the balance will be better if Miss Collison—Faith—stands beside the organ, with Lottie next, then George, then Jamie."

Faith and the children rearranged themselves as directed.

"Good. Now…" Richard looked at the organ and managed to remember what should come next. "Let's start with some scales."

Returning to the musical task at hand anchored him—and, he rather thought, settled the others, too.

Once he was satisfied their voices had warmed, he had them attempt the Lord's Prayer, set to the music he'd found in the vestry. After that, he rearranged his sopranos. Faith remained by the organ—her voice was the strongest and most mature—and Richard moved Jamie next to her, with George beside him and little Lottie at the end of the line. The little girl's voice held a delicate crystalline clarity that, used correctly, would prove achingly evocative. Richard knew of several carols that would benefit from the sound, but first, he needed the music found.

At Jamie's suggestion, they tried one of the carols for which the music sheets had been found in the vestry.

After running through it, they all grimaced.

"That's not at all Christmassy," Lottie said.

Melissa sighed. "It's far too ponderous to use."

No one argued.

"We may as well try the other two we have the music for." Jamie sorted through the music sheets. "We need to know if they're awful, too."

They were.

Richard rested his hands on the keys. He felt frustrated beyond reckoning; like the others, he could hear all the carols he'd sung since childhood in his head, but… He glanced at Faith and found her looking at him. He met her eyes and said, "I just can't play without the music before me."

She smiled gently. "I'm sure we'll find it soon."

"We know it's not at the Swindons'," Melissa said. "The deacon knows of three others who borrowed the book recently, and we'll be visiting them shortly."

"There's still more than a week to go before the carol service," George put in.

Richard managed a weak smile. It was the least he could do when the children were so intent on helping him. Nevertheless, he felt forced to point out, "While as a choir, we can practice using other hymns, we will need at least a few days to work through the carols we hope to perform at the service and..."

"To do that, we need the book of carols." Jamie pulled a face.

Melissa had noticed Lottie eyeing Faith, as if willing her to say something or do something. But while Faith certainly looked concerned and sympathetic toward Mortimer, she didn't seem to have any ideas to offer —to draw Mortimer's gaze back to her.

For all of her life, Melissa had heard references to their grandmother's prowess in promoting ton matches; from what she'd observed of Lottie's interest in Faith and Mortimer, Melissa had to wonder if the predilection for matchmaking was inheritable. And if the trait had come down to Lottie, might not Melissa have it, too?

She racked her brains for some way to forge ahead—to keep Faith and Mortimer in each other's company, albeit with the four of them as chaperons. All she could think of was to extend their practice—to get Mortimer playing and directing them again.

"I was wondering..." She studied the organ's keyboard. "I know two carols by heart—to play, I mean—on the pianoforte. I know it's not exactly the same, piano to organ, but you work off the piano score, don't you?"

Mortimer nodded. "But I need it written down."

Melissa met his gaze and hoped she'd guessed aright. "If I played, could you copy it down—write down the music for yourself?"

Mortimer blinked. For a moment, he stared at the empty organ shelf, then admitted, "That might work." Refocusing, he made various adjustments to the organ, then pushed to his feet. "That's now set to best mimic a piano. Why don't you try out your carols while I fetch a pencil and paper?"

Mortimer headed for the vestry. Melissa slipped onto the organ bench and laid her fingers on the keys. The others gathered about her excitedly.

"Which carols do you know?" Lottie asked.

"'Hark! The Herald Angels Sing' and 'This Endris Night.'" Melissa started playing the former.

Then Mortimer was back, carrying pencil, paper, and a straight-backed chair. He set the chair where Melissa had stood, then sat and looked at her. "'Hark! The Herald Angels'—start at the beginning and stop when I say."

She nodded. "I only know the piano accompaniment."

"That's all we need," Faith assured her. "As long as we have that, we can sing."

The next half hour went in playing and transcribing. Like many musicians, Mortimer had a notation system of his own he used to rapidly write down music. It wouldn't be legible to anyone else, but he could read it, and using it, he could very quickly get down each phrase.

Within a minute of starting, first Lottie, then Jamie and George, started to quietly sing the words that went with the phrases.

Faith glanced at Mortimer. "Does the singing bother you?"

He paused, then looked up—first at her, then at the children. He smiled faintly. "Strangely, no. I suppose because I know the words so well, it actually seems to help me…imagine the music, although imagine is not quite the right word."

After that, Faith added her soprano to the quiet chorus.

From the corner of her eye, Melissa saw Mortimer's lips lightly lift.

Finally, they reached the end of "This Endris Night," and Mortimer jotted down the last chord.

"Right, then." He rose, and Melissa readily traded places. Mortimer settled the pages of his scrawl on the shelf, adjusted several stops, then set his fingers on the keys and played.

His rendition wasn't perfect, but Melissa corrected his mistakes, and he made notations on his score. They went through both hymns, with the children and Faith singing softly along.

At last, Mortimer sat back and smiled—a real and sincere and much happier smile. "At least now, we have two carols we can use." He looked at Melissa. "Thank you."

Melissa grinned back. "You're very welcome."

"All right." Mortimer looked around at his choir. "I'll write these out properly later, but for now, let's see what we can make of them. Back into place, I'll conduct, and let's see what you can remember of the parts."

They all returned to their positions, and after checking they were ready, Mortimer commenced the introduction. He raised a hand, then with a graceful sweep, led them into the choral section.

His baritone rolled beneath Melissa's alto, while the sopranos, led by

Faith, soared above. Gaining confidence, they grinned at each other as the sound swelled and filled the church.

From the rear of the nave, cloaked in shadows, Therese watched, listened, and quietly smiled.

She saw Melissa and Lottie exchange a conspiratorial look; interpreting that look with ease, Therese felt her last lingering reservations as to Melissa's interest in Mortimer fade. Those reservations had prodded her into trudging up to the church, but clearly, her granddaughters saw Mortimer and Faith in the same light Therese did—as a potential match it was their duty to promote.

After a moment, Therese slipped into the nearest pew, sat, and gave herself up to the music—to the sound of her grandchildren's voices rising and twining in the old evocative carols.

Finally, Mortimer declared that morning's practice at an end. He rose from the organ, and the others milled around. Mortimer looked at Faith. "We'll meet again tomorrow at the same time. We can practice with other hymns." He glanced at Melissa. "And thanks to Melissa, we'll have two carols we can use."

"But two carols aren't anywhere near enough for a carol service," Jamie stated. "We need the book—we're going to spend the rest of the day searching."

Mortimer regarded his youthful choristers in sober seriousness. "I wish I could be of some help, but being new to the area..." After a second, he tipped his head toward the organ. "And I've not played as much as I should have over the past months—I need to retrain my fingers, so to speak."

Lottie jigged beside Faith, nudging Faith forward. Melissa, on Mortimer's other side, turned toward the aisle, waved, and started walking.

When the four of them turned in to the aisle, Lottie and Melissa fell back, leaving Faith and Mortimer walking together.

In the back pew, Therese muffled her chuckle; she watched and listened as Mortimer, somewhat hesitantly, asked how long Faith expected to remain in the area.

Therese rose as the children drew level with her position. They noticed her only then and welcomed her with smiles.

Together, they followed Mortimer and Faith onto the church porch. Faith's groom was waiting with the Swindon Hall gig. With her grandchildren about her, Therese watched as Mortimer handed a lightly blushing Faith up to the gig's seat. She thanked him prettily, then he stood and watched the groom drive her away.

Apparently without remembering the rest of his choristers, Mortimer slowly followed the gig down the drive.

Therese didn't mute her smile. She stepped down off the porch, and the children fell in about her, with Lottie and Melissa flanking her. As they walked down the path toward the manor, Therese tapped Melissa's sleeve. "You and Lottie"—Therese smiled approvingly as Lottie turned a happily smiling face her way—"did well in there. Clearly, you've inherited some of my talent."

Lottie positively beamed.

Melissa, too, couldn't suppress her smile, although she quickly ducked her head as if to hide it. But after a second, she murmured, "Thank you, Grandmama."

Her head high, Therese smiled unrestrainedly; when it came to Melissa, she was definitely making progress.

CHAPTER 5

That afternoon, they extended their search to Fulsom Hall.

The day had turned fine, and the children had insisted they could all cram into the gig. Therese managed the reins, with Melissa beside her, juggling Lottie on her lap, while Jamie and George had clambered up behind the seat; they clung to its back as Therese guided the mare—thankfully of stoic disposition—down the manor drive and up the village lane.

Therese was quietly pleased that there had been not the slightest hesitation on Melissa's part over accompanying them. It seemed her older granddaughter now considered herself a committed member of their investigative team; her rejoining of the familial tribe had progressed that far at least.

They reached the entrance to the Fulsom Hall drive without mishap, and Therese turned the gig in under the overhanging trees. "Since Eugenia married Christian and moved to Dutton Grange, Mrs. Woolsey has been in charge of the household here. As Henry is still up at Oxford, managing the Hall's household hasn't overtaxed Mrs. Woolsey—I understand she spends quite a lot of time at the Grange with Eugenia, Christian, and Baby Cedric."

"Mrs. Woolsey probably likes to cuddle the baby," Lottie observed.

"Indeed. But we need to remember that Mrs. Woolsey is not a robust character," Therese said. "We need to question her gently if we're to learn anything to the point."

From the corner of her eye, she saw Melissa take due note.

They reached the forecourt, and Therese halted the gig. Jamie and George jumped down. George went to the mare's head, and Jamie stood ready to help Therese to alight. She nodded approvingly and gripped his hand. "Thank you."

He grinned.

Lottie had scrambled down on the other side, and Melissa descended and shook out her skirt.

One of the Hall's stable lads came running to take charge of the horse. George greeted him by name, as did Jamie. After exchanging several comments, George handed over the reins.

By then, Therese had flicked her skirt straight and settled her coat. "Come, boys." She waved them ahead as she made for the porch and the front door. Melissa, holding Lottie's hand, fell in alongside Therese.

Jamie tugged the bellpull. After several seconds, footsteps approached, then Mountjoy opened the door.

The butler's face creased in a smile. "Lady Osbaldestone." His gaze shifted to Jamie, George, and Lottie, and he gave an unbutlerlike chuckle. "I'd heard that you have your Christmas helpers with you again this year."

"Indeed, Mountjoy." Therese glided into the front hall. She waved at Melissa as she followed. "This is another of my granddaughters —Miss North."

Mountjoy inclined his head to Melissa. "I believe Mrs. Woolsey is in the morning room—"

"No, no, Mountjoy—I'm here." Trailing two woolen shawls and with a knitted scarf loosely draped about her neck, Ermintrude Woolsey came fluttering forward from the rear of the hall. "Lady Osbaldestone! Such a delight to see you again." Mrs. Woolsey halted and surveyed the children, who bowed and bobbed and grinned. Mrs. Woolsey's lined face softened in a gentle smile. "I see you three are back, and you've brought an older sister."

"A cousin," Therese supplied. "Another of my granddaughters, Miss North."

Melissa curtsied. "Mrs. Woolsey."

"Welcome, my dear—indeed, welcome to all of you." Mrs. Woolsey turned bird-bright eyes on Therese. "Have you come to take tea? I fear Henry hasn't yet returned—indeed, I'm not quite sure where he is at present—but he wrote to expect him and several of his friends who came last year. I gather he intends hosting them here for the weeks before Christmas—as he did last year—so I expect that means he and they will be arriving any day."

Mrs. Woolsey turned her gaze on Jamie, George, and Lottie and confided, "Apparently, they—Henry's friends—had so much fun here last year, they begged to come again. I suspect you three feel the same, seeing that you're back in Little Moseley, too."

George and Lottie smiled and nodded, leaving it to Jamie to say, "Indeed, ma'am. Christmas at Little Moseley is quite special."

Foreseeing, from Mrs. Woolsey's expression, a lengthy digression into all the events that had taken place the previous Christmas, Therese stepped in to say, "Actually, it's one of the village's special Christmas events that brings us here—namely, the carol service."

Mrs. Woolsey lightly clapped her hands. "The carols—always so lovely! So evocative in this season, don't you think?"

"Indeed," Therese replied. "But a slight difficulty has arisen, which we're attempting to overcome. The church's book of carols has been mislaid, and we're on a quest to locate it."

Mrs. Woolsey's expression blanked, then she opened her eyes wide. "The book of carols? The red one? *The Universal Book of Christmas Carols?*"

"Yes" came from several throats, and the children nodded.

Therese carefully continued, "We understand you borrowed the book at some point in the recent past and wanted to ask if you still had it."

"Oh no. I only needed it for a few days. After that, I took it back to the church—to the vestry," Mrs. Woolsey earnestly assured them. Then her face clouded, and her gaze grew uncertain. A second later, she frowned. "At least...I think I did." Her frown deepened, then she looked imploringly at Therese. "I must have, don't you think? Quite wrong of me to have kept it..." Still frowning, she tipped her head, and her gaze grew unfocused. "But you see, I don't think I did. Keep it, I mean. Indeed, I'm *almost* sure I put it back on the shelf in the vestry."

Having expected such vagueness, Therese calmly asked, "When you had the book, where did you keep it?"

"Why, in the music room, of course." Mrs. Woolsey waved down one of the corridors leading from the hall. "The pianoforte's in there, so you see, there would be no point in the book being anywhere else."

"Indeed." Therese looked at her grandchildren. "Perhaps, Ermintrude, you and I might repair to the drawing room, and Mountjoy might bring in some tea, and meanwhile, Melissa and the children can look in the music room, just to make sure the book is no longer there."

"Oh yes. What a good idea." Mrs. Woolsey smiled at Melissa, Jamie, George, and Lottie. "Mountjoy, please show these young people to the music room."

"Yes, ma'am." Mountjoy caught Therese's eye. "And after that, I'll bring tea to the drawing room."

"Excellent. Thank you, Mountjoy." With an airy gesture, Mrs. Woolsey led Therese toward the drawing room.

Melissa turned to Mountjoy.

The butler indicated a corridor leading deeper into the house. "If you will come this way, miss"—he directed a smile at the other three —"young gents and lady, I'll show you where you will need to search."

When the butler ushered them into the music room, Melissa understood his phrasing; the room was large and long and boasted a pianoforte and several other wind and stringed instruments arranged about the rectangular space. The room also contained what appeared to be hundreds of sheets of music; they stood stacked on every available surface, cascading from chairs and side tables, and in several instances, spilling and spreading over the floor.

"Good Lord," George said. "We'll be here until Christmas."

Jamie snorted. "It's lucky there are four of us to search."

Melissa, quietly stunned, nodded to Mountjoy. "We'll return to the drawing room after we finish here."

The butler bowed and withdrew, leaving them staring at the challenge before them.

Melissa glanced around, then suggested, "Let's divide the room into quarters and search one each."

The others agreed. Melissa moved to the left of the door.

For the next half hour, they searched, lifting each pile of sheets and checking that no book was hidden among them, poking into cupboards and peering under furniture, and checking every compartment of the various music stools and instrument cases they found discarded and stacked around the walls.

They unearthed no book of carols—not even any loose sheets of individual carols—but—

"Look at this!" Lottie called from the far corner of the room.

Melissa glanced up to see that her youngest cousin had finally reached the end of her section and had lifted a flap of a heavy black cloth thrown over some large piece of furniture and had all but disappeared beneath the covering.

The heavy cloth muffled Lottie's voice as it rose in excitement. "It's a harp!"

The others looked at each other, then left what they were doing and hurried over to see. After ducking and peering beneath the cover and determining that Lottie wasn't imagining things, Melissa worked with Jamie to lift the black material off the instrument, ultimately revealing a full-sized harp.

For an instant, the four of them stared at their find. Then Melissa smiled. "Faith is going to be so pleased."

"Mr. Mortimer, too." Lottie grinned.

Five minutes later, having searched to the point where they felt they could justifiably swear that *The Universal Book of Christmas Carols* was no longer in the Fulsom Hall music room, Melissa led the other three into the drawing room.

At their grandmother's questioning look, she reported, "We didn't find the book of carols, but we found a harp. A full-sized one. It appears to be in working order."

"Oh yes," Mrs. Woolsey said. "That would be Eugenia and Henry's mother's harp. She was quite a talented musician, you know. Most of the instruments in the music room are hers. Other than for the pianoforte, I fear I have little aptitude."

Melissa looked pointedly at her grandmother, but somewhat to her surprise, her grandmother nodded at her to continue. She cast about for the best way to explain, then said, "Mrs. Woolsey, a Miss Faith Collison has come to stay with Mrs. Swindon—Miss Collison is Mrs. Swindon's niece-by-marriage."

"Oh?" Mrs. Woolsey's expression brightened. "It's always nice to have young family visit one at Christmastime."

"Indeed." As Melissa had hoped, the mention of a visiting relative had piqued their hostess's curiosity. "Miss Collison," Melissa went on, "is quite accomplished on the harp, but sadly, she was unable to bring her instrument with her. I daresay you've heard the wonderful playing of the village's new organist—it's been suggested that if a harp could be found for Miss Collison, she might play with the organ during the village's carol service, which would make the service something quite special. We"— Melissa included her three cousins with a glance—"wondered if it might be possible for Miss Collison—well, the church, really—to borrow the harp in your music room, so Miss Collison might play at the carol service."

Melissa had decided that gaining the use of the harp for the carol service had to be their first objective; if she wished, Faith could later ask to move the instrument to Swindon Hall's music room for safekeeping.

Mrs. Woolsey's faded brows had risen almost to her hairline. She blinked, then said, "I can't see why not. No one's played the poor thing in an age. Of course, it's really Eugenia and Henry's property, but neither have ever shown any propensity for playing it, so..." Mrs. Woolsey looked to Melissa's grandmother for guidance.

Her grandmother nodded. "All musical instruments are better for being used. I'll speak to Eugenia about the harp when next I see her, but meanwhile..."

"Indeed, indeed." Mrs. Woolsey turned a smiling face to Melissa and her cousins. "I'll speak to Mountjoy about having the harp suitably conveyed to the church." Mrs. Woolsey blinked myopically, then her face clouded. "I've just remembered. Someone will need to restring and retune it, and I'm afraid I have no idea..."

"I'm sure Miss Collison will know," Melissa rushed to say. "And I'm sure she'll take the very best of care of the harp—she'll be so grateful to have it to play."

Mrs. Woolsey's vague smile returned. "Oh, that's such a relief. I know dear Maude would be delighted that her harp was being used, and for the village's carol service, too."

Melissa was profuse in her thanks and added those of Mortimer, Faith, and her cousins as well.

Therese watched, listened, and approved. Not a hint of reserve or reticence remained in Melissa's manner. All in all, her previously reluctant granddaughter was coming along very well.

The following morning, a minor panic over locating Lottie's coat meant that it was ten minutes past the hour when Melissa and her cousins toiled up the rise to the front doors of the church.

"There's no music." Jamie halted and stared at the closed doors.

"Oh." Lottie halted beside him, her little face transforming into a mask of concern. "Perhaps Mr. Mortimer thought we weren't coming and went away."

"I doubt it." Melissa walked past the pair and on. "Most likely he's sorting through music or some such thing. Come on, or we'll be even later."

The three hurried after her. She reached the door, pushed it open, and quietly walked inside.

Alerted by some sixth sense, she slowed and looked toward the organ corral—then held up a hand in warning to her cousins as they followed her into the nave.

The three clustered around her and looked, too.

Richard Mortimer wasn't sorting music. He wasn't even at the organ, which lay silent beside him. He was helping Faith restring and tune the Fulsom Hall harp.

The pair were speaking in low voices as they worked. Richard's expression was relaxed, and a smile flirted about Faith's lips as she replied to his comments.

Together with her cousins, Melissa remained silent and unmoving in the shadows that shrouded that end of the nave.

After several more minutes of quiet exchanges, the harp was finally fully strung and tuned.

Richard stepped back and studied the picture Faith made seated behind the instrument. She looked up at him and smiled, then ran her fingers lightly over the strings, sending delicate chords rippling through the silence.

As the sound faded, Richard seemed to come to himself. He frowned, pulled out his pocket watch and checked it, then he raised his head and, frowning still, looked up the nave toward the front door.

Jamie reacted first, stepping forward and walking down the aisle as if they'd just entered. "Sorry we're late," he called. "Lottie misplaced her coat, and it took all of us ages to find it."

The others jerked into motion and followed him down the aisle.

Richard and Faith exchanged a swift look. Judging by their identical blushes, both realized they'd had a wide-eyed audience for some little time.

For her part, Melissa assumed an expression of utter obliviousness, and as far as she saw, her cousins did the same.

Richard cleared his throat. "As I understand we have you four to thank for the appearance of this quite exceptional instrument, your tardiness is, on this occasion, excused."

Faith smiled. "We've only just finished tuning it, but it has a wonderful tone."

Melissa returned her smile. "Lovely." She looked at Richard. "Shall we get on?"

He met her eyes briefly, then turned to the organ. "I would like to get your opinion of my rendition of the two carols you taught me yesterday."

He sat at the organ, arranged newly transcribed sheets before him, then set his fingers to the keys and played.

"Hark! The Herald Angels Sing" and "This Endris Night" had never sounded so magical.

When the final chord of "This Endris Night" faded and, brows arching, Richard looked at Melissa, she smiled in sincere delight. "That was absolutely perfect."

"Good." Richard looked at Faith. "We can add the harp accompaniment once we've perfected the choral parts." He glanced at them all and raised his brows. "Shall we?"

They took their previously defined positions around the organ, and Richard led them through the two carols. He proved a stickler for musical precision and had them repeat each carol until not a single note was even fractionally late, much less flat.

At last, he was satisfied. "I believe we can say we have at least two carols in our repertoire." He paused, then grimaced. "Sadly, two carols do not a carol service make. As I understand it, to deliver the traditional village carol service, we need at least eight in total."

"Two is a start," Jamie observed.

"And luckily, we all know most of the carols," George pointed out. "We can practice singing them without the organ. Then when we find the book, we'll just have to put everything together and polish our delivery, and all will be right on the day."

Richard looked as if he wished he could share their optimism.

Melissa volunteered, "We now know the book of carols isn't with either the Swindons or Mrs. Woolsey. We only have two more places to search—it must be with either the rector of East Wellow or at Dutton Grange."

"It won't take us much longer to hunt down the book," Jamie said, his tone determined.

"And then," Lottie put in, "we'll have to decide which eight carols to sing."

Her serious tone made everyone smile, which, judging from Lottie's small swift grin, had been her intention.

Young as she is, Melissa thought, *she knows how to help people along.*

"Never fear." Jamie struck a crusader's pose. "We will find the book of carols and save the carol service from being far too short."

"And dull," George said. "Definitely dull, even with our singing."

Richard had to smile. Faith, Melissa noted, watched him, her gaze soft and faintly concerned.

"There's no reason for dejection," Melissa said as she rewound her scarf about her throat. "We still have a full week before the carol service. That's more than enough time to track down one book, especially in such a small village."

Richard hesitated, but then inclined his head. He looked at Faith. "Are you free to work on the harp accompaniment to 'Hark! The Herald Angels' now?"

Faith nodded. "Yes. I can stay for a while longer."

Melissa smiled and bade the pair farewell and, smiling even more definitely once she'd turned away, led her cousins out of the church.

That afternoon, after much discussion over the luncheon table, Melissa, Jamie, George, and Lottie persuaded their grandmother that, in furtherance of their hunt for the book of carols, it was imperative they visit Dutton Grange.

Having secured the loan of the harp and having heard what they and their voices could create with just two popular carols had strengthened their determination to unearth the book, and the realization that only a week remained before the carol service lent urgency to their quest.

Melissa hadn't visited Dutton Grange before. Although, apparently, the Grange was close—just down the manor drive, across the lane, and up the Grange's winding drive—her grandmother, who these days walked with a cane that she sometimes even used, insisted on taking the gig. Melissa's cousins laughed and ran ahead; smiling at their carefree state, she was tempted to follow, but decided that the dignity of her years required that she accompany her grandmother in the gig.

"Here." Already settled on the seat, her grandmother held out the reins as Melissa clambered up. "You drive."

Taking the reins—feeling honored to be trusted in even such a minor way—she sat, arranged the reins in her hands, then released the brake and concentrated on guiding the plodding mare along.

After an uneventful and untaxing journey, she drew the gig to a halt in the forecourt before the front porch of the Grange. A stable boy, apparently having been summoned by George and Jamie, was waiting to take the reins. He bobbed his head to Melissa and her grandmother. "Miss. Your ladyship."

Jamie came to help their grandmother down.

"We're likely to be an hour or so," she said to the stable boy.

"Aye, ma'am," the lad returned. "We'll keep her in the yard. Send when you're ready, and I'll bring her around."

Melissa walked up the porch steps beside her grandmother. George had beaten Jamie to the bellpull; as Melissa stepped onto the porch, the door opened to reveal a mountain of a man in a tweed coat rather than the customary butler's garb.

"Good morning, Hendricks," her grandmother said. "Are your master and mistress receiving?"

The mountain smiled. "I believe so, your ladyship, but please come in, and I'll endeavor to rally them."

Her grandmother chuckled, and Melissa followed her inside. As Hendricks showed them into a lovely drawing room, Melissa reflected that the more relaxed manners that prevailed in the village were refreshing.

Soon, she was making her curtsy to Eugenia Longfellow, a lovely young matron who was cradling a gurgling baby in her arms. Eugenia's husband, Christian, Lord Longfellow, followed her into the room; he greeted the boys and Lottie with cheerful ease, ruffling the boys' hair and smoothing his hand over Lottie's head.

Lottie caught his hand and grinned up into his scarred face. "You haven't met our cousin, Melissa, before."

"No, indeed." Lord Longfellow looked at Melissa and smiled warmly. "Welcome to Dutton Grange, Miss…"

Melissa found herself returning his smile. "North. But please"—she included Eugenia with a glance—"call me Melissa."

Within minutes, as they all settled, not to say sprawled, in the comfortable chairs and sofas, Melissa realized that of all the houses in the village, this was the household her grandmother and her cousins felt most…not so much at home in as attuned with. Even the children were encouraged to call their host and hostess by their first names, although ingrained manners being what they were, the boys and Lottie instinctively reverted to "sir" and "ma'am."

Undemanding, inclusive warmth was very much a feature of Dutton Grange.

Eugenia held out the baby—Cedric, apparently only a few months old —to Lottie. "He was awake, so I thought you might like to hold him."

Seated on the sofa between Melissa and Eugenia, Lottie looked uncertain.

Very accustomed to taking charge of infant cousins, Melissa held out her arms. "I'll hold him, and you can entertain him."

Smiling again, Lottie nodded. Melissa carefully settled the baby in her arms, angled so that Lottie could chatter to the tiny person.

Therese looked on approvingly as, with Lottie absorbed, Melissa spoke with Eugenia over Lottie's head, readily answering Eugenia's queries as to how long she expected to be in the village and where she normally lived.

As Therese and the children had visited the Grange only days before, the talk quickly turned to their purpose in calling.

"The church's book of carols?" Jamie had broached the subject with Christian, who now looked across at Eugenia. "Yes, we had it, but the rector of St. Aloysius in East Wellow arrived in pursuit of it, sent on by Deacon Filbert."

Eugenia nodded. "We put the book of carols into his—the rector's —hands."

The children sighed. George asked, albeit with little hope, "And the rector definitely took the book with him? He didn't leave it here?"

Eugenia regarded George in faint amusement. "Yes, he definitely took it away. I gathered that the entire purpose of his trip to Little Moseley had been to fetch the book—he wouldn't have left without it."

"Well," Jamie said in more bracing fashion, "that just means we'll need to travel to East Wellow and call on the rector and see if he still has the book."

"I take it"—Christian looked from face to face—"that your search is occasioned by the upcoming carol service."

"Yes," George said. "We need the book so Mr. Mortimer can play—if we can't find the book, he won't be able to play, and the village won't have a carol service."

"Great heavens!" Eugenia looked at Therese. "I hadn't realized the book was so vital. I can't recall Mrs. Goodes using it…" Eugenia broke off, then grimaced. "Well, she might not have used the book during the service, but presumably she'd already learned the carols from it."

"Most likely," Therese allowed. "But sadly, Mr. Mortimer, while a quite superlative organist playing-wise, needs the written music before him in order to deploy his genius. In short, he can't play the required carols without the book, and if he can't play…"

"Oh dear." Eugenia looked at Christian. "I can't remember—did the rector mention returning the book to the church?"

Christian shook his head. "Not that I recall." He looked at Jamie. "Perhaps the rector still has the book, although I understood he only required it to copy three carols. That shouldn't have taken long. It was weeks ago that he had the book from us."

Jamie grimaced. "He could have brought it back to the church and put it on the vestry shelf, and someone else might have borrowed it." He looked at George, then at Lottie and Melissa. "We might have to ask around more widely."

The four looked rather cast down. In an attempt to lighten their mood, Therese caught Eugenia's eye. "One improvement to the carol service brought about through all the searching is that we've discovered a harpist —Miss Collison, who is Major Swindon's niece and has come to live with them while her parents are abroad. And while searching for the book of carols in the music room at Fulsom Hall, the children uncovered a harp that was apparently unused and gathering dust."

Eugenia's eyes lit. "Mama's harp."

"So Mrs. Woolsey informed us. We asked, and she agreed that the church could borrow the instrument. I understand it's been restrung, retuned, and is now sitting in pride of place beside the organ in the church. I told Ermintrude I would mention the loan to you in case you had any reservations."

"No. None at all." Eugenia was all smiles. "I'm delighted to know Mama's favorite instrument will be played again."

"In that case," Therese replied, "you will have even more reason to look forward to the carol service. Miss Collison—Faith—will be joining with Mr. Mortimer in playing the accompaniment to the carols."

"How lovely!" Eugenia said. "I will, indeed, look forward to hearing that."

Cedric had fallen asleep, and Lottie's mind had wandered. Frowning, she asked, "When is the Nativity play? Will it be held again this year?"

Christian smiled. "You mean the village pageant, which includes the re-enactment of the Nativity scene. Yes, indeed—it's a village tradition, too—but this year, we've moved it ahead of the carol service. The pageant will be held as usual on the village green at eleven o'clock next Wednesday."

"Will Duggins be there?" George asked. To Melissa, he explained, "He's the Grange's donkey and played the role of the donkey who carried Mary to the stable."

"'Played' being the operative word." Christian shook his head in mock morose resignation. "I fear Duggins remains the only donkey in the parish, and so his services will, indeed, be required again this year. We can only hope that, after his efforts last year, he'll stick to his lines rather better."

The children laughed and asked about the village youngsters who might be selected to play the various roles. Courtesy of their sojourn in the village the previous year, they were acquainted with many of the younger inhabitants.

"Actually"—Eugenia exchanged a glance with Christian, then shifted on the sofa to meet Melissa's eyes—"I heard your little choir singing this morning while I was walking Cedric past the church, and I had a thought which I mentioned to Christian, who's helping organize the pageant this year." Eugenia included Lottie, Jamie, and George with her gaze. "Your combined voices sounded so lovely, I wondered if we might persuade you and Mr. Mortimer to add an extra appearance to your season's calendar. If you could manage a short a cappella performance during the pageant, perhaps as the angels' chorus given how very like angels your choir sounds, it would add another layer of wonderment to the re-enactment."

"That," Therese declared, lightly tapping her cane on the floor, "is an excellent idea!"

Both Jamie's and George's faces lit. "Yes!" Jamie said. "Why not? We have to practice every day, anyway."

"And," George said, "Mr. Mortimer has the music for lots of other pieces—not carols—that we could use. When we tidied the vestry music shelf, I saw the sheets for some choruses and triumphals. There's sure to be some that would fit."

Lottie tugged Melissa's sleeve and, when Melissa looked down, asked, "What does a cappella mean?"

"It means singing without any instruments accompanying," Melissa explained.

"Oh." Lottie looked intrigued. "So it will be just our voices."

Melissa nodded.

"Have you sung that way before?" Lottie asked.

"No."

Watching her elder granddaughter, for a moment, Therese wondered if she would balk, but then Melissa looked at Jamie and George and said what, for their family, were the magic words. "It will be a new challenge."

To Therese's continuing delight, Melissa raised her gaze to Therese's face and said, "I'm sure if we put our minds to it, we can persuade Mr. Mortimer and Faith to agree."

CHAPTER 6

$\mathcal{T}$he next morning, Melissa, Jamie, George, and Lottie made a point of being prompt to choir practice. They walked into the church as the clock in the tower above pealed for ten o'clock.

The song that greeted them halted them at the top of the aisle. Pure and sweet, Faith's soprano wended its way through a light country air, soaring and dipping, then falling, only to rise in splendor again. The sound was simply beautiful. The sight of Faith standing by the organ, one hand resting on the side of the keyboard, her gaze on Richard while his eyes were wholly for the music before him, touched something inside Melissa and kept her silent and still; from the corner of her eye, she saw her cousins were similarly affected.

As a group, they waited, willingly enraptured, until, on a strong clear note held by Faith as the organ faded, the piece finally came to an end.

Spontaneously, the four of them burst into applause.

Faith heard and looked up the aisle as Richard lifted his hands from the keys and swung around.

Smiling delightedly, the four from the manor came quickly down the aisle, little Lottie skipping ahead to exclaim, "That was lovely!"

The others echoed the sentiment.

Faith was pleased that, this time, she didn't blush so hotly. When she glanced from beneath her lashes at Richard, she saw that he wasn't blushing at all.

After greeting the others and accepting their accolades with a panache

Faith could only envy, he directed them all to their places, and in businesslike fashion, they started going through their scales.

Singing scales was something Faith could do without thought; while she kept pace with the others, following Richard's directions, she allowed herself to savor those moments when she'd been able to justifiably look at him and drink in all she could see.

His was a quiet, understated handsomeness that appealed to her far more than that of the dramatic beaux who strutted through London's ballrooms. As her gaze had lingered on Richard's face, she'd recognized what she saw in him—something enticingly close to her ideal—but she had no idea whether he found anything at all attractive in her.

Well, other than her voice; she felt certain he appreciated that, along with her skill on the harp. But when his gaze fixed on her—when he seemed to see past her spectacles, past all veils, to her inner self—what was it he saw? A lady to whom he might grow romantically attached? Or simply an unusual lady, one who piqued his curiosity in a purely academic way?

From their first meeting, she'd sensed that he possessed a particular aloofness she'd learned to associate with academics, who tended to view life as if from one step removed. As if matters didn't touch them in the same way as they impacted other people.

To her, Richard Mortimer was temptation and fascination, and although the thought remained distant, hovering just beyond her ability to believe it, there was a chance he might also be her salvation. That he might represent connection and a future—one her inner self desperately wanted, but that she'd thought she would never have.

Yet as Richard took his hands from the keys and reached for some music sheets, saying they would try another choral piece for practice, Faith lectured herself against reading too much into his encouragement over the contribution she could make to their performances.

Melissa had been watching Faith and Richard's interactions with unalloyed interest. Even though she had no intention of speaking to her grandmother on the subject, had she needed to make a report, she felt she could say that matters between the pair were progressing well.

Judging by Lottie's expression and the glances she, standing beside Faith, kept directing between Faith and Richard, Melissa's young cousin thought so, too.

Melissa, Jamie, George, and Lottie had agreed to wait until the end of the practice before broaching the idea of an a cappella performance at the pageant, reasoning that the more confident Richard and Faith, too, grew over the ability of their small choir, the more likely they were to agree. Finally, after running through the two carols in their repertoire twice each, Richard declared the practice done. He glanced around at their faces. "You've done very well. Those harmonies were really quite outstanding." Focusing on the cousins, he said, "I take it you've sung together before—within your family."

"Sometimes at family gatherings," Jamie admitted. "But we've never done anything formal like this."

"Speaking of which," Melissa said, "we visited Dutton Grange this morning, and Lady Longfellow gave her permission to use the harp."

"Oh, excellent!" Faith's smile was relieved. "I'd hoped she wouldn't object."

"She was very happy to know the instrument was being used again." Melissa seized the moment. "She also had a suggestion to make. She heard us practicing yesterday and wondered if we might possibly do a short a cappella performance as part of the village pageant. It's to be held next Wednesday and revolves about a re-enactment of the Nativity—Lady Longfellow's suggestion was that we might provide the angels' chorus to celebrate the Savior's birth."

Richard looked faintly alarmed, but Faith was interested. "I haven't heard about this pageant."

Jamie, George, and Lottie chimed in with a colorful description of last year's event.

"It's the village's other major Christmas event," Jamie informed Richard.

"It's as important to the village as the carol service," George added, and his siblings nodded emphatically.

Richard still looked uncertain.

"We wouldn't have to use carols," Melissa pointed out. "George said he saw the music for several choruses in the vestry."

Reluctantly, Richard inclined his head. "Yes, we do have the music for several such pieces, so we could practice...and I suppose, as the performance itself will be a cappella..." He glanced at Faith.

She met his gaze and, lips firming, nodded. "I think we should do it." She waved at the others and included herself. "We're all guests in the village, and it would be a nice contribution for us to make to the village festivities."

Richard glanced at Jamie, George, Lottie, and Melissa. "The chorus might not be—indeed, won't be—the right one for the Nativity. Those pieces are, I'm told, included in the back of the book of carols."

"As long as it's a triumphal chorus," Melissa said, "I don't think anyone will mind."

Richard looked at them, clearly weighing the issue, then he glanced again at Faith.

She was waiting to catch his eye. "I really think we should. Whether the book of carols is found in time or not, this is something we can do for the village—a contribution we can make."

Melissa felt like applauding, but contented herself with watching as Richard held Faith's gaze for a moment longer, then he faced Jamie, George, Lottie, and Melissa and capitulated. "Very well." He studied their faces, then, eyes narrowing in thought, said, "But if we're going to do this, we should do it properly." He focused on her cousins. "You three know the program—when are the most appropriate moments for us to sing?"

A lively discussion ensued, and they eventually agreed on two points in the proceedings that would most benefit from choral support.

Apparently having set aside his reservations, Richard nodded. "I'll look out the music for the most suitable choruses, and we'll start practicing them on Monday."

Jamie and George cheered.

Faith smiled—indeed, beamed—at Richard when he glanced at her.

Melissa's smile was a trifle smug as she and Lottie exchanged a satisfied look. At that moment, in their corner of Little Moseley, all was going well.

They reported to their grandmother over the luncheon table.

Therese listened to her grandchildren prattle about how well they felt the two carols they already had music for—thanks to Melissa's efforts— were coming along, how Faith's harp accompaniment had blended so wonderfully with the organ, and how they'd managed to secure Mortimer's agreement, along with Faith's, to their small choir providing an a cappella performance at the pageant.

Therese waited. When neither Melissa nor Lottie volunteered any further information, Therese baldly asked, "And how are Miss Collison and Mr. Mortimer getting on?"

Lottie shot a quick look at Melissa, then offered, "Faith was singing when we got to the church—Mr. Mortimer was playing for her."

"It was a lovely performance—they both seemed pleased." Melissa paused, then gave Therese what she wanted. "They seem to be getting along well—they were more at ease with each other than they were yesterday."

"They didn't blush as much," Lottie said.

And that, Therese thought, was what she'd *most* wanted to know—that her granddaughters, both of them, were awake and aware as to the potential for romance between Richard Mortimer and Faith. Indeed, it seemed as if both were exercising a degree of discretion over when to push and when to appear oblivious.

Jamie and George had kept their heads down, busily cleaning their plates. Setting down his knife and fork, Jamie said, "Even though we don't absolutely need the book of carols for the pageant, it would be better if we could find it in time to use one of the Christmas choruses instead of just any old one."

Melissa nodded. "We need to find the book even more urgently given the pageant is on Wednesday at eleven o'clock in the morning."

Four pairs of eyes fixed on Therese.

George stated, "Our next step has to be to go to East Wellow and ask the rector of St. Aloysius if he still has the book."

"And if not, what he did with it." Jamie looked pointedly at Therese.

She narrowed her eyes, but then—somewhat to her own surprise, sincerely regretfully—shook her head. "Sadly, my dears, I won't be able to go with you—I have an appointment with my man-of-business this afternoon. As our meeting has been arranged for weeks and he's coming down from London expressly to see me, I can't put him off."

The four faces around her table predictably fell.

Thinking further, she frowned. "I was going to suggest you venture to East Wellow regardless, but I fear that, today, your journey would be in vain." She looked at their puzzled faces. "It's Saturday, and it's already after one o'clock. I can guarantee the rector will be far too busy arranging everything for tomorrow morning's service to attend to your query."

It was amazing, Therese thought, how, without seeming to move, children could slump. All four looked as if all energy had drained from them.

"However," she said, straightening and, purely with her tone, bringing them back to full attention, "there's no reason you can't spend the afternoon eliminating other possibilities and widening your search. I agree that with the carol service, let alone the pageant, so rapidly nearing, there's no time to lose, and that it would be folly to waste a whole afternoon. That said, I believe you should rethink your strategy."

Jamie frowned. "How so?"

"When you started on your hunt for the book of carols, we assumed the book would be found with one of those known to have borrowed it recently. We've now eliminated three of the four known borrowers, and realistically, while I agree you must ask the rector of East Wellow in order to eliminate him, he more than anyone else would appreciate the importance and significance of the book of carols to this village." She shook her head. "I really can't imagine that he would have kept it. I'm sure he'll tell you he brought it back and, indeed, returned it to the vestry. I've met the man once, and he's a punctilious sort." She paused, then summarized, "So I agree that he must be asked, but I would advise against pinning your hopes on him having the book."

George was now frowning, too. "So we should think of where next we should search."

"Exactly."

"But we know of no one else who borrowed the book," Melissa said.

"And that," Therese said, "is my point. When you first started your search, you kept the actual searching to yourselves, which seemed perfectly reasonable at the time because we assumed the book would be easily found. Sadly, that hasn't come to pass, and given the increasing urgency, I therefore suggest that it's time to involve the whole village in the quest."

It was Lottie who asked, "How do we do that?"

Therese smiled. "By asking for their help." She glanced around the table. "Everyone in this village from the eldest to the toddlers knows about the carol service and what it means to the village. They might not have seen the book of carols themselves, but chances are the adults, at least, will know of it. As we don't know if anyone else borrowed the book, asking around can't hurt. And there's also the fact that many of those in the village have sons or daughters who work at the larger houses. Asking if they or anyone they know have seen the book is a way of double-checking that the book wasn't—for example—in Mrs. Woolsey's bedroom, and some maid found it and put it in the library because she thought that was where it belonged."

Jamie brightened. "I hadn't thought of that."

"Indeed. But as the possibilities for such happenings are well-nigh infinite, the only way to address the issue—to find out if someone in the village knows where the book is—is to ask everyone. Absolutely everyone. Once you tell them that the carol service is at stake, I predict they'll do everything they possibly can to help."

Therese looked around the table and saw determination once again in all four faces. "In pursuit of your goal, I suggest that the four of you could best spend this afternoon enlisting the help of all the villagers. You can take the gig and visit all the homes, farms, and businesses and ask if anyone has any idea of where the book might be." She paused, then added, "You won't need me for that."

Melissa looked uncertain; she met Therese's eyes. "Will they talk to us—will they take our questions seriously?"

"If it was just the younger three, perhaps not, but with you to lead the delegation..." Therese arched her brows. "I'm sure you've learned enough from your mother to know how to elicit information from shop-keepers and villagers."

Melissa blinked; her expression stated that having never tried, she wasn't sure.

Therese patted Melissa's hand where it rested on the tablecloth. "Trust me—you'll manage." Therese felt certain she would—that when faced with a challenge, Melissa would step up and meet it.

With the other three looking at her expectantly, Melissa swallowed her doubts and nodded. "All right." She glanced at the clock. "It's almost two—if we're to go around the whole village, we should start straightaway."

"Yes!" Jamie and George pushed back their chairs.

Lottie slipped from hers, rounded the table, and caught Melissa's hand. "Come on—let's go!"

Melissa had to laugh. She got to her feet, inclined her head to their highly amused grandmother, and allowed Lottie to tow her from the room.

Courtesy of their visit the previous year, Jamie and George knew the village well.

"There's no point calling at the Grange, or at the church or the vicarage, or at Deacon Filbert's cottage," Jamie said as he tooled the gig up the village lane.

Seated beside him with Lottie in her lap, Melissa nodded. "The people at all those places know we're hunting for the book." They'd turned right out of the manor drive and were heading into the village proper. "So, who's next along the lane?"

"Not who," George replied. "It's a what."

Melissa's heart sank as Jamie turned the gig in to the yard of the Cockspur Arms. "But it's a public house." She couldn't keep the dismay from her voice.

"Don't worry." Jamie was already tying off the reins. "Mr. and Mrs. Whitesheaf are nice, and anyway, we'll probably speak with one of their sons—Rory or Cam."

Reluctantly climbing down from the gig, Melissa did not find that information reassuring. But with the other three waiting for her to lead the way, she had little choice but to push through the open door of the pub and walk in.

The first person she saw was a red-haired girl only a few years older than herself. The girl was wiping down tables not far from the door; she looked up and smiled brightly. "Can I help you, miss?" Then she saw Jamie, George, and Lottie, and her smile brightened. "Hello, you lot." The girl's gaze went from the three to Melissa, then back again, then she looked at Melissa. "Are they with you?"

Melissa glanced at her cousins. "Yes. They're my cousins."

"I thought you must be related. I'm Ginger. So what can we do for you?"

Melissa found herself saying, "We're trying to find the church's book of carols." To her considerable surprise, the details of the book and why they needed to find it rolled easily off her tongue.

Ginger's expression changed to one of concern. "Gracious goodness! We can't do without our carol service!"

"We wondered if you could possibly ask all the members of your family if they'd seen the book—it has a red cover with writing and a design in black ink—anywhere. Anywhere at all. We've asked at the obvious places, you see, and no one knows where it might be."

"It's possible the book got left somewhere by accident," Jamie put in. He glanced at the various tables around the taproom. "Even in here."

"But really, it could be anywhere about," George said.

Ginger nodded. "I'll spread the word. And I'll get Da and my brothers to do the same among our regulars—whoever comes in tonight." She tipped her head to two old men huddled over pints by the fire and grinned. "I'll even ask them. Like you said, sounds as if the book's wandered accidental-like and might turn up in any old spot."

Melissa thanked Ginger for her help, and they parted on excellent terms.

As she climbed into the gig and took Lottie back onto her lap, Melissa observed, "People here are very friendly—and they really do want to help."

After their success at the Cockspur Arms, Melissa found no difficulty in knocking at the doors of the next two cottages along the lane, then walking into Butts's Bakery, followed by Bilson's Butchers and Mountjoy's Stores, and pleading their cause. At all the premises, they were met with attention and, once they'd stated their purpose, unstinting support. At Mountjoy's, they were lucky enough to meet two of the wives from an outlying farm who promised to spread the word.

"We'll ask around and let you know after church tomorrow," they promised.

Back in the gig, the cousins traveled around the curve in the lane, stopping at each cottage. Eventually, they rolled past the entrance to the Fulsom Hall drive and turned down the track to Tooks Farm. As they rattled along, Jamie, George, and Lottie told Melissa the tale of their adventures the previous year, when they'd led the hunt for Farmer Tooks's missing flock of geese. Melissa admitted to being duly impressed.

She was even more impressed by the welcome accorded them when they reached the farm gate. Nothing would do but that they should all go into the farm kitchen and be regaled with tea and Mrs. Tooks's homemade scones.

When, in between bites of luscious scone topped with fragrant raspberry jam, Melissa explained their current quest, Farmer Tooks swore he'd ask around his friends that very evening. Not to be outdone, the Tookses' children and Mrs. Tooks vowed the same.

"It's Saturday," Mrs. Tooks explained. "We often get together, several families of us, of a Saturday night for our meal. We'll be able to ask those who come to join us from the big houses, too."

"Thank you." In sincere appreciation, Melissa held up the last bite of her scone. "And for the scones, too."

From Tooks Farm, Jamie turned the gig south, onto the lane that ran past Swindon Hall. "There's no other village houses farther out that way." He waved northward.

"That's the way to East Wellow," George said.

There were several cottages on the opposite side of the lane from Swindon Hall. As it was Saturday afternoon, most men as well as the housewives were in. Melissa found everyone she spoke with highly receptive to their plea.

After gaining promises to search and ask all around, they continued south along the lane, calling in at Witcherly Farm and Crossley Farm along the way. Finally, they came to three cottages facing the other end of the village lane. After knocking on the doors and speaking with the three couples who lived in the cottages, Jamie declared that they'd come full circle.

"Those farmwives you spoke with in Mountjoy's come from Milsom Farm," he said, "so we don't need to go down there, and that's the last farm in the village."

Melissa nodded and climbed back into the gig. As Jamie turned the mare's head into the village lane, she noticed another thatched roof through the trees. She pointed. "What about that cottage?"

"That belongs to the church, and Richard is staying there now," George said, "so we don't need to call there, either."

The Dutton Grange drive appeared on their left, and then Jamie was turning right into the manor's drive.

As the shadows of the trees closed about them, Melissa realized how late it had grown. She swiveled to look west, but the sun must have set; there were no slanting rays to be seen. "It must be after four o'clock." The chill in the air was rapidly deepening.

Jamie set the mare directly for the stable. "We only just finished in time, but that's a good job done."

Melissa had to agree. And she'd led their little band without mishap or any embarrassing stumbles.

As she helped Lottie down, then took her cousin's small hand and, with the boys, raced for the manor's kitchen door, she found she was smiling—and laughed.

Therese wasn't surprised that the children's spirits sank somewhat as night fell and the realization impinged that another day had gone by and they'd yet to gain any clue as to the book's whereabouts.

When, as was their custom, they rose from the dining table and followed her into her private parlor—her inner sanctum that she rarely invited any others to share—she was ready with her arguments to bolster their flagging confidence.

She took in their sober, serious faces as Melissa and Lottie settled on the sofa and the boys sprawled on the hearthrug. They didn't, she noticed, drag out their box of games and soldiers. Bracingly, she said, "Buck up! You still have five days before the carol service, and thankfully, it seems Mortimer doesn't need days of practice to play superbly."

Jamie shifted. "He just needs the book, but we still don't have it."

"And we've asked everywhere," George said.

"Well, except for the rector of St. Aloysius," Melissa pointed out.

"The book will turn up," Therese maintained. "How could it not in such a small village? But I commend you for your efforts today—you've spread your net wide, and now, you need to wait to see what information you glean."

"But we do need to speak with the rector," Jamie said.

"Indeed." Therese nodded. "I agree that he and St. Aloysius are next on the list for investigation." She glanced around at their still-uncertain expressions. "Let me think how best to approach the rector. Now tell me, what are you and Faith and Mr. Mortimer planning for the pageant?"

That distracted them. Their faces brightened, and they happily launched into a description of the two choruses they'd decided to perform, one as Mary and Joseph rode to the stable and the other after the three kings arrived and the re-enactment reached its climax.

"We thought those were the best places to sing," Lottie informed Therese.

"Mr. Mortimer will have music for both pieces, but if we find the book of carols in time, we can switch one of the Christmas choruses for the second piece. The one we have now is not just for Christmas but more general," George explained.

"But it will do." Jamie glanced at his siblings. "I wonder who will be Joseph this year."

"And who will be Mary," Lottie said.

The three younger children started exchanging opinions on the potential candidates.

Melissa sat quiet and contained. Therese glanced at her assessingly. Apparently, Melissa hadn't been distracted by talk of the pageant; her expression as she sat relaxed in one corner of the sofa suggested that her mind had remained firmly fixed on their goal—on their hunt for the missing book of carols.

Therese considered her elder granddaughter for a moment more—considered the resolution and determination in her face—then, faintly smiling, returned her attention to the younger three and their increasingly humorous speculation.

CHAPTER 7

*A*ccompanied by her grandchildren, Therese toiled up the rise to attend Sunday morning service at St. Ignatius on the Hill. On entering the church, she walked down the aisle and sat in the middle of the front pew on the left, the pew closest to the organ. Mrs. Colebatch and the Swindons occupied the pew across the aisle; Therese exchanged smiling nods with her neighbors while the children arranged themselves on either side of her. Then Reverend Colebatch arrived and took up his stance before the altar, and she and her brood all dutifully gave their attention to him—or at least pretended to.

In reality, their gazes flicked constantly to where Faith had joined Mortimer in the organ corral. When Mortimer wasn't playing, Faith sat in a chair alongside the organ, but when Mortimer set his long fingers to the keys, she stood beside his bench and turned the sheets for him—an act which, if the smile he directed her way was any guide, he found exceedingly helpful.

Lottie and Melissa, along with Therese, were fascinated by the interplay.

There'd been no choral practice for the children and Faith and Mortimer that morning, but as a group, they put their heart and soul into the hymns, leading the congregation with enthusiasm. Therese and, indeed, everyone else, was left in no doubt as to how much they all— Melissa and Faith and Mortimer included—loved to sing.

Therese spent the hymns watching Mortimer play; she still found it exceedingly curious that a professional organist of his caliber was so dependent on written music. Yet he plainly was. She had to wonder if his dependency was more imagined than real.

She spent most of Reverend Colebatch's sermon pondering all she'd ever heard about the peculiar sensitivities of brilliant musicians. Then a whispered conference between Faith and Mortimer distracted her. In glancing across at the pair, who were juggling music sheets, from the corner of her eye, Therese caught the expression on Melissa's face. Melissa was smugly pleased by the sight of Faith and Mortimer with their heads bowed together.

Therese lowered her gaze to Lottie, seated between Therese and Melissa, and found a more juvenile yet similar expression on Lottie's face, too.

Smiling with amused satisfaction, Therese faced forward. Quite aside from being gratified by the evidence that her talents and inclinations had been passed down through the generations, she felt increasingly confident that by the time Melissa left Little Moseley, she would have turned a corner and would be…not a different girl, although undoubtedly, she would have changed, but more the girl—the emerging young woman— she had the potential to be. As Reverend Colebatch concluded his teaching and exhorted the congregation to pray, Therese was not too proud to bow her head and thank the Almighty for His help.

After another hymn, the reading, and a final hymn, the service concluded. The congregation made its slow, shuffling way out onto the lawn to mill and mingle as was customary. In the dull light of the gray day, neighbor chatted with neighbor, farmer to farmer, housewife to housewife.

With her small tribe about her, Therese paused to one side of the lawn. She'd invited the Longfellows, the Colebatches, the Swindons and Faith, and Mortimer for luncheon. As her staff were the most experienced and enjoyed employing their skills, she often hosted luncheons and dinners, viewing the activity as a contribution to village life and the maintenance of harmony—not that Little Moseley needed much help with the latter. Today, she was hoping that the luncheon would nudge a romance along; while she frequently dabbled in encouraging romance, it wasn't often she got the chance within the bounds of Little Moseley.

While she waited for the other couples to move through the crowd and join her, Therese graciously nodded to Mrs. Mountjoy and exchanged a few words about a recently arrived grandson.

Then Mrs. Mountjoy's son, Dick, came up. After ducking his head to Therese, Dick turned to Melissa, who had been standing silently beside Therese. Dick nodded to Melissa. "Wanted to let you know, miss, that we asked around all those we know in the village, and no one's seen that book you and the others are after."

Melissa blinked, then covering her surprise, responded, "Thank you, Mr. Mountjoy."

"Aye, well." Dick grimaced. "We're all wanting our carol service to be the best it can be, so seems it's us should be thanking you and the youngsters for hunting for the book."

With another nod, Dick moved away, leaving Melissa staring after him.

"Miss!" Mrs. Tooks came puffing up. She, too, dipped her head to Therese, then focused on Melissa. "I'm right sorry to have to tell you that we haven't found hide nor hair of that carol book. We asked all our neighbors and all our boys and girls who work at the big houses." Mrs. Tooks tipped her head toward the other side of the lawn, indicating a large gathering. "We've just been sharing what we've learned, which I'm sorry to say is nothing."

"Thank you for checking, Mrs. Tooks—you and all your family and friends." With easy grace, Melissa inclined her head to the farmwife.

"Well," Mrs. Tooks huffed, "seems as if, if we want our carol service, the least we can do is help you find the blessed book."

After dipping in a rough curtsy, Mrs. Tooks lumbered off.

Her place was filled by a small procession of locals, all coming to report to Melissa that, in response to her inquiry the previous day, they'd looked and asked about, but hadn't turned up any hint as to where the book of carols might be.

Cam Whitesheaf, a tall, gangly youth, regarded Melissa with something like awe while his sister, Ginger, related their failure to find anyone who knew anything of the book.

After Melissa thanked them, and Ginger all but towed Cam away, Melissa glanced around, but no one else was waiting to report. She turned to Therese and, finally, let her amazement show. "I really hadn't thought they would stir themselves to the degree they have, not just on my say-so —because I asked."

Therese suspected Melissa had underestimated her impact. "From what they've let fall, you were obviously successful in impressing on them that, without the book of carols, the carol service will be, at best, severely abbreviated or, more likely, not held at all. The villagers value their Christmas traditions, and the prospect of one not eventuating is more than enough to move them to action."

Melissa blinked again. "Apparently."

Along with Melissa, Therese turned as the Longfellows came up, closely followed by Faith and the Swindons, along with Mortimer, who had been chatting with them.

After smiles and greetings were exchanged, Eugenia said, "Christian and I will take Cedric back to the Grange, then we'll join you at the manor."

Therese stroked Cedric's downy cheek with the back of one finger, smiled, and nodded. "We'll see you shortly."

Turning to gather her remaining guests, Therese saw Mortimer speaking with Melissa and the three children. Faith joined them as Mortimer said, "We'll need to practice in a concerted fashion tomorrow. For singing a cappella, we need to become accustomed to each other's voices anew, and we should also ensure we have the two carols we have music for as polished as they can be." Mortimer's gaze went over the children's heads. He scanned the dispersing crowd, then grimaced. "Even then, how we're going to construct a carol service if you don't find the book, I simply don't know."

"We'll find the book." Faith lightly touched Mortimer's sleeve, drawing his gaze back to her and the other four.

Jamie nodded, his expression firming. "It has to be here somewhere."

"Somewhere within reach—where we can lay our hands on it," George added.

"It can't have vanished," Lottie observed.

"And," Melissa put in, "the whole village has now been alerted, and everyone's on the lookout for the book. Someone will find it."

Therese hid her smile. From near dejection the previous evening to firm resolution and confidence in the face of adversity this morning; it was amazing how having someone more anxious and in need of assurance than they brought out certain traits in her descendants.

Mrs. Colebatch joined them, greeting all with a smile and a nod. "Jeremy will be with us shortly." She focused on the children. "Still no luck?"

"Not yet," Jamie replied. "We're going to call at East Wellow next."

Just then, Reverend Colebatch, having shut up the church and seen his last parishioner on their way, came striding up. "Another Sunday service done!" He beamed at all the faces. "And how is everyone?"

Everyone smiled and responded.

Deciding that it was time to make a move, Therese raised her arms in a gathering motion. "And now, Mrs. Haggerty has a roast waiting to sustain us. Shall we go?" She directed the group onto the path down the rise.

Readily—even eagerly—the Swindons and Colebatches started off arm in arm.

Mortimer turned to Therese and offered his arm. "Thank you for inviting me, ma'am."

"The pleasure is mine." Therese took his arm and allowed him to lead her in the other couples' wake. The children skipped beside her, and Melissa and Faith brought up the rear.

As Therese strolled beside Mortimer, she was visited by the same elusive notion that had afflicted her days before—that she *should* know Richard Mortimer or at least know of his family. In ton terms, she should know who he was. Her inability to place him irked like a social failure—more, a failure in an arena in which she'd long considered herself unchallengeable.

She glanced at Mortimer's face, but there was nothing in his serious features that triggered any recognition.

As they reached the lane, she waved her cane toward the entrance to the manor's drive. "Have you spent much time in London, Mr. Mortimer?"

"No, ma'am," Mortimer answered, apparently without reserve. "I've spent more of my time in Oxford than in the capital."

Perhaps that was why she simply didn't know him.

As the manor came into sight and thoughts of the upcoming luncheon rose higher in her consciousness, Therese allowed her various puzzlements over Mortimer to sink beneath the surface of her mind.

As Melissa had only recently graduated to her parents' table when they were dining with company, she was pleased to have been included at her grandmother's board as a matter of course. She was somewhat surprised to find Jamie, George, and Lottie also at the long table, but apparently, through their activities the previous year, the trio had earned the interest and, indeed, the respect of the adults gathered, none of whom seemed to think the children's presence odd. All the adults interacted freely with the three children and with Melissa. As the questions and chatter ranged back and forth, she relaxed and joined in and found herself enjoying the meal and the company much more than she'd anticipated.

Although an attempt was made by the ladies to steer the conversation along unfraught paths, with Reverend Colebatch, Christian, and Richard at the same table, inevitably the talk turned to the upcoming Christmas events.

Richard had tried to keep his mind from the sense of impending failure that haunted him over the carol service, which seemed destined to be canceled because of his inability to play without written music. To say he felt guilty on multiple counts was an understatement; he wished there was some way for him to give the best performance of his life to the village that had so readily taken him in, but...without the music, that wasn't going to happen.

Whether by luck or by design—and he suspected the latter—Lady Osbaldestone had placed him beside Faith Collison in the middle of one side of the long table. That had certainly helped in keeping his mind off the carol service and the missing book of carols; with her sweet face, her pretty eyes framed by her spectacles, and her gentle, compassionate, yet determined nature, Faith effortlessly fixed his attention and lured his senses.

With their conversational scope widened by being in general company rather than alone in the church, they chatted over inconsequential things —what sort of trees each liked, whether they preferred country or town to live in, whether they liked to ride and what sort of horses each favored; they shared preferences and experiences and discovered they had many of the former in common. Looking past the glint of Faith's spectacle lenses and smiling into her eyes, he managed to forget about the dark cloud that hovered over his and the village's collective head.

Then Reverend Colebatch sobered and said, "Many of the villagers mentioned how concerned they are over the possibility of the carol service not going ahead." His expression anxious but, as ever, mild, he looked around the table. "I took it upon myself to assure them that, even if we have to make do with only a few carols, the service, as such, will take place." He looked at Melissa, Richard, Faith, Jamie, Lottie, and George, all seated along the opposite side of the table, and went on, "I thank Heaven that we decided, this year, to switch the order of the carol service and the pageant. That will allow us two extra days—indeed, until Friday afternoon—to find our missing book."

For a second, silence reigned, then Melissa heard Richard, seated beside her, give a soft sigh.

His tone one of sincere contrition, he said, "I cannot apologize enough for not being able to play without the book. Most organists would be able to play most carols from memory, but I fear that, music-wise, my mind doesn't work that way."

Several adults—Lady Longfellow, Mrs. Swindon, and Mrs. Colebatch as well as the reverend—leapt in to assure Richard that the fault was not his.

"I certainly don't recall playing by memory being a stipulation when the parish hired you to the organist's position," Mrs. Swindon said.

"Indeed." Mrs. Colebatch nodded. "Quite right. It's the parish's responsibility to provide the music, and really, that book of carols ought to be in the vestry. If any fault exists, it's one shared by all the village for not ensuring that book was where it should be long before this."

Reverend Colebatch coughed, then muttered, "Indeed, my dear." More loudly, he said, "And the fact remains that we *do* have the book of carols—it's simply been misplaced, and we just have to find it."

In her mind, Melissa heard, as she was sure everyone else did, the words Reverend Colebatch had left unsaid. *In time.* They had to find the book of carols by Friday.

She glanced around the table. Despite the bracing comments, all present were concerned—increasingly so—over the continuing mystery regarding the whereabouts of the book of carols and the looming prospect of a regrettably short carol service.

Reverend Colebatch's initial comment might have been a touch tactless, but he hadn't been wrong. The prospect of a poor carol service was weighing on the village as a whole.

To her left, from beyond where Richard sat, Melissa heard Faith's soft voice reiterating the others' assurances that he was not to blame for the situation.

Richard sat half turned toward Faith; Melissa couldn't see his face, but Mrs. Swindon, seated opposite, was watching and taking note.

Then Richard sighed again, this time resignedly. Melissa heard him softly say, for Faith's ears rather than the whole table's, "The village has been so very welcoming, I don't want to let people down. If I had my way, I would strive to give them the best carol service they've ever enjoyed."

"That's a laudable aim," Faith immediately responded, "and when we find the book of carols, you'll be able to do precisely that."

The stalwart certainty in her voice gave Richard pause, then he chuckled. After a second, he said, "Thank you. I will place my trust in our youthful helpers and hold myself ready to give my all *when* they recover the book."

Any doubt Melissa or Mrs. Swindon—or indeed, Melissa's grandmother, who she now saw had been closely observing Faith and Richard, too—might have harbored regarding the reality of a romance between Faith and Richard Mortimer was, Melissa judged, laid to rest. That Richard had paid most attention to and placed most credence in Faith's words—that she had reached him more effectively than any other and lightened his dejection—spoke volumes; even Melissa knew that.

As conversations started up on less-fraught topics, Melissa pondered Richard's sentiment of repaying the village for its welcome and inherent succor and felt a wave of corresponding emotion—and determination—rise inside her. Little Moseley might be a tiny village in rural Hampshire, but something about it made it special. Her cousins knew it; that was why they'd insisted on returning. She herself had sensed it—as if the village somehow cleared the mind and shone light on the path to becoming the person one really should be.

More than anything else, it was the people who lived there who made the village what it was. And she, too, could embrace the goal of returning the village's favor by finding the missing book and making the village carol service the most splendid in living memory.

She glanced at Jamie, seated on her right.

He met her eyes and mouthed, "We have to find the book."

She nodded and whispered back, "As soon as we possibly can."

The rest of the luncheon passed in easy camaraderie.

When, eventually, replete and smiling, Therese's guests departed, she sighed, waved to Crimmins to close the front door, and turned to find her grandchildren regarding her, impatience writ large in their faces and the missing book of carols on their minds.

She waved them to her parlor. "Come—let's sit and see where we are."

The four duly followed her into her inner sanctum and settled in their customary spots—the girls on the sofa and the boys on the hearthrug. As

Therese sank into her armchair, all four fixed their gazes expectantly on her.

She took in all she could see in their faces—the resolution, the determination, and the worry that ran beneath the more positive emotions. "It seems that by widening our net and informing the villagers of the consequences of not finding the book, we've spread concern over the matter, but in reality, that couldn't be helped. They needed to understand so they would be moved to check, and at least we now know that the book isn't sitting, forgotten, on some cottage dresser."

"But we need to find it and soon," Jamie stated.

Therese inclined her head. "Indeed. And to that end, I suggest you four should focus all your energies on tracking down our elusive tome. As we've already discussed, speaking with the rector of East Wellow is the necessary next step." She frowned lightly, then in a considering tone, went on, "As it happens, Sunday afternoon is not a bad time to accost a rector. His duties for the week will be done with, and I daresay, in this season, you will find him relaxing at home. He will be most amenable to questioning"—she glanced at the clock on the mantelshelf—"over the next few hours."

She allowed her frown to deepen and edged her tone with regret. "Sadly, after my meeting with my man-of-business yesterday, I must write and dispatch several important letters in relation to my financial affairs. The letters won't wait." She paused, seeing frustration bloom in all their faces. "However"—she tapped the chair's arm smartly—"I can't see any reason the four of you shouldn't take the gig and drive over to East Wellow and inquire of the rector whether he still has the book— unlikely, as I believe we've agreed—and if not, to whom or where he returned it."

Melissa blinked. "The four of us...without you?"

Therese opened her eyes wide. "I can't see why not. Dealing with a country rector should be well within the scope of your abilities." She paused, then added, "If in doubt, simply behave as your mother or I would in the same circumstances."

Therese watched Melissa weigh the challenge Therese had deliberately laid at her feet against her desire—and that of her cousins—to push ahead with finding the missing book.

Therese flicked a glance at Jamie, George, and Lottie. All three had their lips firmly shut, no doubt biting back demands that Melissa should take on the role of leading their expedition and could they go? *Now?*

Therese hid a smile. She was proud of the three; they were learning in leaps and bounds, and this was definitely a decision for Melissa alone.

Therese was unsurprised when, after several more seconds, Melissa refocused on Therese's face, on her eyes, then nodded. "All right. I'll try."

Melissa smiled weakly when her cousins erupted into cheers. To her way of thinking, she had precious little choice. They needed to push on with their search for the book of carols, and if approaching the rector herself was the only way to move forward immediately, then she had to try.

The fact that her grandmother believed she could carry off the encounter bolstered her confidence. Besides, if she wanted her part in finding the book to stand as her thank-you gift to the village, then her role had to cost her something, didn't it?

After regarding the cheering three with a fond smile, their grand-mother turned her obsidian eyes back to Melissa, viewed her—also fondly—for a moment, then arched her brows. "Well? What are you waiting for? The clock is ticking."

Melissa drew in a breath, rose, and looked at the other three. "Come along, you lot. Let's get on the lane to East Wellow."

CHAPTER 8

$\mathcal{M}$elissa stood in the lane outside the cottage they'd been told was the home of the rector of East Wellow. Jamie had asked a farmer walking beside his plodding horse, and the farmer had pointed to the neat cottage sitting behind a low stone wall.

After staring at the door—a daunting sight—Melissa drew in a determined breath, raised her chin, and marched forward. Jamie fell in beside her, and when she paused before the gate, he reached out and opened it for her, then followed her through and up the path; Lottie and George fell in behind.

There was a single shallow step before the small porch. Melissa stepped up, reached for the brass knocker, and rapped smartly. She'd been rehearsing what she should say to the rector—how she should address him—all the way from Little Moseley.

Yet when a thin, peevish-looking man opened the door, looked out at them with open disfavor, then, before Melissa could even open her mouth, declared, "You've come to the wrong door—I have no time for children," every rehearsed phrase fled her head.

Along with the other three, fanned out behind her, she stared, momentarily shocked by the rector's rudeness.

Something of her reaction must have shown in her face. The rector—assuming it was he—shifted on his feet and primed his lips, then irascibly inquired, "Well, what is it? I'm a very busy man, you know."

"Indeed." Melissa managed not to make the word a challenge.

Remembering that one caught more with honey than vinegar, she summoned a pleasant smile and politely said, "I'm Miss North. We've come from Little Moseley, and on behalf of the church—St. Ignatius on the Hill—we're trying to trace the movements of the church's book of carols with a view to determining the book's current whereabouts." She felt pleased with that opening statement, and indeed, it seemed to have given the rude rector pause. She went on, "Deacon Filbert recalled that you had wanted to borrow the book some weeks ago, and Lord Longfellow confirmed that he and his wife gave the book—which they'd had at the time—into your hands."

Now, the rector was halfway to scowling. "Yes, I borrowed the book and fetched it from the Longfellows. What of it? As far as I can see, it's no concern of yours."

His dismissive tone and the way he edged back as if to close the door in her face snapped the last thread of Melissa's reserve. She stiffened, and her grandmama's advice rang in her head: *Simply behave as your mother or I would in the same circumstances.*

Melissa straightened to her full height—making her nearly as tall as the rector—tipped up her chin, and infused her voice with her mother's haughty tones. "I see." She paused to allow those two, distinctly icy words to register, then went on in the same, exceedingly intimidating, clipped-accents vein, "You might like to know that we're residing for the season with our grandmother, Lady Osbaldestone, in Little Moseley, and as the village as a whole has very kindly included us in all its activities celebrating Christ's birth, we"—she waved at her cousins, who had stiffened, too; their expressions stony, they'd closed ranks about her—"my cousins Viscount Skelton, his brother, and his sister Lady Charlotte, and I—are attempting to assist the village by locating the church's missing book of carols, without which the village will not have a proper carol service this year."

She fixed her gaze—cold and haughty—on the rector's now-wide eyes. Obviously, adopting a superior tone and indulging in name-dropping had succeeded where politeness had failed. She continued, "I'm sure that's what our parents—the Earl and Countess of Winslow and Lord and Lady North—would wish, indeed, expect us to do."

She waited, steadily looking down her nose at the rector—and with some relief, saw him swallow, then he cleared his throat and half bowed.

"Ah—yes. I see. My apologies, Miss North, for my somewhat hasty assumptions." The rector cast a measuring glance at Jamie and the other two.

I can do this! Clinging to her haughty mien, Melissa inclined her head. "And the book of carols?"

The rector returned his gaze to her face. "I borrowed the book early in November—I picked it up from Dutton Grange, as you've learned."

She nodded. "Lord and Lady Longfellow had borrowed the book in preparation for the christening of their son, Cedric."

"I wanted the book to copy out three carols," the rector continued. "That didn't take me long. I only had the book for a week."

"To whom," Jamie asked, doing his best imitation of his father, "did you return the book?"

The rector regarded Jamie for a moment, then replied, "Deacon Filbert had told me the book was kept in the church vestry, so I took it directly back to the church. As it happened, Reverend Colebatch was polishing the candlesticks. We chatted, then he took the book from me— he said he would return it to the right shelf in the vestry for me."

Melissa exchanged a glance with Jamie, then looked at the rector. "Do you know if he did? Were you still in the church when Reverend Colebatch carried the book into the vestry?"

The rector frowned. "No. But when we parted and he turned away, he had the book in his hands, and he walked toward the vestry door."

Melissa couldn't think of anything more they needed to ask. She glanced at Jamie and arched her brows, but he shook his head fractionally.

Turning back to the rector, Melissa clung to her aloof and haughty demeanor, mimicking her mother and grandmother as she thanked him. Then gathering her cousins with a glance, she turned and led the way back up the path to the lane.

The rector watched them go, then, still frowning, he stepped back and shut the door.

Melissa exhaled. On reaching the gig, she leaned against its side.

Lottie looked up at her and grinned. "He wasn't very nice or helpful —not until you started sounding like Aunt North."

George grinned at her as well. "That was a good trick—and very effective." He waved her into the gig. Melissa turned and climbed up, then sat, and George lifted Lottie onto her lap.

After settling Lottie, Melissa resumed her haughty expression and, in chilly tones, instructed, "Home, James."

The others looked at her, then burst out laughing.

Melissa smiled. "Well, at least let's head back to Little Moseley."

The others snickered, and she let her act—her façade—slide away. She hadn't known she could so effectively mimic her mother. Another talent Little Moseley and her time there had revealed to her.

Before they even reached the lane leading south to Little Moseley, they'd all sobered. They were, Melissa knew, thinking about what they now knew about the book of carols.

Frowning as he turned the gig into the lane, Jamie said, "The rector had to have given the book back, and Reverend Colebatch must have returned it to the vestry shelf, because as far as we know, the rector was the second person to borrow the book over recent weeks."

"That's right." From his perch behind the seat, George continued, "Cedric was born at the beginning of October, so late October or early November was when the Longfellows must have had the book, and then the rector took it from them."

"*Then*," Melissa said, "the rector saw Reverend Colebatch take the book to the vestry, and he must have put it back on the shelf—"

"Because," Lottie piped up, "Mrs. Woolsey and Mrs. Swindon both borrowed the book as well."

"Yes, they did." Melissa narrowed her eyes in thought. "But did they borrow the book after the rector or before the Longfellows?"

"Mrs. Swindon said she had it sometime in November," Jamie said. "So most likely she borrowed it after the rector had returned it."

"But"—George leaned forward between Jamie and Melissa—"we didn't ask Mrs. Woolsey when *she* had the book."

"We need to find out," Melissa said.

Jamie nodded. "Did Mrs. Woolsey have the book last? Or was it Mrs. Swindon who last had the book at Swindon Hall?"

"If so," George pointed out, "that means that Reverend Colebatch is the last person known to have had the book in his hands."

"We need to map the movement of the book," Melissa said with decision as the northern end of the village lane appeared on their right. "We need to work out who had the book when and follow the trail to who had the book last—"

"And," Jamie said, determination ringing in his voice, "find out what happened to the book after that."

∾

Immediately after dinner that evening, Therese's grandchildren gathered in her private parlor and got to work on a list of the places the book of carols had been, organizing the list by date.

Secretly amused, Therese looked on as Melissa led the other three in a comprehensive review of their search to date.

"If we want to be able to sing the proper chorus at the pageant," Melissa concluded, "as if we're the angels announcing Christ's birth, then we have less than three days to find the book of carols and get it into Richard's hands."

Jamie nodded decisively. "We need to find it, and if at all possible, we need to find it tomorrow."

"Exactly." Melissa looked down at the notes she'd taken while they'd conducted their review.

Deciding to push matters along, Therese asked, "So what do you propose to do?"

The four children looked at her.

Then George looked at Melissa and said, "I vote we start by accepting everything the rector told us as fact."

Melissa nodded and scribbled something on her notes. "Extrapolating from that, the book was back on the shelf in the vestry—"

"Assuming Reverend Colebatch actually put it there," Jamie said.

"Yes," Melissa agreed, "assuming that, but at least we can be certain that the book is not at the Grange with the Longfellows, nor in East Wellow. The book went back to the church after both those households had borrowed it."

"Right." Jamie nodded.

"I suspect," Therese said, "that it's safe enough to assume that Reverend Colebatch did, indeed, return the book to the vestry shelf. Given he was already in the church and heading toward the vestry, and by the sounds of it, there was no one else there to distract him along the way, then most likely he did reach his intended destination and put the book back."

The children looked dubious—they had already seen more than enough of the good reverend's vagueness to be wary of drawing conclusions as to his actions—but then George's face cleared, and he pointed out, "Reverend Colebatch must have put the book back then, because we know Mrs. Swindon, at least, borrowed it after that."

"True." Melissa made an addition to her notes. "We know Mrs.

Swindon had the book sometime in November, and that must have been after the rector returned it to the church."

Jamie was peering over Melissa's shoulder. "But what we don't know is when Mrs. Woolsey borrowed it. Did she have it before the Longfellows, or between the rector and Mrs. Swindon, or after Mrs. Swindon?"

"And that"—Melissa tapped her pencil on her notes—"is what we must find out next." She looked at the others, then at Therese. "If Mrs. Woolsey was the last person to have the book, then the chances are that it's still at Fulsom Hall."

Therese couldn't fault their logic; she nodded in agreement. "So what do you propose?"

Melissa paused, then glanced at the others. "The pageant is nearly upon us, and once we find the book, we'll need time to practice whatever carols we choose to sing before the carol service. Richard might be able to play faultlessly by sight, but we'll need to run through our harmonies a few times at least."

"Yes," Lottie and George both said.

"So…" Melissa looked at Therese and met her eyes. "Given Mrs. Woolsey is such a…well, dithery sort, I could easily imagine her forgetting and leaving the book in the linen press, or some such place, and yet being quite sure that she'd returned it to the church, because that's what she'd intended to do."

Therese arched her brows. "I can't say you're wrong. But how do you think to assess that prospect?"

Melissa drew breath, glanced one more time at her cousins, then said, "Given we are running out of time, I suggest we visit Fulsom Hall tomorrow morning and ask Mrs. Woolsey when she had the book. But regardless of what she says, I think we must search the house—everywhere we possibly can, high, low, and everywhere between—to make absolutely certain that the book isn't somewhere at Fulsom Hall."

Therese considered, then inclined her head. "That proposal sounds a touch drastic, but in the circumstances, I agree that might well be the most decisive way forward. But how do you imagine mounting an effective search of a house as big as Fulsom Hall?"

"I thought that as the staff now know about the book being missing and what it will mean if we don't find it, then we could enlist their help. We"—Melissa glanced at her cousins—"can probably manage searching the reception rooms, but the staff will know better than anyone else where to search through the rest of the house." She met Therese's gaze. "They live with Mrs. Woolsey, after all."

Therese pressed her lips together to stop them twitching into a smile.

"Even if Mrs. Woolsey thinks she wasn't the last to have the book," Jamie said, his brow furrowed, "I think we still should search." He, too, met Therese's eyes. "We really don't have time to be going back and forth from house to house, not being able to strike any place off our list."

She considered, then said, "I understand your point, and I suspect that if you ask nicely, Mrs. Woolsey will happily allow a thorough search— you might say it's to establish once and for all that the book is not at Fulsom Hall."

"We could point out," George offered, "that if we don't search every-where, and the book isn't found, and the carol service doesn't go ahead, or only in a poor way, how awful people will feel if they later find the book sitting on some shelf somewhere unexpected, gathering dust."

Therese nodded encouragingly. "That's an excellent notion. Invoking people's emotions in such a way will recruit any villager you wish to the search."

George basked in her approval for a second, then fixed his blue eyes on Therese's face. "So tomorrow, we'll go to Fulsom Hall." A statement, not a question.

"After our practice with Faith and Richard," Melissa said. "We can't miss that."

George nodded. "But as soon as that's over, we should head to Fulsom Hall."

With almost-grim determination, Melissa nodded. "And if we find nothing there, after lunch, we'll move on to Swindon Hall."

The following morning, when Richard walked into the church at five minutes before ten o'clock, he found Melissa, Jamie, George, and Lottie waiting—transparently impatiently—beside the organ.

They'd already loosened their coats and unwound their scarves; as he approached, he saw that they'd even sorted the music sheets and placed them on the organ shelf, ready for him to play.

George followed Richard's gaze to the neatly regimented sheets and sighed. "I suppose you'll want to start with scales, anyway."

Richard's lips twitched, but he nodded. "Indeed." He was about to suggest they wait for Faith before commencing when the church door opened and she came hurrying inside.

She saw them all gathered before the organ and started unwinding her muffler as she bustled down the aisle. "I'm sorry—I didn't realize I was late."

"You aren't." Richard returned his gaze to the other four. "This lot were early."

"Only by a few minutes," Jamie said, almost reproachfully.

"We have things to do afterward," Lottie informed Richard, "so we don't want to be late *finishing*."

"Ah, I see." Richard wasn't at all sure he did, but faced with such candid matter-of-factness, admitting that seemed unwise. But Lottie's words were clearly a prod to get started, so with Faith taking her place beside Jamie and Lottie moving to her position on the other side of George, Richard slid onto the organ bench, adjusted the organ and got it going, then played middle C. "Right then. Scales."

He took them through a rigorous set of scales, then they started on the first chorus they intended to sing a cappella at the pageant.

All four of Lady Osbaldestone's grandchildren had been gifted with particularly fine voices, and all four had been well trained. Faith's soprano was strong and clear, and Richard's baritone anchored the result. It was a pleasure listening to the interweaving harmonies, and all of them knew how to work with a conductor to make the sound soar, then sough and fade; he was starting to believe that their contribution to the pageant would be a highlight well received by all.

His suspicion that the four younger members—with their patent wish to be done with the practice so they could be elsewhere—might have started to lose interest in the choir was banished within minutes of commencing the first song. The way the four sang, with their hearts and souls in their voices, testified to how much they enjoyed the activity and how committed they were to their ultimate performance.

He wondered if their apparently urgent task had something to do with their search for the book of carols. They hadn't volunteered the information, and he elected not to ask. His anxiety over the carol service was mounting, and he'd decided that his rightful role was to prepare for the worst and do all he could to fashion a service around the two carols—possibly three if he used one of the more ponderous ones—for which he had the music.

At the conclusion of the a cappella choruses for the pageant—the latter of which they hoped to replace if the book of carols was recovered in time—Richard paused and regarded his choristers. "I don't believe we could possibly do better with either of these pieces—we just need to ensure we keep our standard high."

Faith tipped her head. "You don't think the sound is a little too light? Overwhelmed by the sopranos?"

Richard acknowledged the comment with a dip of his head. "I agree we could use more male voices to balance the tone, but I can't imagine where in this community I might find male voices that are suitably trained. I gather the previous choir under Mr. Goodes was heavy on sopranos as well, and to blend with this choir, we need polished voices. I seriously doubt my ability to dragoon Lord Longfellow into performing, and their wives have informed me that Reverend Colebatch and Major Swindon can't hold a tune to save themselves."

He studied the faces before him and realized that, youthful though the children were, all of them understood singing. "Truth to tell," he admitted, "unless we can find trained voices, I would prefer to maintain the quality of our sound, somewhat unbalanced though it is."

They all nodded in agreement, and Richard tapped a finger on the organ shelf. "Let's go through the two carols we definitely have in our repertoire."

With unwavering focus, they worked through both carols, with Richard suggesting and Faith and Melissa attempting separate, more taxing parts. The result elevated the simple carols to something quite special—a result that had all of them beaming.

"I suggest we call it a morning—ending on a high note." Richard grinned at the muted groans his pun elicited.

He sorted the music sheets while Faith and the children redonned their coats, scarves, and mittens.

Richard started to play a processional, experimenting with various stops. The children chatted, then called their goodbyes. Without looking around, Richard raised a hand and briefly waved. As the four from the manor turned up the aisle, from the corner of his eye, he saw Faith glance at him and hesitate.

If he turned his head and smiled, she would stay. They could talk, and he could revel in her presence.

But to what end?

Was it fair to encourage her…

Why not?

Richard's eyes continued to track the music, and his fingers continued faultlessly depressing the keys, while his mind ventured into a heretofore unexplored landscape.

Yet if he wished to honorably pursue Faith, to pursue the possibility of a marriage with her, he would have to admit his deception, wouldn't he? How would she view him then?

Faith dithered, but when Richard showed no hint of encouraging her to stay—when, indeed, his gaze remained fixed on the music in front of him—she gave up, swung around, and followed her second impulse, namely to question Melissa and the three children as to whether they'd discovered any clue at all as to where the book of carols might be.

Faith hurried up the now-empty aisle. She knew the prospect of a dull and drab carol service was weighing heavily on Richard, and she felt compelled to do all she could to fix the problem and free him from the burden.

She pulled open the heavy front door to find the four from the manor conferring on the porch. Although the sky was clear, the sunshine was anemic, and there was a biting chill in the air. Her breath fogged before her face as, letting the door close behind her, she asked, "Have you got any further in finding out where the book of carols is?"

Melissa and the younger three turned to her. After a second's pause, Melissa replied, "Not as such, but we've established that the book might be at Fulsom Hall." Succinctly, with interjections from Jamie and George, Melissa explained their conclusions after their visit to the rector at East Wellow and how that had led to their present direction—their intention to search high and low at Fulsom Hall.

Melissa glanced at her cousins, then looked at Faith. "We're about to set off for Fulsom Hall. Would you like to join us?"

Faith could hear the organ filling the church. She nodded. "Yes. I would like to help."

She'd driven the Swindon Hall gig to the church. At her suggestion, the others piled in, then Faith took up the reins and turned the old mare down the drive toward the lane.

CHAPTER 9

"Well…" Mrs. Woolsey blinked myopically and lightly wrung her hands. "I'm not sure, really…"

Melissa exchanged a glance with Faith. They stood in the front hall of Fulsom Hall. Melissa had just inquired of Mrs. Woolsey as to when—over what dates—she'd had the book of carols in her possession.

As well as Melissa, her cousins, and Faith, Mountjoy, the Hall butler, stood nearby and, no doubt inured to his mistress's vagueness, looked on impassively.

Mrs. Woolsey's brow furrowed as she plainly wrestled with her memory. "You know, dear, I can't be certain when I had the book. Was it October or November? I really can't recall. However"—the old lady straightened—"I'm sure I must have returned it. I would have, surely?"

Melissa was saved from having to respond by the sound of heavy footsteps approaching along a corridor giving off the hall. She and the others watched as a sturdy young gentleman with curly blond hair led three other well-dressed young men out of the shadows.

"What-ho?" the first gentleman exclaimed. "What's this, then?"

"Henry!" Jamie beamed and bounded forward, closely followed by George and Lottie. They swarmed the young gentleman—who, from their greetings, Melissa took to be the owner of the Hall, Sir Henry Fitzgibbon—and he, in turn, beamed back at her cousins and returned their greetings with equal vigor. "Excellent to see you three back here. Staying with your grandmama again, no doubt. Couldn't keep away, heh?"

Jamie nodded. "Last year was fun, so we came back—at least for a few weeks."

"We have to go home for Christmas this year," George explained. "But we'll be here for all the events."

"No skating this year," Lottie said, including the three other young gentlemen with her innocent smile. "Mr. Mountjoy—the other one—says it hasn't been cold enough, and there's really no ice."

The three other gentlemen and Henry exchanged glances.

"Perhaps that's just as well," one of the gentlemen—the one with straight dark hair and a wickedly handsome face—said.

Then that gentleman looked at Melissa. "But who are your other callers, Mrs. W?"

At the question, Mrs. Woolsey fluttered into action, introducing everyone—even Jamie, George, and Lottie, who the newcomers clearly knew—to everyone else in a flurry of names and, somewhat to Melissa's surprise, titles.

The dark-haired gentleman—who appropriated her hand and bowed gracefully over it—proved to be Viscount Dagenham, the eldest son and heir of the Earl of Carsely and a friend of Henry's from Oxford.

"Like your young cousins," Dagenham said, demonstrating that he'd paid attention to Mrs. Woolsey's disjointed introductions, "we were here last year for the weeks before Christmas and had such a good time, we begged Henry to allow us to return."

"Well, there were four of them last year," Henry said, "but Roger Carnaby had to stay back and swot, don't you know."

Melissa smiled and retrieved her hand from Dagenham's grasp; he seemed to have forgotten he still held it, absorbed as he was in staring at her face.

"But it sounded as if you're after something." Henry grinned at the children. "On the hunt again, I take it. Last year, it was the geese. What's it this time?"

"The church's book of carols," Jamie promptly replied. He started the tale, but soon appealed to Melissa. She took over, with Faith, George, and Lottie adding various points.

When they explained the likely outcome if the missing book of carols wasn't found—namely that the carol service would be either very short or canceled altogether—even the visiting gentlemen looked shocked.

"I say," the gentleman introduced as Thomas Kilburn exclaimed, "that would be a crying shame. The carol service was a highlight last year."

The other gentlemen-visitors nodded earnestly.

Henry was appalled. "Good Lord! We can't have that. No carol service..." His tone suggested that such a happening was unthinkable. Abruptly, he refocused on Jamie, then looked at Melissa. "But you're on the book's trail, and you're here. Do you think the book might be somewhere at the Hall?"

Melissa explained—with distractingly vague interjections from Mrs. Woolsey—why they thought it was necessary to mount a search of the Hall. "We're running out of time, you see, and as matters stand, with Mrs. Woolsey unsure, if we don't search thoroughly, we can't cross the Hall off our list of places the book might be."

"Yes, of course. Entirely understandable." Henry looked past Mrs. Woolsey to Mountjoy. "We need to organize a search, Mountjoy—one that covers every possible nook and cranny in this house."

Mountjoy bowed, his ready acquiescence suggesting he agreed. "I will summon the staff, sir. It might be best were you to speak with them."

"Yes, of course." Henry nodded his permission, and Mountjoy departed.

Dagenham, who had remained beside Melissa, caught her eye. "We'll help as well, of course."

She dipped her head in apparent acceptance. She couldn't stop him helping, but she was already finding him distracting. Perhaps he would go off and search with his friends.

In less than a minute, Mountjoy returned with the rest of the staff at his heels.

Henry smiled genially and, once his household troops had gathered around Mountjoy at the rear of the hall, addressed the company. "Miss North and her cousins are searching for the church's book of carols, which has gone missing somewhere."

Many nodded their understanding; it was clear the villagers had, indeed, spread the word far and wide.

Henry glanced at Melissa, and she stepped forward and said, "As you know, we"—with a wave, she indicated herself and her cousins—"have been here before. We searched for the book in the music room, but nowhere else." Remembering George's suggestion from the previous evening, she went on, "Since then, we've asked everywhere the book was known to be. In the other cases, we can be certain it was returned. But when the book left here is unclear. Given that, we feel that if we don't make every effort and search everywhere, and the book isn't found and the carol service doesn't go ahead, but then sometime later, someone finds the book lying on a shelf somewhere... Well, just think how dreadful that person and that household are going to feel."

Murmurs rippled through the staff; from their faces, they could readily visualize the scenario she'd painted.

From behind her, Dagenham murmured, "Nice touch."

She ducked her head and hoped she wasn't blushing.

Then Henry said, "I think Miss North makes an excellent point. We don't want Fulsom Hall to be the household that had the book but failed to find it in time. So!" Henry rubbed his hands together and surveyed his troops. "I believe we need to search the Hall."

"High and low and everywhere between," Jamie put in.

Henry inclined his head. "Indeed. We need to search now—this minute—and as I appreciate you all have duties to perform, let's see if we can organize ourselves to be thorough, but also quick." Henry looked at his butler. "Mountjoy?"

Mountjoy was ready to meet the challenge. "I would suggest, Sir Henry, that if you and your guests could search the reception rooms, we —the staff—will search all the rooms above stairs. Although it's unlikely the book made its way into the areas the staff inhabit, we will search there as well."

Henry nodded in agreement. "We'll take the rooms down here while you look everywhere else."

With a bow, Mountjoy turned to the staff.

Henry swung to face his guests. "We should split up into pairs, two pairs of eyes always being better than one." He proceeded to pair everyone up—all except Mrs. Woolsey, who he quite tactfully suggested should hold the fort in the drawing room so that each pair could report there once they finished searching their allotted room.

Given Dagenham was standing beside her, Melissa couldn't protest when he and she were paired. Not that she wanted to protest—not exactly. But he was broad-shouldered and lean and a good head taller than she was, which was unusual and, in an odd way, put her on her guard.

They were assigned to search the library, along with Henry and George Wiley. Faith went off with Thomas Kilburn to search the morning room before moving on to the drawing room, and the three children stuck together, intending to search the music room once again and then the dining room.

Melissa glided beside Dagenham in Henry and George Wiley's wake.

The pair turned through a door, and Dagenham stood back and waved Melissa in. She walked into the library—and realized why Henry had decided all four of them would be needed to search the room. The library was large—probably the largest room in the house—and boasted a lot of bookcases. Sadly, the bookcase shelves were only partially filled with books, more or less neatly arranged. The rest of the shelf space hosted an assortment of objects—knickknacks to hunting trophies and everything in between, including stacks of loose pamphlets.

The four of them stood just inside the door and surveyed the challenge.

"What does this book of carols look like?" Dagenham asked.

Melissa described it.

"Well, at least it isn't bound in leather." Dagenham waved Henry toward the other end of the room. "We'll take this end. Why don't you two start down there?"

Melissa turned, walked to the nearest bookcase, and started to poke through the detritus that littered the section of the shelves that was not filled by leather-bound tomes.

Dagenham trailed after her. After a second of observing her industry, he said, "Perhaps if you concentrate on the shelves from the middle to the floor and I search the higher shelves, we'll get along faster."

Melissa had to admit that was a sensible suggestion. She nodded. "Good idea."

They proceeded to move from bookcase to bookcase, working their way around their half of the long room.

Melissa's senses flickered every time Dagenham reached over her to an upper shelf, or when he moved around her, of necessity close enough for his boots to brush her hems.

Temptation whispered, and when she thought he wouldn't be looking her way, she shot a glance at him—expecting to see his undeniably aristocratic profile. Instead, she discovered that he'd chosen the same moment to glance swiftly—assessingly—at her.

Their gazes clashed. A second later, they both looked away. She felt heat rise in her cheeks and vowed not to succumb to temptation again.

Besides, he was at least six years older than she and possibly even older.

Admittedly, she was often taken for several years older than she was, so he might think...

She stifled a snort. As she flicked through another stack of pamphlets

—this time about harvesting and crop rotation—she sternly lectured herself that, regardless of whatever Dagenham was thinking with respect to her, with his ruffled dark locks, pale-gray eyes, and mobile lips, let alone his wickedly charming smile, he was just the sort of young gentleman who had impressionable young ladies casting themselves at his feet, and she had no intention—none at all—of being so foolish over any gentleman and especially not one like him.

With her armor thus bolstered, she adopted a cool, calm façade and had the pleasure of seeing him glance, faintly puzzled, at her.

Clearly, he'd anticipated her swooning at his well-shod feet. Ha!

Yet she couldn't fault his behavior toward her, which remained rigidly correct in every degree.

Several minutes later, he said, "I had no idea pigs could be trained to fetch."

She looked up to see him reading a pamphlet he'd discovered on the top shelf. He noticed her looking and showed her the front of the pamphlet, which did indeed show a pig standing on its rear trotters with a pair of slippers in its mouth. She couldn't hold back her laugh.

He smiled. "Indeed." He looked again at the pamphlet, then shook his head and returned it to the shelf. "What will people think of next?"

Of course, she then felt compelled to share the next silly pamphlet she found—one touting the benefits of the water used for boiling eels for easing boots from swollen feet.

He frowned at the pamphlet. "Wouldn't the water make the leather cling even more?"

"So one would think." She replaced the pamphlet and moved on to the next bookcase. "While we might laugh at the contents of these pamphlets, I have to wonder who it was who saved them."

"Indeed." He followed her to the new bookcase, and they continued their searching in strangely companionable accord.

They met Henry and George Wiley by the fireplace in the middle of the long inner wall.

"Nothing," Dagenham reported.

Henry grimaced. "It was a long shot, but with it being a book, I could imagine one of the maids or footmen finding it and thinking it belonged in here."

The same idea had occurred to Melissa. She looked along the top of the mantelpiece, but there were no books lying on it.

Dagenham had pulled out his watch. "We've been searching for nearly an hour." He tucked the watch back into his waistcoat pocket and looked at the others. "Let's head for the drawing room and see if any of the others have struck gold."

"I doubt it." Henry turned toward the door. "If they had, I'm sure we would have heard."

His assessment proved correct. When Melissa preceded the three gentlemen into the drawing room, a sea of glum faces greeted her. From the lack of hope in everyone's expression, no one had imagined the library would have provided richer pickings.

"No book," Jamie reported, dejection in his voice. "Not anywhere. The staff finished just a few minutes ago, and Mountjoy came and told us."

"It wasn't in the library, either." Henry walked to the fireplace and took up a stance before it. He frowned. "I can't think of anywhere in the Hall we haven't looked—nowhere such a book might be."

Melissa, Dagenham, and George Wiley had halted at the edge of the rug, facing the fireplace.

Seated on the end of the sofa closest to the hearth, Mrs. Woolsey stirred. Raising a hand to her throat, she glanced up at Henry. "What with all this hunting and searching, I've been wondering..." She broke off, looked down at the rug, and tipped her head, much like a curious bird.

Melissa saw Henry press his lips together, no doubt suppressing the urge to prompt his aging relative. Dagenham shifted, but just thrust his hands into his pockets and held his tongue. It seemed that all present were acquainted with Mrs. Woolsey's mental meanderings.

Sure enough, after a moment, with a faint frown forming on her face, Mrs. Woolsey resumed, "I have to wonder, you see, if in returning the book, I might have called first at the Grange." She looked up at Henry. "To see dear little Cedric. I've made a point of dropping by every time I venture into the village, so I suppose I must have called there...perhaps before I went to the church." She opened her old eyes wide and looked around at the gathering. "Might I have left the book there?"

No one thought to answer; they were all too busy exchanging glances.

Eventually, Henry drew breath and said, "Right-o! We'll go and find out." He turned to check the clock on the mantelpiece, then looked back as all those who had been sitting, bar Mrs. Woolsey, got to their feet. "We've time before luncheon to call on m'sister at the Grange."

With no more ado, they all filed out of the drawing room and headed for the front door.

～

They rattled up the drive of Dutton Grange in a small convoy of gig and curricles.

Melissa and Lottie traveled with Faith, but the boys eagerly scrambled up into Dagenham's curricle, along with Thomas Kilburn, while Henry and George Wiley brought up the rear in Henry's curricle.

Melissa, Lottie, and Faith reached the front door first and waited for Henry to join them. He strode up the steps with Dagenham at his heels, with the others clattering up behind them.

Henry tugged the bellpull.

Hendricks must have been alerted by the thunder of feet on the steps; he opened the door only seconds later and looked out at their company with interest. His gaze swept over them, then came to rest on Henry. "Yes, Sir Henry?"

"Good morning, Hendricks…well, it's afternoon, I suppose." Henry grinned at Hendricks. "Is my sister at home? Or Longfellow?"

"Sadly, sir, Lord and Lady Longfellow are out for the day. We aren't expecting them to return until after dark."

"Oh." Henry looked taken aback, but then said, "It's about this missing book of carols, you see. Aunt Em thought she might well have called in on her way to return the book, and instead of taking it with her when she went on to the church, left it somewhere here."

Hendricks nodded. "Aye—her ladyship had the same thought. She had all the staff hunt everywhere in the house—upstairs and downstairs and through every room. Mrs. Wright—our housekeeper—knows what the book looks like, so we knew what we were searching for. But although we found other things we'd misplaced, we didn't find the book of carols."

The deflation that afflicted their company was evinced by downcast expressions and slumping shoulders.

Hendricks grunted. "Sorry to disappoint, but the book isn't here."

Henry nodded. "Regardless, it's useful that you and the staff searched." He looked at Melissa and Jamie. "We can strike Dutton Grange off the list of places the book might be."

Somewhat glumly, they nodded.

After farewelling Hendricks, the company trod back down the steps and walked across the forecourt to the carriages. They milled about the horses' heads.

George was frowning. "Maybe we're on the wrong track"—his frown deepened—"but what other track is there?"

Jamie shook his head. "The book can't have vanished."

Dagenham softly added, "Ergo, it has to be somewhere. The question is where."

Melissa shared a glance with Faith, then looked at the others and said, "There's one last place where we know the book was for at least a few days. Exactly when—before or after Mrs. Woolsey had it—we don't know, but clearly, we now need to ask."

"Indeed," Faith said. "We need to hold to our path and be thorough. Aunt Sally is sure she handed the book to Reverend Colebatch, but as I understand it, we've yet to confirm that he definitely had the book with him when he left Swindon Hall."

Melissa looked at Jamie. "Actually, one place we haven't searched is the vicarage."

His jaw firming, Henry nodded sagely. "Very rambling, is our good reverend. He could well have carried the book off, forgotten what he was carrying, and taken it back to his study, then put it on his desk and left it there. If so, the book might well be buried under his papers. Every time I've been in his study, the entire desk is covered in piles of letters and sermons and such. The book could very well be hidden there."

Jamie's eyes lit. "That sounds promising."

Just then, the *bong* of the church clock rang out over the village, a single midrange note.

"It's lunchtime," Melissa said, "and we're expected back at the manor." She looked around the circle of their now-expanded search party. "I say we all go and have lunch, then reconvene and stick to our plan and move on to Swindon Hall. We can talk to Mrs. Swindon and, hopefully, search there, and if we still find nothing, and thus prove the book isn't at the Hall and that Reverend Colebatch took it away, then we go to the vicarage and ask to search there."

Henry nodded, and Dagenham said, "That sounds like a solid, straightforward plan."

Everyone agreed.

Faith offered to drop Melissa and the children back at the manor before driving on to Swindon Hall. She said she would speak with her uncle and aunt over luncheon and that the others should come to Swindon Hall at half past two, prepared to search.

With that decided, everyone scrambled into gig or curricle and rattled back to the lane.

CHAPTER 10

*W*hen at fifteen minutes past two o'clock, Jamie tooled the manor gig down the drive to the lane, Melissa spied Dagenham in his curricle idling about along the verge. Thomas Kilburn was with Dagenham, while Henry and George Wiley were in Henry's curricle, waiting a little farther up the lane.

On seeing them, Dagenham smiled and raised a hand in greeting. "Henry knows the way, of course, but we thought we'd wait for you and go all together." Holding his high-spirited horse on a tight rein, Dagenham waved Jamie past. "Go ahead. We'll follow."

Jamie grinned and proudly did.

Sitting in Melissa's lap, Lottie squirmed about to look up at Melissa's face, but Melissa continued looking forward and refused to meet Lottie's gaze.

Eventually, Lottie gave a soft huff and turned to face forward again.

With Dagenham trotting his horse immediately behind the gig and Henry following Dagenham, they proceeded at a clipping pace around the corner and into the lane that led north to Swindon Hall.

They reached the Hall forecourt to find grooms waiting to take charge of the horses. The Swindons' butler opened the door to them and, unsurprised, bowed them all into the house.

They filed into the front hall and discovered that Faith, waiting to meet them, had paved their way with her uncle and aunt, too; Major Swindon and Mrs. Swindon came out of the drawing room to greet them.

Viewing them all—including the younger gentlemen—the Major nodded approvingly. "We all know how much the carol service means to the village. Your efforts to find this missing book are commendable."

Everyone looked faintly bashful.

Mrs. Swindon smiled upon them all. "Faith has pressed your cause—quite unnecessarily, because as Horace says, we all know how important the book of carols is at this time. You have our permission to search the ground floor rooms, and Colton has already organized for the staff to search the rooms upstairs." She cocked a brow at the butler. "I believe the staff are doing so as we speak."

Colton bowed. "Indeed, ma'am."

When the company looked back at their host and hostess, Major Swindon gestured expansively. "Search as you will. Mrs. Swindon and I will take refuge in the drawing room. Do let us know how you fare."

The searchers quickly conferred, and once again, Melissa found herself partnered with Dagenham in searching the library in company with Henry and Kilburn. The others, too, had largely stuck to their previous assignments, except that this time, George Wiley went with Faith.

They searched assiduously, even moving furniture and peering behind the leather-bound tomes, but were forced to accept that the book of carols had not been secreted in the library.

Or, as it transpired, in any of the other downstairs rooms.

Dejected again, the company gathered in the front hall, where Colton waited. He, too, didn't look hopeful, and sure enough, when the house-keeper came to report on the search upstairs, it was to confirm that no book of carols had been found.

They all looked at each other, then Jamie asked, "So shall we go on to the vicarage?"

Melissa frowned, then shook her head, in puzzlement rather than disagreement.

Dagenham, standing beside her, had been studying her face. "What is it?" he asked.

Melissa grimaced, then looked across at Jamie. "I know Reverend Colebatch is sometimes vague and forgetful, but he's not as dithery as Mrs. Woolsey. If he left here with the book of carols under his arm, then…" She frowned more definitely and turned to Colton. "Colton, I assume it was you who opened the door for Reverend Colebatch when he left the house?"

Colton nodded. "Yes, miss. I remember doing so quite clearly. Reverend Colebatch doesn't call that often—he hasn't been here since that day."

"Excellent." Melissa focused all her attention on Colton. "If you would, please think back—try to picture Reverend Colebatch as he left the house."

Colton frowned slightly, but judging by his expression, he obediently thought back. "Yes, miss?"

"When Reverend Colebatch walked out of the front door and onto the porch, did he have a book with a red cover in his hand or under his arm?"

Colton stared into space for several heartbeats, then he blinked and looked at Melissa. "No, miss. I can see him clear as day in my head. He didn't have the book with him."

"And," Melissa said, triumph in her tone, "as I understand it, the book of carols is too big to be put into a pocket."

"Right!" Henry's exclamation was the verbal expression of the surge of enthusiasm that shot through them all.

"That's more like it." Dagenham caught Melissa's gaze and smiled admiringly. "Sharp thinking."

She colored.

"My goodness!" Colton was still blinking. "But...that means the book must still be here." He glanced at Faith, then at Major and Mrs. Swindon; alerted by Henry's exclamation, they'd emerged from the drawing room to see what was happening.

Colton licked his lips and looked at Melissa. "I don't understand, miss. If the book didn't leave the house with Reverend Colebatch, and yet we haven't found it even though we've searched every room, where is it?"

"Somewhere we haven't yet looked," Dagenham murmured, softly enough that only Melissa heard.

Faith echoed Colton's puzzlement. "Where could Reverend Colebatch have left it?"

Melissa shook her head. "I don't know, but..." She regarded Mrs. Swindon. "You gave Reverend Colebatch the book of carols while you were both in the music room."

Mrs. Swindon nodded. "He was holding the book when I left him there—I was called away to the laundry, and he waved me off, saying he knew the way to the front door."

Melissa was imagining the scene. "So Reverend Colebatch was in the music room with the book in his hands. We've searched that room twice, so we know he didn't leave the book there." She transferred her gaze to Colton. "Could Reverend Colebatch have gone somewhere else in the house before he came into the front hall and you showed him out of the door?"

"Well," Major Swindon said, "if the good reverend was in the music room, he would have had to come all the way along the corridor to reach the front hall, so I would say the answer to your question is yes."

"So," Henry eagerly summarized, "Reverend Colebatch, carrying the book, could have gone somewhere else in the house and, for whatever reason, left the book there."

"Wherever that somewhere is," Dagenham said, "it has to be a spot that hasn't yet been searched."

"But we've searched everywhere," Jamie said.

"No. We haven't." Melissa suddenly realized what might have happened. She looked at Major Swindon. "Could we possibly assemble all the staff? Not just those who work above stairs but all those who work in the house?"

The major studied her for a second, then nodded. "Excellent notion." He looked at his butler. "Colton?"

"At once, Major." Now as determined as anyone to get to the bottom of the mystery of the missing book, Colton strode for the door at the rear of the hall. "I'll summon everyone."

Within minutes, staff members started filing in. Soon, what Colton assured them was the entire complement of indoor staff stood clustered around him at the rear of the hall.

Melissa and the others had turned to survey them, making several of the maids rather nervous.

The major harrumphed and stated, "We're still looking for the missing book and have a few questions." He turned to Melissa and inclined his head. "The floor is yours, m'dear."

Melissa had been thinking furiously about how to lead the staff's minds in the direction she wished. "I would like you all to think back to the day when Reverend Colebatch last visited this house. It was several weeks ago." She paused, then said, "Mrs. Swindon, who had been with the reverend in the music room, was called to the laundry, leaving Reverend Colebatch to make his own way from the music room, along the corridor, and so to the front hall. Do any of you know if, at that time,

Reverend Colebatch went anywhere else in the house? Anywhere other than the music room, the corridor, and the front hall?"

All the staff Melissa could see looked at each other, then shook their heads. Mumbles of "No, miss" reached them.

Then Dagenham, still standing beside Melissa, tapped her arm and pointed. "At the rear of the pack."

Melissa went up on her toes and, past the shoulders of two footmen, saw a small hand waving. "Yes?"

The rest of the staff looked around, then shuffled aside to allow a short, rotund woman in a flour-dusted apron to be seen.

The woman nodded at Melissa. "Mrs. Higgins, miss. I'm cook here. And if you're speaking of the day a few weeks ago when Reverend Colebatch called at the house, then he came to the kitchen to give me a message from my sister."

The major made a chuffing sound. "There's a door to the kitchens along the corridor between the music room and the front hall."

Mrs. Higgins nodded. "Aye, that's the way he came. Past the butler's pantry and the housekeeper's room, through the servants' hall and into the main kitchen."

"So," Henry said, rising excitement in his voice, "he could have put the book down anywhere along there."

Colton cleared his throat. "Begging your pardon, Sir Henry, but those rooms are constantly in use. If the book was there, we would have found it long since and handed it back to Mrs. Swindon." Colton glanced at his fellow staff members, all of whom nodded in agreement.

Mrs. Colton, the housekeeper, spoke up. "I believe I can assure you, Major, Mrs. Swindon, Miss North, that the book of carols is nowhere in those rooms."

Disgruntled, Henry humphed and subsided.

Melissa looked again at Mrs. Higgins. "So Reverend Colebatch came into the kitchen via that route and gave you the message from your sister. Did he leave by the same route?"

Mrs. Higgins frowned, then nodded. "Eventually."

Melissa arched her brows. "Eventually?"

Rather sheepishly, Mrs. Higgins admitted, "I asked him to help me get down my Christmas jelly molds. He did, then he left, going the same way he'd come."

Everyone, staff included, turned to stare at the cook.

Colton asked, "Why ever did you ask Reverend Colebatch for help with such a thing?"

"Well, he was there, wasn't he? And I needed those molds, and he's such a long, lanky thing"—she spread her arms—"and look at me."

Mrs. Higgins was barely five feet tall.

"I needed the molds right then and couldn't reach them," she went on, "but he could, and he was happy to help, so he got them down for me, and that was that."

"Where were the molds?" Melissa asked.

"On the top shelf in the pantry. On account of not being used but once a year."

Dagenham glanced swiftly at Melissa, then looked at Mrs. Higgins. "Did the reverend have a book with him when he came into the kitchen and spoke to you?"

Mrs. Higgins frowned. "I can't say as I noticed, sir." She screwed up her face in thought. "He *might* have been carrying something, but I didn't really look." She paused, then her expression firmed. "But I know he had nothing in his hands, nor under his arms, either, when he reached up to the pantry's top shelf and lifted down the molds, then held them out to me. He had to use both hands, so of that I can be sure—he wasn't carrying any book then."

"Then." Melissa could all but see what must have happened. She shared a quick glance with Dagenham, then said to Colton, "We need to search the pantry."

Colton glanced at Major Swindon, who gave a brusque nod.

"Yes, indeed," the major said. "The good reverend might have set the book down. We have to check in there."

The rest of the staff, now as interested as anyone, drew back to allow Colton to lead the way. Mrs. Higgins followed. The major waved Melissa forward. With Dagenham, Henry, and all the other searchers on her heels, she quickly caught up to the cook.

Colton led them down the corridor to the music room, but halted at a door set into the wall midway along. He glanced at Melissa. "This is the way Reverend Colebatch went from the music room to the kitchen." Then Colton pushed the door open and continued on.

Melissa followed Mrs. Higgins past the butler's pantry and the house-keeper's room, through the servant's hall and into the kitchen. At that point, Colton stepped aside, and Mrs. Higgins marched past him to a tall, narrow door set into the kitchen's side wall.

Mrs. Higgins hauled the door open and propped it wide, then stood back and waved Melissa and the searchers forward. "Right at the end on the left, on the very top shelf, was where the jelly molds were stored."

Melissa halted on the pantry's threshold and surveyed the space. With the door open and illumination from a small skylight in the ceiling at the far end, there was enough light to see the five rows of deep shelves that lined the walls on both sides of the long, narrow room. The recesses of the highest shelves were only just within the reach of a very tall man. Virtually every inch of shelf space was packed with packets and bags and containers of foodstuffs, from hessian bags of flour, barley, and oats to packets of sugar and salt and pots of treacle to glass and pottery jars of preserved fruits from the Hall's orchards.

The others in their search party had gathered around and behind Melissa, all doing their best to survey the pantry. Faith stood close by Melissa's shoulder. Lottie, George, and Jamie had wriggled through the press to fetch up behind Melissa and now peered around her.

Henry, craning his neck to look in from beside Dagenham, on Melissa's other side, huffed in disappointment. "There's only space enough for three between the shelves—and it needs to be our tallest three." Which meant not Henry.

All the company glanced at each other, then Dagenham lightly touched Melissa on the back, and she stepped forward. Dagenham joined her just inside the pantry and waved her down the room. From the rear of the group, Thomas Kilburn eased past the others and joined them. They were the tallest of the searchers.

Melissa faced the shelves on the left-hand wall below where Mrs. Higgins had said the jelly molds had been. Melissa couldn't see what was on the top shelf and could only scan the top of things arrayed on the next shelf down.

"Just like in the library," Dagenham said. "I'll search the top two shelves while you take the other three."

Melissa nodded and started searching. She and Dagenham, working side by side, started at the far end of the pantry, and Kilburn started from the end closest to the door; they concentrated on the left-hand shelves. Melissa and Dagenham covered more ground than Kilburn, who had to search all five shelves. When they met, they looked at each other, then his tone flat, Dagenham stated, "Nothing."

Those gathered about the pantry's door shifted restlessly.

The three in the pantry exchanged a glance, then as one, they turned to the right-hand shelves. Melissa walked the two steps back to the end of the space, and Dagenham followed, and they started diligently searching again.

Melissa didn't want to think that they might not find the book or of what their next step ought to be, given they knew the book had been at the Hall and hadn't left the house—

Dagenham made a strangled sound. Melissa looked up to see him push aside various packets and reach to the back of the second-highest shelf.

When he drew back, he was holding a book—one with a dull red cover with a black design and black lettering—in his hands.

He stared almost reverently at it, then he looked at her and held out his find. "Is this it?"

Melissa took the book between her hands. She didn't dare look up, into Dagenham's eyes—courtesy of the confines of the pantry, they were far too close. She had to turn the book around to be certain of the ornate lettering on the cover. Then in a firm clear voice, she announced, "This says it's *The Universal Book of Christmas Carols.*"

Unable to keep a beaming smile from her face, she looked toward the door as a cheer went up from all those gathered outside the pantry. Shifting so she could be seen past Dagenham—who, helpfully, put his back to the shelves—Melissa held up the book, displaying the cover for all to see.

More cheering and whoops erupted.

"Come out"—Henry waved them out—"and let us all see."

Kilburn led the way, followed by Dagenham, and with the book held high, Melissa triumphantly brought up the rear.

A near-carnival atmosphere abounded as the delighted staff joined the relieved searchers, and thanks and accolades and congratulations rained down on everyone.

"At least now we'll have a proper carol service," Mrs. Colton said.

After thanking Mrs. Higgins, the Coltons, and the rest of the staff for their help in unraveling the mystery and hunting down the book, flown on high spirits, the search party made their way back to the front hall.

There, they found the Swindons, who had heard the cheering and were waiting expectantly to have the good news confirmed.

Melissa showed Mrs. Swindon the book.

A smile wreathing her face, Mrs. Swindon nodded. "Yes. That's the one. *The Universal Book of Christmas Carols.*"

"Where, exactly, was it?" the major asked.

As a group, they explained where they'd found the book and speculated that Reverend Colebatch, wanting to lift down the jelly molds, had placed the book on the shelf to free his hands and then forgotten it and left it there.

"I suspect," Dagenham said, with a glance at Melissa, "that Mrs. Higgins or one of her helpers, all unable to see the book given the height of the shelf, had subsequently put packets into the space in front of the book, pushing it farther back into the shadows. They wouldn't have known the book was there."

Mrs. Swindon beamed at them all. "The Colebatches, the Longfellows, Mrs. Woolsey, and indeed, everyone in the entire village is going to be so very pleased."

"And relieved," the major added. "That was quite a black cloud looming on the village's horizon—not having our usual carol service."

There was, in fact, a great deal of relief mixed in with their exuberant triumph.

"So," Henry said, "what now? Do we rush the book back to Reverend Colebatch?"

Melissa was still holding the book. She studied it—and thought of something her mother had said when packing her off to Little Moseley. *One sign of wisdom is learning to make the most of whatever life sends one's way.*

So...

With sudden decision, Melissa looked up and scanned the searchers gathered in a loose circle in the hall. Faith was standing between Henry and Kilburn and, along with all the others, was smiling and watching Melissa expectantly.

Melissa stepped across the circle and held out the book to Faith. "I think you should take it—it was found here, after all. You can bring it with you tomorrow morning when we meet at the church for our last practice before the pageant—you can give it to Richard then."

Faith looked faintly stunned; she looked at the book, but didn't move to take it.

Melissa continued to offer the book and swiftly marshaled her arguments. "There's no point giving the book to Richard immediately. He would only stay up half the night playing the carols, but he doesn't need to practice—we all know he plays perfectly by sight. So tomorrow morning, at practice, will be the time to present the book to him. Then we can practice the replacement chorus for the pageant, and afterward, we can choose what carols we'll sing for the carol service."

Faith blinked and met Melissa's eyes. "You seem to have thought things out, but it was you—you and your cousins—who started the search for the book. It was you who led the search—even here, today. If you hadn't pushed on—"

"But it was you who helped to hold us to our purpose when we didn't find the book at the Grange," Melissa replied. "And besides, we'll all be there tomorrow to back you up and share the credit when you give Richard the book."

Faith was plainly torn. When she continued to hesitate, Melissa reached out, took one of Faith's hands, and pressed the spine of the book into it. "Trust me," Melissa said, her tone one of brooking no argument. "It'll be best if you bring it."

Melissa glanced at Mrs. Swindon, who was standing near.

Mrs. Swindon responded to Melissa's wordless appeal and stepped forward, replacing Kilburn at Faith's side. Mrs. Swindon patted Faith's arm. "I think you should do as Melissa suggests."

Lottie popped up beside Melissa. "Melissa's right—it's a good plan."

Faith tried to protest again, but Lottie's words prompted all the others to support Melissa's right to organize what next to do with the book, and finally, Faith had to give way.

At last, with the pale light of the winter's day fading around them, the rest of the searchers left Faith on the Swindon Hall porch. She still held the book of carols, cradling the precious tome, and the Swindons flanked her, smiling and waving the triumphant company on their way.

Melissa was very aware that, more or less throughout their time at the Hall, Dagenham had remained by her side; she'd been conscious of his taller, heavier, harder frame perpetually beside her. His nearness had impinged on her senses constantly through the hours; she'd almost grown accustomed to the effect—like a rippling caress over her nerve endings. Now, he matched his graceful, long-legged stride to hers—almost as long and definitely as graceful—as, with Lottie's hand in hers and Jamie and George in tow, Melissa walked toward the manor's gig, which a groom was holding farther along the gravel forecourt.

Henry, Kilburn, and Wiley ambled a pace or so behind, on their way with Dagenham to claim the two curricles other grooms had stationed facing down the drive in front of the gig. The three paused when, on reaching the gig, Dagenham halted and gallantly offered Melissa his hand.

It was prettily done without any overt show, as if it was merely a polite gesture from a gentleman to a lady.

She held her breath and laid her fingers across his palm. His fingers closed about hers—surprisingly gently, as if she was made of porcelain. She kept her gaze down as, very correctly, he helped her up into the gig. He balanced her until she sat, then he released her hand and turned with a smile to Lottie, who had hovered close.

His smile deepening, Dagenham bent and lifted the little girl up to Melissa's lap.

Melissa settled Lottie, then raised her gaze and met Dagenham's gray eyes. "Thank you."

He tipped his head to her, but didn't look away, instead lightly resting a hand on the gig's front board. "Actually"—with a glance, he drew Jamie and George, who had scrambled up from the gig's other side, George perching behind the seat and Jamie sitting beside Melissa and picking up the reins, into the conversation—"you mentioned a practice session at the church with Mortimer. Can I ask what that's in aid of?"

Dagenham's gaze returned to her face, but Melissa allowed Jamie, George, and Lottie to explain about Richard Mortimer's idea of a special guest choir to add strength and something extra-special to the carol service. "And now," Jamie added proudly, "we're to sing a cappella at the pageant, too."

While the others had been talking, Melissa had been thinking. Debating and weighing up whether or not to speak. But she owed it to the village, and Richard Mortimer, too, to make the most of what life had sent her way. As the others fell silent, she met Dagenham's gaze and said, "Mr. Mortimer has bemoaned the lack of trained male voices to balance the sopranos." She glanced at Henry, Kilburn, and Wiley, including them in her subtle invitation. "Faith is a strong soprano, you see, and Jamie, George, and Lottie sing that part as well, which leaves only me—I sing alto—and Richard, who is a baritone, on the other side of the scales, so to speak."

The four young gentlemen exchanged glances, wordless questions in their eyes.

Then Dagenham turned back to Melissa. She felt a frisson of expectation as he met her gaze for a silent second, then, his expression easy, he dipped his head and said, "In that case, I might look in at the church tomorrow morning. I'm said to have a decent voice—perhaps Mortimer can find a use for it."

"That's a jolly good idea," Henry said. "We'll be attending those events, anyway. Why not do our bit there as well?"

"Especially after joining the hunt and being in at the end," Kilburn said.

Wiley smiled and nodded. "I remember enjoying the carol service last year. A strong choir to lead it will make it even better."

Dagenham pushed back from the gig. As he retreated, his eyes again sought Melissa's, and he angled his head in a graceful salute. "It seems we'll see you at the church tomorrow morning." Satisfaction edged his smile.

Melissa was conscious of a fizzy, bubbling sensation in her middle. With what she hoped was a coolly gracious smile, she inclined her head to Dagenham, then extended the courtesy to include the other three gentlemen as Jamie set the mare trotting past their curricles and on down the drive.

She traveled the lanes to the manor in something of a distracted daze.

They'd almost reached the manor drive, and Jamie and George were arguing over the species of a bird they'd spied in the bushes, when Lottie twisted around, nudged Melissa in the ribs, then leaned close to whisper, "Viscount Dagenham's sweet on you."

Melissa managed to arch her brows in a show of being haughtily unimpressed, yet inside…

Inside, she was giddily, dizzily, really quite sillily smiling.

～

The following morning saw all of the choristers early to the church. Melissa, Jamie, George, and Lottie just beat Faith to the top of the rise. They waited on the porch while she parked the Hall's gig and tethered the horse, then George pushed open the door, and they all trooped inside.

Faith had wrapped the precious book of carols in brown paper to protect it during the journey; the five of them sat in the front pew, and she unwrapped it. The others huddled close on either side as she opened the book. Together, they started flipping through the pages, exclaiming over how many of their favorite carols were included.

The door opened. They all looked up and around.

But it was Henry, Dagenham, Kilburn, and Wiley who whisked inside and shut the door behind them.

They came hurrying down the aisle.

"We saw Mortimer at the bottom of the path," Henry explained. "He's just started up the rise."

Melissa and Faith exchanged a glance, then Faith suggested, "Let's take our usual places and be ready when he comes in."

The children led the way, filing past the organ and the harp, which was set immediately to the organist's left, to line up on the other side of the harp—Jamie closest, then George, and lastly Lottie, with her piercingly sweet voice, at the end of the row.

Faith went to settle behind the harp, but Melissa tugged her sleeve. "Later. You have to give him the book first."

Faith stared down at the book, then turned and sat on the organist's bench with the book held in her lap.

Melissa took up her usual position on the organist's right. She looked at Dagenham and the other gentlemen and waved at the space to her left. "I think Richard will want you four on this side."

They obediently lined up beside her, Dagenham, as usual, claiming the spot by her side.

They'd only just got into position when the door opened, and Richard entered. Having no doubt seen the carriages outside, he looked expectantly toward the organ. When he saw them all waiting, males and all, he smiled and walked down the aisle. "I take it we have some new recruits to our special guest choir."

"Indeed." Henry rubbed his hands together. "Although I'm not strictly a guest, I've never sung in the village choir, and like this crew"—with a wave, Henry indicated the other three gentlemen—"I have been trained to sing."

"We all sang in our school choir," Wiley informed Richard as he reached the end of the aisle and turned toward the organ corral.

Faith stood as Richard neared, revealing what she'd held in her lap. His gaze was drawn to the book she continued to hold between her hands. His steps slowed, and he halted on the other side of the wooden railing.

Faith drew in a breath and held out the book. "*The Universal Book of Christmas Carols*. We found it."

For several seconds, Richard simply stared, then he came around the railing, accepted the book from Faith's hands, stared at it for a second more, then simply said, "Thank God."

He slumped onto the organist's bench. For a moment he appeared lost for words, then he exhaled long and hard and said, "And my thanks to all of you. This…is *such* a relief."

He couldn't seem to drag his eyes from the book. A second later, he was flipping through it, scanning the contents. "Good." He turned more pages and paused, then with rising excitement in his voice, exclaimed, "Excellent!"

They allowed him a minute more to leaf through the book, then Jamie prompted, "So what do you think?"

Richard paused in his flicking and looked at Jamie. Then he extended his glance to all three children, and to Faith, now seated behind the harp. Then he swiveled on the bench and looked at Melissa, Dagenham, Henry, Kilburn, and Wiley. Then Richard smiled in a way he hadn't for months and months—with all his heart and soul.

"I think," he said, "that now that I have this book, which includes all the music we could possibly need, and a decent choir of talented voices, that we, together, will put on a carol service that Little Moseley will never forget."

The passion in his voice fired theirs. Spontaneously and in unison, they all cheered.

Richard took in their eager faces, all glowing with commitment and enthusiasm, and felt his own commitment to their plainly shared goal harden even as his enthusiasm swelled. "Right, then. Let's get cracking." He surveyed the four new additions. "I believe the first task on our list has to be settling you four into place. So!" He swung to the organ and started it up, then nodded at the young men. "Scales."

The others sang, too, and Richard listened, picking out each voice, noting range and tone. Sorting through them didn't take long, then he stopped playing and directed them into the correct positions to best blend their voices. Dagenham was possessed of a lovely rich tenor; Richard left him next to Melissa. Henry and Kilburn were baritones. Richard waved them into a second line behind Melissa and Dagenham, adjusting the positions of the two in front so Richard could see the two behind. George Wiley, who was, somewhat surprisingly, a resonant bass, Richard placed at the end of the line beyond Kilburn.

Richard surveyed that side of his choir with unexpected satisfaction, then turned to where Faith sat, with Jamie, George, and Lottie lined up beside her. "Although there are fewer of you, your voices should easily rise above the harmony of the others. You won't need to sing with any more strength than you usually do. Don't strain."

The three children nodded soberly.

Richard suppressed a smile, then his eyes met Faith's. He saw her happiness—that they'd found the book and could now forge ahead to give the villagers the best performances they'd ever heard—and in that moment, he realized he had never been so simply happy.

More than anything else, because he was sharing the moment, the experience—the satisfaction—with her.

He blinked and forced himself back to the task at hand. "Very well. Now we're organized and your voices are warm, let's start with the first chorus for the a cappella performance at the pageant tomorrow morning. I propose we get that polished to perfection, then move on to the Christmas triumphal chorus from the book—that, we'll need to go through in detail and get each part correct and working together." He looked to either side and saw nothing in their faces but eagerness. "Given how much we have to get through today, I suggest we put off choosing our pieces for the carol service until tomorrow. The pageant, I'm told, begins at eleven o'clock on the village green—we can gather here at ten o'clock as usual, choose our carols, then warm up, run through the a cappella pieces, then walk across in good time for our performance." It was helpful that the village green was located just north of the church.

Richard paused, but sensed from his choristers nothing but impatience to get on with his agenda. He smiled and focused on the newcomers. "Gentlemen, if you would merely listen the first time through, we'll then work on your parts before blending all together." He put his fingers to the keys, saw Melissa draw in a breath—then he played, and his established choir sang like angels.

From the rear of the church, in the shadows about the door, Therese watched and listened and allowed a satisfied smile to curve her lips.

Remaining still and silent—unobserved—she drank in all she could see.

The interaction between Faith, behind her harp, and Richard Mortimer, with his gaze flicking frequently to her face, was nothing short of inspiring, a testament to what might be between them. With any luck, that seed was now so well planted and nurtured, it would bloom without further ado.

While that result was pleasing, evaluating the romance between Faith and Richard Mortimer was not why Therese was there. Lottie—whether innocently or deliberately, Therese couldn't be sure—had mentioned that Melissa had a beau.

Therese had noticed a glow in Melissa's cheeks, but had put it down to pleasure over her successful role in leading the search for the book of carols. Lottie's comment, however, had jarred Therese to focused awareness, and she'd realized that Melissa was also showing signs of distraction.

The sort of distraction that, in a girl of Melissa's age, as Lottie had observed, usually meant only one thing.

As Therese couldn't imagine Melissa developing a tendre for any of the villagers or any of the staff at the surrounding houses, much less for the rector of East Wellow, that had left Henry and his visitors.

Now, as with her old eyes narrowed, she watched the interactions taking place between the choristers in the pauses between the songs, she realized just whom Lottie had identified as Melissa's unexpected beau.

"Well, well," Therese whispered. Relaxing, she considered the prospect, then lightly arched her brows. It would be interesting to see if anything came of a first love of such standing.

With the question of Melissa's would-be beau's identity resolved, Therese shifted her attention to the music swelling and rolling through the church. The organ and the harp blended perfectly, the former played with superb and unerring touch, the latter with responsive feeling. And above both instruments, the voices swooped and soared, fell and sighed and thundered and rumbled, weaving an evocative aural tapestry.

Therese remained until she sensed the hour's practice drawing to a close. Choosing a moment when the choir was distracted, she eased the church door open and slipped outside. On the porch, she paused, then she smiled and set out to cross the graveyard to the vicarage—to bear tidings of great joy to the Colebatches.

CHAPTER 11

$\mathcal{F}$aith had never before experienced a village festival quite like the Little Moseley Christmas pageant. It seemed that everyone in the village and all the surrounding farms had made their way to the village green, eager to watch the children's re-enactment of the Nativity and enjoy a few hours of celebration in company with their neighbors.

"I suppose," she said to Richard, close beside her as they eased their way through the throng, "in this season, there's not so much to do on the farms, and they can spare the time to cheer on their offspring."

Richard huffed in agreement. "And the day's fine, thank goodness."

The heavens had chosen to cooperate, and the sun shone palely from a clear, ice-blue sky. Everyone was rugged up against the chill carried on the crisp air, but the absence of wind and clouds definitely contributed to the crowd's smiles and the good-humored atmosphere.

The focal point for the massed villagers was the makeshift stable to which Mary and Joseph would soon come and in which the Christ Child would be laid in the manger and visited by various shepherds, animals, and the three kings.

The special guest choir was to supply the voices of the heavenly host.

While Reverend Colebatch marshaled the children, Christian Longfellow, standing on a wooden crate, directed the crowds. He saw Richard and Faith approaching and waved. As they neared, Christian raised his voice to be heard above the hullabaloo. "We've staked out an area for the choir on the rise below the vicarage wall." He pointed.

Richard looked and nodded. "Thank you. We'll assemble there."

"Do you know your cues?" Christian asked as Richard guided Faith past.

"Yes," Richard replied. "Reverend Colebatch explained the program to us yesterday afternoon. We'll commence the first chorus as Mary and Joseph start through the crowd on the donkey, and the second when Reverend Colebatch reaches the end of his narration."

"You won't be able to see Mary and Joseph until they get closer," Christian said. "If you keep an eye on me, I'll wave when they appear, so you'll know when to start your first piece."

Richard nodded his understanding.

Faith wove through the crowd, denser on the rise, which afforded a good view of the stable. Her nerves felt just a little taut, tensed in expectation of the upcoming performance. Ahead, she glimpsed the others— Melissa and the children and Henry and his friends—already in the staked-off enclosure; they saw her and Richard and waved madly. Hendricks stood nearby. Although the choir had set off from the church in a group, the others had forged ahead; Hendricks must have spotted them and directed them to the improvised choir-corral.

"This is exciting!" Lottie chirped. "Last year, we were down there"— she waved at the seething throng before the stable—"and I couldn't see it all. I can see much better from up here."

"I wonder if the animals will run amok at the end," George said. "Like they did last year."

Jamie replied, "I heard Lord Longfellow talking to the farmers about being on hand to grab their animals at the end, so probably not."

From Jamie's tone and George's reception of his news, Faith couldn't tell whether the boys thought the new arrangements a good thing or not.

Regardless, judging from their expressions and the way the children jigged and Melissa and the four gentlemen shifted on their feet, every one of them was prey to the same nervy excitement that had infected Faith. She knew that, before a performance, such tension wasn't a bad sign, and indeed, after all the hard work they'd put in practicing, they had every reason to feel confident.

Yesterday morning's practice session had run late, and as they'd all been reluctant to call a halt, Henry had suggested that, after luncheon, they should continue working on the second a cappella chorus—the one from the book of carols—and all had agreed. Given they'd been expected at their separate homes for luncheon, they'd dispersed. As Richard's cottage lay along the route to Swindon Hall, Faith had offered to take him up in the gig, and he'd accepted.

The interlude alone, just him and her behind the plodding horse, had been...pleasant. A moment in time when they'd set aside music and spoken of other things—observations of the village and, for each, their plans for the coming days.

Richard had been waiting in the lane by his cottage gate when she'd driven back to the church at two o'clock; she'd laughed and taken him up again, and they'd beaten the others back to the organ.

Those moments alone with him shone in her mind and warmed her with their remembered glow.

But now, it was nearly time for them to sing; the rising anticipation of the crowd was palpable as all craned their heads to look back toward the far end of the vicarage wall around which, Faith understood, the children playing the roles of Mary and Joseph would come, Mary perched upon Christian's donkey and Joseph leading it. As aware of the approaching moment as she, Richard marshaled the choir into order, then waited, watching Christian, who, from his vantage point, was looking over the crowd's heads.

Then Christian turned, looked at Richard, and waved.

Richard faced Faith and the others. "Right, then. This is it." He raised his hands, one holding a thin conductor's baton, and looked at Melissa. "Ready?"

Melissa was the one who would sing the first note. Eyes wide and trained on Richard, she nodded. Richard gave her the beat, then she filled her lungs and started—and the others joined in, fluidly and faultlessly blending their voices into the swelling sound.

As one, the crowd turned to look at them, and smiles spread over every face. After several seconds, the collective attention swung back to the small procession that was wending its way along a path through the crowd that the Whitesheaf family worked to keep clear. The path led to the stable, and the choir's combined voices sang the couple and the donkey along.

The chorus came to an end on a high, sweet note—held by Faith, Lottie, Jamie, and George—then, at Richard's direction, the sound faded and thinned, until a profound silence engulfed the scene, and a shiver of expectation, of anticipation, rippled over and through the onlookers.

Even the choristers felt it; they exchanged glances, delighted to have elicited such a frisson purely with their voices, then, along with everyone else, they gave their attention to the re-enactment as, before the stable, Mary scrambled down from the donkey's back.

It was as though their music had spun and cast a magical web over the scene; despite the inevitable moments of high drama—when the geese took exception to a nosy lamb, and when Mary's sleeve got caught on the manger and she nearly dumped her child on the ground while struggling to get free—the underlying meaning of the re-enactment shone through, and when the full cast of children held their final pose and the choir filled their lungs and gave voice to the triumphal Christmas chorus, the uprush of feeling was so glorious it brought tears to many an eye.

Their voices soared and, at the last, blended in one powerful and ecstatic *Hallelujah*! The choir fell silent, and Reverend Colebatch stepped forward and, in the almost-eerie quiet, ended the pageant with a special benediction.

With smiles of delight on every face, the crowd milled, talking, laughing, and exclaiming, gathering children and beasts, and making much of all who had played a part. Many villagers made a point of fighting their way through the throng to congratulate and thank the special guest choir and Richard most especially.

When he attempted to disclaim, Mrs. Tooks patted his arm. "But without you, it would never have happened."

To the choristers' delight, the comment left Richard with nothing to say.

A few minutes later, after conferring and agreeing to meet later that afternoon to start practicing for the carol service, the choir dispersed, the members moving into the crowd to find and talk to others. It was going on for noon, and the sun continued to shine, albeit weakly; no one was in any hurry to quit the green.

As the others wandered off, Faith found Richard by her side.

"I think I spied your uncle and aunt over there." He pointed to the other side of the crowd.

Faith glanced in that direction, then returned her gaze to his face.

He was looking at her. He met her eyes…

In that instant, Faith realized that, after years of thinking love had passed her by, she'd finally started to believe—in her heart, she'd finally started to hope—that at last, she'd found a gentleman she could trust. A gentleman who saw past her spectacles and recognized and valued the person she was.

A truly estimable gentleman in every way.

She smiled and didn't care if her feelings showed in her eyes. "Thank you," she said. "I'd best find my way to them."

Immediately, he offered his arm. "Allow me." His eyes said much more—spoke of much more—than merely escorting her across the green.

Faith smiled and laid her hand on his sleeve, and Richard guided her down the rise.

Richard was amazed at the intensity of the hopeful anticipation that surged within him. He couldn't recall the last time he'd felt so positive about his life, so eager to go forward.

Having Faith Collison on his arm—having her look at him with gentle encouragement and seeing the support he always seemed to find in the soft green of her eyes—was, he knew, a large part of what drove that wonderfully uplifting feeling. Doubtless, the echoes of their performance bolstered the emotion; they'd done remarkably well. In his humble opinion, their performance had been worthy of St. Martin-in-the-Fields or even King's College in Cambridge.

While he guided Faith through the joyful crowd, with he and she stopping and being stopped every yard or so by someone wanting to congratulate them and tell them of how moving they'd found the choir's performance, or when they met a child they wished to congratulate and encourage in turn, he debated taking the risk of telling Faith all.

He had never been so drawn to a lady—indeed, to any other person. Her practical, no-nonsense style combined with her instinctively caring personality attracted him on a level deeper than the norm and with a power he couldn't deny. With her by his side, he felt complete and, being so, that he could take on any challenge and win.

Even the challenge awaiting him—the one he'd run from.

Perhaps he'd been meant to run—to take refuge there, in Little Moseley, so he would meet Faith and find his salvation.

Those who believed in Fate would certainly deem that likely.

But if he told her all, what would she think?

How would she respond?

What would she say or feel about him once she learned that he'd deceived her and, indeed, the whole village?

Admittedly, he hadn't truly lied, but he'd certainly been guilty of omissions.

Major omissions.

Meaningful omissions.

When Faith learned who he truly was and of the duties awaiting him...

Would she turn from him, or would she understand and at least give him a chance to prove himself?

He should make a decision soon, but luckily, both he and Faith were fixed in Little Moseley for the immediate future. The carol service was looming, and—together with the members of his quite amazing special guest choir—he wanted to make the occasion and their performance the very best it could be. A gift to all in the village who had accepted him so welcomingly.

At the thought of his time in the village coming to an end—as it inevitably would—the specter of his family and all else he'd left behind rose in his mind. Returning would be another hurdle—one he wasn't all that well equipped to handle.

What would his family say when he informed them that Faith was his chosen bride?

Richard paused for an instant among the happy, chattering villagers. A chill passed over him as if a cloud had crossed before the sun, but when he looked up, the sky remained clear.

Then Faith tugged his sleeve.

He looked down, into her glowing eyes and joyful face.

"Uncle Horace is over there, speaking with Lord Longfellow." Faith waved to their left, then tipped her head as if sensing he'd been thinking of other things and more gently said, "We should join them."

He banished all thoughts of his family and returned her smile—returned his mind to enjoying the day. "Yes." He closed his hand over hers on his sleeve. "Let's see what they thought of our performance."

Therese passed slowly, regally, through the crowd. Despite the gentle, almost-vague smile on her lips, she was watching, listening, and observing intently.

In many ways, for her, Little Moseley and its inhabitants now featured as an alternate society, one she visited from autumn to late winter before she returned to the hothouse of the ton. She was who she was; she'd been a grande dame for most of her life, and while she probably could rein in the associated impulse to meddle in people's lives, she didn't really see why she should.

She always acted in the best interests of those involved.

Of course, her attention was even more intently engaged when it was family she had in her sights.

She glimpsed Melissa and Dagenham through the crowd and paused to take covert stock. Henry, Kilburn, and Wiley were part of the group, and, Therese noted with amused approval, Lottie was holding firmly to Melissa's hand. Therese's younger granddaughter was looking up, watching the interplay between Melissa and Dagenham—watching Dagenham especially—indeed, as acutely as Therese herself.

She had met Dagenham on and off since his infancy; her gaze resting on him, she had to admit that she'd never seen him so...not shy—never that—but unsure of himself. Cautious and wary of putting a foot wrong— yes, that was it. Interesting. And, she suspected, rather revealing.

Melissa, in contrast, was as cool as a cucumber, quietly assured in the way she responded to Dagenham and the others—always appropriately and with not the slightest hint of encouragement thrown Dagenham's way.

Naturally, her apparent imperviousness was the equivalent of issuing a challenge to Dagenham; regardless of whether that was Melissa's intention, he appeared to be growing ever more fixated on her.

And in Therese's expert opinion, that was even *more* interesting.

She should probably inform Henrietta—Melissa's mother—of the unexpected acquaintance. Nothing might come of it, and indeed, nothing could come of it for years yet, not until Melissa was considerably older, but there was no denying that for a young lady like Melissa, Viscount Dagenham, heir to the Earl of Carsely, would be a perfectly acceptable, not to say quite brilliant, match.

Imagining Henrietta's reaction to such news, Therese smiled and moved on through the crowd. She was keen to assess the status of the budding romance between Faith and Richard Mortimer; she finally spotted the pair chatting with the major and Christian Longfellow.

She paused some yards away, screened by the bodies passing between her and the group as the villagers started slowly returning to their homes and businesses. The pageant had been a huge success with nary a major glitch, and most had been inclined to linger and wallow in the associated glow.

Therese studied the way Richard Mortimer stood with Faith's hand anchored beneath his on his sleeve. Studied the way he angled his head and gazed at Faith as she responded to Horace's and Christian's comments.

In particular, Therese noted the glow in Faith's face and the quick glances she directed at Richard, meeting his gaze.

All in all, matters between the pair appeared to be progressing smoothly. Therese could see no reason to interfere; with luck, all would proceed in the customary fashion, and soon, Richard would be calling at Swindon Hall to seek counsel from the major over contacting Faith's parents.

Therese was smiling somewhat smugly to herself when Sally Swindon halted by her side. Glancing at Sally, Therese saw that Sally's gaze, too, was focused on the young couple speaking with her husband.

"It will do, won't it?" Sally didn't shift her gaze from Faith and Richard Mortimer.

"Oh, I think so." Therese paused, then added, "We might not yet know a great deal about Richard Mortimer's background, but he is indubitably a gentleman, and his behavior speaks well of him. Other than his initial reclusiveness—which Faith has largely cured—there's little I've seen to fault."

Sally nodded. "My thoughts exactly." She met Therese's gaze. "Shall we join them?"

"Indeed," Therese returned.

Together, they negotiated the intervening yards. After being dodged by racing young Foleys from Crossley Farm and pausing to compliment Mrs. Mountjoy on her new hat, they fetched up between Christian and Faith.

Therese smiled at a beaming—thoroughly satisfied—Christian and thought how far he'd come since the previous year. The scars marring his face no longer seemed to impinge on his awareness, any more than they influenced the way others truly saw him. He was such an inherently commanding personality—one who commanded by character, as it were—that all others looked to him to take charge, and this year, he'd been the primary organizer of the pageant. She caught his eye. "You should be proud—this year's event has set a new and very high standard."

He looked mock-concerned. "That sounds as if I should commence planning next year's festivities this afternoon."

She laughed and patted his arm. "You'll come up with something even better now that you have the reins in your hands and have taken your team once around the park, so to speak."

Christian chuckled, and his gaze moved to Richard. "Mortimer's contribution was the standout addition."

"That was Eugenia's idea," Therese pointed out. "You will have to thank her."

Christian's smile grew fond. "Oh, I will."

Sally Swindon was speaking with Faith, discussing their plans for the rest of the day.

Therese looked at Richard Mortimer and succeeded in capturing his gaze. "I wanted to thank you, Richard, for your exemplary work in forming and guiding your special guest choir. Not only was the performance evocative, not only did it contribute in a very real way to the village's enjoyment of the event, but your enterprise has kept my grandchildren occupied in a thoroughly unexceptionable way. I fear you, being a bachelor, will not properly appreciate the favor you have done me, but I do sincerely thank you from the bottom of their mothers' hearts."

Everyone laughed.

Smiling, Richard inclined his head in response. "I will only note that leading a choir of such talented people is, in itself, an honor, and the result was more their doing than mine. Such voices are a blessing, and it's to all the choristers' credits that they were willing to put those voices to use and to devote the time needed to practice." He met Therese's eyes. "I was impressed with the dedication shown by all of them."

She felt quite ridiculously pleased—almost as if they were her own children. Apparently, grandchildren could fulfill the same role. "I was speaking to Christian about the new standard he'll be expected to better next year. You, too, won't be allowed to rest on your laurels—we'll all be looking forward to your choir's a cappella performance next year."

A cloud passed through Richard's eyes; Therese saw it clearly, but then he blinked, and it was gone, and after the slightest of hesitations, he smiled—although now the gesture seemed a trifle strained. But "Indeed" was all the reply he made.

Therese's instincts twitched rather violently. Was Richard not expecting to stay in the village? That, she felt certain, was what she'd sensed behind his sudden reservation.

But before she could frame any probing question, Faith turned to Richard with a sweet smile. "Aunt Sally wondered if you would care to take luncheon with us. I explained that we had a choir practice scheduled for this afternoon, but we could drive back in the gig—we would be back in good time."

The warmth returned to Richard's face, then he looked past Faith to Sally Swindon and half bowed. "I would be honored to have luncheon at Swindon Hall."

Therese concealed the sudden whirl of her thoughts behind a parting smile as the group broke up—the Swindons heading for their coach with Faith still on Richard's arm, while Christian turned to deal with an inquiry from Bilson, the butcher, who had been in charge of dismantling the stable.

When Christian returned his attention to her, Therese briskly patted his arm. "I'm going to go and speak with Eugenia and see how young Cedric enjoyed his first pageant."

Christian grinned and pointed out his son and heir, cradled in his wife's arms as she stood beside Cedric's pram close to the opening in the vicarage wall that would allow them to skirt the rear of the vicarage and the church and reach the Grange stables. Hendricks stood nearby with Duggins the donkey's leading rein in his hamlike fist.

"I note that Duggins behaved like an old hand this year," Therese observed.

Christian snorted. "Perhaps the singing calmed his inner beast."

Therese laughed, waved, and started up the rise toward Eugenia.

Looking down as she managed her skirts, Therese found her mind swinging back to what, somewhat to her surprise, was fast becoming "the vexed question of Richard Mortimer."

The hesitation she'd sensed in him minutes ago—and the uncertainty that had raised regarding his commitment to the village and the post of church organist—had reminded her of all the questions about who he was to which she had yet to find answers.

Head down, she muttered, "No matter how exemplary his behavior and his outward character, as he presents at this time, Richard Mortimer, as the youngsters are apt to say, simply doesn't pass muster."

As she toiled up the rise, Therese concluded that the only explanation for all she'd seen and sensed in Richard was that he was hiding something. Quite what, she had no idea. "And I still find it difficult to believe he is villainous in any way. But what is his problem?"

Regardless, with his concern over the carol service resolved and that weight lifted from his shoulders, he and Faith seemed to be growing ever closer...

Therese absolved Richard of any intention to hurt Faith in any degree whatsoever. Yet… "I do hope," she murmured beneath her breath, "that he knows what he's doing."

The truth was that, in the matter of Richard Mortimer, she was honestly unsure whether she needed to be concerned—whether she needed to take a more definite hand in his and Faith's evolving romance. For Therese, when it came to promoting desirable marriages, uncertainty was an unusual and unwelcome feeling.

Finally gaining the plateau where Eugenia was waiting, Therese set aside all thoughts of her "vexed question," released her skirts, raised her head, and went forward with a delighted smile to greet two-thirds of the product of her previous year's Christmas meddling.

The following morning, in something of a state, Mrs. Haggerty popped her head around the door of Therese's parlor to report, "I've just come back from the shops, my lady, but I'll have to go out again. I was planning on using honey for glazing the ham, but the children have raided my honey supply and made a honey-and-lemon drink—for their throats, apparently, so Mrs. Crimmins says—and they've left me only a smidgen."

Therese considered her flustered cook. As Therese had arranged to host a special celebratory dinner tomorrow evening after the hopefully wildly successful carol service, she felt somewhat responsible for Mrs. Haggerty's stress. Mrs. Haggerty was a perfectionist, a fact Therese and her guests appreciated.

Setting aside the letter she'd been perusing, Therese glanced at the window, confirming that the day remained fine. "I was intending to stroll outside and get some air at some point. There's no reason I can't go now and stroll in the direction of Mountjoy's." She grasped the head of her cane and pushed to her feet. "Will a single jar be enough?"

"Oh, thank you, m'lady!" Mrs. Haggerty gushed. "That'll allow me to get on with plucking the goose. And yes—one of Mountjoy's large jars will be plenty."

"Consider it on its way."

With a bob, Mrs. Haggerty rushed back to her kitchen.

Reflecting that a honey-and-lemon drink for her four choristers' much-used throats was arguably just as important as the glaze for Mrs. Haggerty's delicious ham, Therese walked to the bellpull to call for

Orneby to fetch her coat, gloves, thickest scarf, and bonnet. Judging by the way the branches were whipping, the breeze today was brisk.

After allowing Orneby to fuss and wrap her up in multiple layers of wool and to firmly tie on her bonnet against the breeze, Therese set off for the village's general store. She saw no reason to rush. Despite the season, the clear weather had left the drive and footpaths firm underfoot; she reached the lane in excellent time and crossed to the footpath that followed the lane north to the village proper.

A few yards along, she reached the entrance to the church drive. The voices of angels spilled down the rise and wrapped around her. She halted and listened, smiling as she recognized Melissa's alto and then heard Lottie's piping voice soaring over all. Seconds later, Therese picked out Jamie's and George's clear, boyish sopranos, blending well with Faith's more mature voice.

Dagenham's tenor was distinguishable, but at this distance, the other men's voices were a rumble.

And supporting all, the organ and harp laid down a complex, inter-weaving accompaniment that was rich beyond measure.

Therese smiled to herself and walked on. Sadly, the glorious sound faded rapidly, blown in the opposite direction by the brisk northerly breeze.

Therese had passed the village green and was nearing Mountjoy's Store when she looked ahead and saw a familiar face—one that seemed entirely out of place. The old lady—a few years Therese's junior, yet still old—was standing in the middle of the lane between Mountjoy's and Bilson's Butchers and looking about as if she was completely and utterly lost.

Or at a loss. Given who it was, Therese wasn't willing to guess which.

A carriage that was plainly the lady's was drawn up outside one of the cottages a little farther along.

The lady had glanced back in that direction; now she turned fully that way and looked north up the lane—away from Therese.

Therese continued on, then halted outside Mountjoy's and raised her voice. "Maude Helmsley—what on earth are you doing in Little Moseley?"

Maude swung around so fast she nearly toppled. She caught her balance, stared at Therese, then Maude's shocked expression dissolved under what seemed a veritable tide of relief. "Lady Osbaldestone! I had no idea I might find you here." Maude quickly approached and halted two paces away. She glanced around, then asked, "Are you visiting?"

"No," Therese said. "My dower house is here…"

She suddenly knew of whom Richard Mortimer reminded her—namely, the Helmsleys. Therese kept her eyes from narrowing and maintained an even tone as she asked, "But what brings you here, dear? You appear quite lost. Perhaps I can help."

"Oh, I do hope so…" Apparently recollecting to whom she was speaking, Maude suddenly looked wary. But after two seconds of internal debate, she sighed and met Therese's eyes. "You're sure to hear all about it in short order once the news gets out—as it inevitably will if we don't succeed in running the boy to earth and getting him back where he belongs."

Therese allowed her brows to arch high. "Boy?" She certainly wouldn't have labeled the man who called himself Richard Mortimer a boy—but perhaps that was part of the reason Maude had lost him. Assuming it was he Maude was searching for. "Who, precisely, are you looking for?"

Maude sighed resignedly. "The rest of the family and I have been trying to locate the new head of the junior branch—my nephew, Richard —and Totty Firbanks wrote to tell me she was sure she'd spotted him when she drove through Little Moseley on her way to her cousin's house in the New Forest."

Therese folded her hands over the top of her cane. "How old is this nephew?"

Maude compressed her lips, but then reluctantly admitted, "Richard is thirty-one."

"Indeed?" Therese's brows couldn't get any higher. "If you don't mind me saying, Maude, thirty-one seems a trifle old to be running away from home." Therese tipped her head. "Is he touched in the upper works or…?"

"Good God, no!" Maude stared at Therese.

Therese waited.

Again, Maude's reluctance to say more was excruciatingly clear.

With her expression revealing nothing more than polite interest, Therese waited for Maude to realize that she had no choice but to explain all if she wanted Therese's help.

Eventually, Maude softly huffed and said, "As you no doubt realize, by 'family,' I mean the Shropshire Helmsleys."

Therese nodded. The Shropshire Helmsleys were the junior branch of the same family that held the earldom of Montcargill.

"What most don't know is how very wealthy the junior branch is—not in land but in funds and other investments. My oldest brother, George, has done well by us all and grown the estate, as it were, significantly during his tenure."

Therese frowned. "George is still alive." She opened her eyes wide. "Or is he?"

"Oh, George is still there, sitting in Shropshire, but he's very old and feeble now, which is why it's us younger ones—my sisters and I—who are trying to find Richard."

"But why are you trying to find Richard? He's a grown man, and his older brother..." Therese saw a glimmer of light. "Ah—so it's true." She fixed her gaze on Maude's face. "Richard's older brother, Roddy—a profligate rake if ever one was born—was the idiot who cuckolded Lord Denbigh and the man Denbigh subsequently dispatched in a duel that has been as hushed up as a duel ever was."

Maude gritted her teeth and nodded. "Yes. Roddy died a week after the duel, and no one thought it right to lay his demise at anyone's door but his own. Truth be told, the family viewed Richard—who is a much more sober sort—stepping into Roddy's shoes as George's heir to be the silver lining to that dark cloud."

"Hmm." Therese had to agree. "So what went wrong? Why did Richard bolt—as I assume he has?"

Maude exhaled gustily. "We—the family—thought we knew Richard. He was always so much quieter than Roddy—indeed, he hid behind his flashier older brother and devoted himself to the study of music. He was a Fellow at Cambridge, you know. But after Roddy's death, Richard had to come home, of course. And then... Well, from what we've pieced together from the little the family's man-of-business—who seems quite devoted to Richard now—deigned to tell us, apparently, Richard discovered that George had let go of the reins years ago, and Roddy's depredations had made a sizeable impact, and although I gather there's still plenty in the coffers, things about the house and elsewhere are in a serious mess. However, if I understood Phillips—the man-of-business—correctly, he believes that the changes Richard has made should see all right again shortly. Consequently, I fear that money—the managing of and responsibility for it—isn't the issue that sent Richard fleeing." Maude met Therese's eyes and announced, "I suspect it's marriage, you see."

Therese's brows rose to new heights. "Indeed? How so?"

Maude paused as if to marshal her thoughts, then went on, "Naturally, Roddy's unexpected death acted as a powerful reminder of mortality, to George especially." She tipped her head in admission. "And on the rest of the family, too. We all depend on the estate for the bulk of our incomes, and if Richard was to meet with some accident… Well, other than my other brother, Harold, who is a confirmed bachelor now in his eighties, there isn't another heir. The estate would revert to the principal line after Harold's death—which might occur sooner rather than later. Given his gout, Harold might even go before George."

Therese narrowed her eyes. "And once George and Harold are gone, you don't believe the principal line—the earl, in fact—will continue the payments to you and your sisters."

Maude primmed her lips, then parted them to confide, "As you know, Cecil is the current earl, and we know he'll do right by us girls. But his son…" Maude's features pinched in disapproval. "He would cut us off without a farthing and laugh while he was doing it."

"I see." Therese did, indeed, understand; she'd recently had the misfortune to meet the Earl of Montcargill's only son, a spendthrift and gamester just waiting for his father to die to gamble away every last sou. "Sadly, I fully comprehend your dilemma. However, that doesn't explain why Richard fled his home."

Maude colored. "I'm afraid that might have been due to us—my sisters and I." She twisted her gloved fingers together. "We were so desperate to have Richard wed and start his nursery that we…might have pushed a little."

Therese eyed Maude. "Don't you mean that you and your sisters pushed rather a lot?"

Maude looked guilty. After a moment, in a small voice, she said, "We might have been a tad insistent—but *really*." Her voice gained in strength. "Richard's obsession with music to the exclusion of all else was utterly insupportable. How he could hope to find a suitable chit when all he would do was attend the most academic of concerts and spend all his spare time—the time he should have been strolling in the park or dancing at balls and chatting at soirees—playing music or meeting with other musically minded gentlemen, I simply do not know."

Therese studied Maude's now-flushed face. "You might as well confess—what did you do?"

Maude drew in a long, slow breath through her nose, then in a tone of righteous indignation said, "We organized a house party—it was to run this week. We invited the pick of the suitable, unmarried young ladies and their mamas. Everything was in train—all Richard had to do was come downstairs, look them over, and make his choice." Maude huffed. "But no. He vanished weeks ago—the day after we told him of our plan. I left my sisters to cope with writing to all our guests, claiming we'd had an outbreak of illness and putting them off, while I set out for London to find Richard and, if necessary, haul him home by his ear!"

Therese's gaze could not have been more chillingly severe.

Seeing it, Maude abruptly deflated. In an almost childish whine, she countered, "Well, what else am I to do?"

"For a start, you might reflect that applying such an attitude to a thirty-one-year-old gentleman who has, it seems, very capably organized his life until now might not be the wisest course, no matter the appropriateness of the outcome you desire." Therese paused, then asked, "Did he leave any note or communication?"

Maude sniffed. "Richard was always the soul of consideration—which is why we were so overset by his kicking over the traces. He left a letter with Phillips. In it, Richard wrote that he was leaving for a time to sort out what he wanted in his life—how best to balance our demands with his own wishes. By which, of course, he means music. He said—and Phillips confirmed—that all decisions that needed to be made for the next months have been dealt with, and there's no reason the estate can't function normally until after next quarter day."

Therese thought rapidly—of Richard and Faith and all that might be —while Maude again looked around. Eventually, Therese returned her gaze to Maude's face. "Where are you staying?"

"I'm expected at Totty's for the night." Maude waved to the north. "Her house lies east of Romsey."

Therese thanked the Almighty that the wind was blowing the music emanating from the church in the opposite direction. If Maude heard it, even she would guess...

Maude's eyes narrowed on Therese's face. "Totty was certain she'd spotted Richard in this village, and she's met him often enough to be sure it was him." Maude's expression grew suspicious. "Have you seen him?"

"As to that..." Therese paused, still considering, then slanted a knowing look at Maude. "I can assure you that Richard—who I don't believe I had previously met—has not sought refuge with me. However, I do know where he is, and"—she raised her voice to override Maude's demand to be taken to him immediately—"if you will do as I say, I'll arrange for you to meet with him."

Maude studied Therese, saw the resolution in her face, and somewhat grudgingly capitulated. "Yes, of course." Maude looked at Therese expectantly.

She nearly smiled in anticipation; it took effort to keep her expression unrevealing. "Meet me in this lane, outside the vicarage"—she turned and pointed at the sprawling house on the other side of the green—"at precisely ten minutes to six o'clock tomorrow evening, and I will take you to your nephew."

Maude looked at the vicarage, then at Therese. "You will?"

Therese inclined her head. "You have my word." Which, as Maude well knew, was good enough for kings.

Maude heaved a huge sigh. "Well, at least I've found him." She nodded. "I'll do as you ask."

"Bring no one else," Therese warned. "And to that end, I would counsel you not to tell Totty you might have found your errant nephew. Better you wait until after you've met and spoken with him to decide who you wish to know all."

Maude looked suitably aware of the danger. She nodded. "I'll keep mum until after I meet him."

"Good. And I would also suggest that you climb back into your carriage and head over to Totty's with all speed—were I you, as regards this village and its environs, I would play least in sight until ten minutes to six o'clock tomorrow evening. The last thing you want is for Richard to glimpse you and vanish again."

"Oh dear me, no." Maude bobbed. "Thank you for your help, Lady Osbaldestone. I'll meet you outside the vicarage as arranged tomorrow evening."

With that, Maude turned and started hurrying up the lane to her carriage.

Then Therese called, "Maude?"

Maude halted and turned back. "Yes?"

"I strongly suggest that, tomorrow evening, you wear a veil."

"Oh. I see. Yes, all right." Maude bobbed again and went.

Therese remained in the lane until Maude's carriage rattled off, then she arched her brows, spent two seconds in abstracted thought, then turned and entered Mountjoy's Store, intent on acquiring a large jar of honey.

CHAPTER 12

*H*aving laid her plans, the following evening, Therese was waiting patiently outside the vicarage when a heavily veiled Maude Helmsley came hurrying across from the Cockspur Arms yard, where her coachman had sensibly drawn in.

Darkness had fallen, but flares set along the lane and the path to the church acted as beacons; the wind had died, allowing the flames to cast a steady light and illuminate the way of the faithful.

Many villagers had already streamed past Therese to climb the path to the church, but a goodly number were still flowing, increasingly quickly, along the footpath, through the lychgate, and up the rise; rugged up against the icy chill, the adults smiling and the children excitedly skipping, all hurried to secure a seat or at least a good spot from which to watch and listen.

Maude glanced distractedly at the people moving past her, then, with her gaze, followed the line of bodies moving up the rise to the church. Halting beside Therese, where she waited, out of the rush, in the space before the vicarage gate, Maude asked, "What's happening?"

Therese gently smiled. "It's a village tradition, one that has great meaning for the villagers and those who live round about."

Maude caught snippets from a mother and two children as the trio hurried past, then Maude glanced at Therese. "It's a Christmas carol service?"

"Indeed." Therese picked her moment, gripped Maude's arm, and tugged her into the stream of people. "Now come along." Therese released Maude and tightened her grip on her cane. "I promised to take you to your nephew, and I shall."

Therese was well aware of how adamantly people could refuse to see a reality that didn't suit them; she had to wonder if Maude had ever truly seen the Richard that Therese was about to show her.

The church bells started pealing as Therese and Maude passed through the lychgate. With nods and smiles, others flowed around them as, two elderly ladies together, they trudged up the rise to the open church door.

Richard stood in the organ corral and looked out at the gathering congregation. The inside of St. Ignatius on the Hill was bathed in the golden glow shed by a great many lamps hanging from the ceiling and dotting the stone walls. Screens erected around the still-open front door shielded those inside from the cold that seeped in.

The swelling crowd was chattering good-naturedly, neighbor hailing neighbor, children laughing and grinning and taking in everything with wide eyes.

For his part, Richard felt more nervous than he could remember ever feeling. Admittedly, as a musical scholar, in recent years, he'd performed only rarely, and then only for an audience of peers and colleagues. He couldn't recall the last time he'd performed in public—and he knew this public had high expectations.

In his mind, he reviewed his preparations—his and those of his special guest choir. He'd practiced for hours alone, late into the night on both Wednesday and Thursday, until he felt unshakably assured that his playing of their chosen carols was and would be utterly flawless. Faith had been unstinting in devoting the hours necessary to marry the harp and the organ, and Richard harbored no doubts on that score, either. As for the choir, they'd exceeded his expectations of their commitment to the performance; in the wake of the pageant, they'd dutifully presented themselves for practice on Wednesday afternoon and had spent most of Thursday and this morning, too, rehearsing the nine carols they'd elected to sing— seven from the book of carols plus the two Melissa had earlier taught him and that they'd already perfected.

Perfecting the other seven had been an act of devotion in its own right.

Richard felt confident the choir wouldn't let him or themselves down, much less their avid audience.

Nevertheless, he still felt nervous, hope and the desire to deliver an amazing performance leaving a knot of nerves in his gut. On top of that, he felt humbled and a touch unworthy; he should have led the hunt for the missing book of carols himself, but in his head, he'd deemed finding the book the responsibility of the parish—of Deacon Filbert and Reverend Colebatch.

Melissa, Jamie, George, and Lottie—and Faith, Henry, and the other three young men who'd so readily joined the hunt—had taught Richard a valuable lesson in community, in what being part of a community meant, what belonging to a group entailed, and how one responded to a shared need.

Accepting responsibility for anyone other than himself was still new to him, still something he was finding his way with.

And family—the large extended sort—was, in fact, just another community.

Indeed, thinking of community, he also wanted tonight to be a rousing success for his special guest choir, each of whom had played a part in making the evening happen. He wanted the performance to be perfect for them, too.

With Melissa, Faith had been checking the tuning of the harp. Now, as Melissa returned to the other side of the organ, Faith came to stand by Richard's side and look out at their eager and excited audience.

He glanced at her face and let his gaze linger. During the past days of working closely with her, he'd realized that, like him, she was a musician at heart, but her station precluded her from ever taking any public stage—as was the case with him. He and she didn't just share a love of music; they also shared the constraints the stratum of society into which they'd been born placed on indulging that love.

Yet tonight…he noted the delighted smile on her face; she, like he, was looking forward to playing for those who had come with hearts and minds wide open to listen to their music. An audience so ready to appreciate their talents was musician's gold.

Just having her near settled his nerves. More, her presence made him feel they could conquer any challenge.

Faith glanced at him and met his eyes. "Ready?"

He nodded. "I am."

He glanced behind him and found all his choristers present. Lottie, George, and Jamie were clustered on the other side of the harp, while Melissa had joined Dagenham, Henry, Kilburn, and Wiley, who had been waiting in a group, quietly chatting, on the other side of the organ. The bells had been pealing for a few minutes now; soon, Reverend Colebatch, Deacon Filbert, and the altar boys would appear and walk down the nave.

Richard cast a last, sweeping glance over the congregation; the pews were full to bursting, and latecomers stood packed along both side walls and in the shadows at the rear of the nave. Then he drew in a deep breath and turned to face the organ and his choir.

The others had been waiting; they all looked at him expectantly.

"Time to get into position."

They quickly arranged themselves; he could sense that their nerves were as taut as his—that their hopes were as high.

"We all know the order we settled on. There are no last-minute changes." He met each pair of eyes briefly, then, in a voice that wouldn't reach the pews behind him, said, "We all know how much this service means to the people of Little Moseley. There are many here this evening who will only darken the church's doors once or twice a year, yet despite the cold, tonight, they're here. They've come to hear us sing and to raise their voices with ours. We each have a wish to give back to this village, to these people as a community. We each have a talent we've brought with us tonight, honed and polished. Collectively, we have the ability to deliver a great experience to this congregation." With his gaze, he swept the line of his choristers one last time. "We've practiced. We're ready. And now we're going to sing." His lips easing, without looking around, with his head, he indicated the congregation behind him. "For them."

They all beamed at him, then impatiently shuffled as Richard stepped around the organ bench and sat.

Any minute now.

From her position beside the organ, Melissa raised her head and peered down the nave.

Beside her, Dagenham murmured, "Reverend Colebatch hasn't yet entered."

"It won't be much longer," Henry said from his position behind Melissa.

"It better not be," Thomas Kilburn, beside Henry and behind Dagenham, warned. "Our audience is getting restless."

"So are we," George Wiley said from the end of the line beside Thomas.

Melissa swallowed a nervous giggle. She was so keyed up and knew the others—all the others, even Richard—were, too. It was a curious sort of camaraderie, this intensity of expectation in the minutes and seconds before their performance would start.

Before them, the church was packed to capacity. She saw many families, children on laps or tucked close to their mothers and fathers to allow others to squeeze into the pews. All the young faces, and many older, shone with excited anticipation.

In that instant, like a spring bubbling up, joy filled Melissa's heart; she was so glad she was there to be a part of this. That she'd helped find the book of carols, that she'd been a part of this choir, that she'd come to Little Moseley.

This—being part of an endeavor that brought joy and pleasure to others—was surely a large part of what Christmas was about.

Then the bells slowed and halted; the last echoes of their summoning peal died away.

A few latecomers scurried inside as Richard set his hands to the keys, and an expectant hush swept over the congregation.

Tugging Maude Helmsley with her, Therese slid into the rear pew on the left, into the seats that Mrs. Crimmins had saved.

They were just in time, having slipped through the door immediately ahead of Reverend Colebatch and his acolytes. Indeed, she'd timed their entrance perfectly; Richard had already been facing the organ, his back more or less to the congregation. There was no chance he had glimpsed his aunt entering the church.

She and Maude barely had time to sit before the notes from the organ swelled in the deep, opening chords of a processional, and the congregation rose as the two altar boys, each carrying a heavy candlestick, preceded Reverend Colebatch, resplendent in his robes, down the aisle.

The music surged and swirled, then, once the procession reached the altar, came to a resounding end, and facing the congregation, Reverend Colebatch raised his arms and bade all welcome before God to the service dedicated to His glory and in gratitude for His sending Jesus Christ to be the savior of all mankind.

Everyone sat. The reverend glanced at the organ corral, smiled, and turned back to the congregation and explained that, this year, they were to be led in their worship by a choir of special guests assembled under the auspices of the village's new organist, Mr. Richard Mortimer.

The name jerked Maude to attention; a second later, eyes wide, she leaned from the pew and peered toward the organ. After staring for a long moment, she pulled back, looked at Therese, and in a horrified whisper said, "He's the organist in a village church?"

Therese took in Maude's scandalized expression and quashed an urge to grin. "Wait" was all she said.

Reverend Colebatch rolled on, naming each chorister and paying special tribute to Faith on the harp, before explaining that certain carols would be performed by the special choir alone, while for others, the entire congregation would sing, led by the choir.

A familiar introduction played softly beneath Reverend Colebatch's instruction that the first carol, to be sung by all, was to be "Christians Awake!"

Therese smiled as, along with the rest of the seated congregation, she got to her feet; quizzing glass in hand, she quickly flicked through her personal hymnal for the correct page. Deploying her quizzing glass, she held the book up where Maude could see. Maude fumbled with her pince-nez, perched them on her nose, and peered at the page.

Then the organ swelled, and the harp joined in, and everyone drew in a breath.

And the most glorious delivery of the opening lines Therese had ever been privileged to hear rolled out from the choir at the front of the church. The congregation had come prepared to sing, and heartened and enthused, as one, they gave voice, and the sound expanded and filled the church. The volume was remarkable, the enthusiasm undeniable—sparked by the essence of unrestrained and confident joy coming from the choir; the result was powerful and moving.

That first carol—a resounding success—was followed by a riveting performance of "The First Nowell," sung by the choir in fine harmony. Faith's harp, rippling beneath and twining with the voices, lent an unearthly quality to the piece.

Therese hadn't expected to find herself captivated, yet she was. The music—orchestrated by Richard and created by Faith, the young men, and Therese's grandchildren—was evocative, compelling, and tugged at the heart. She was as enthralled as any when, after a stalwart rendition of

"Good Christian Men Rejoice" sung with gusto by all, Melissa's rich alto combined with Dagenham's tenor to weave magic into a hauntingly lovely version of "The Holly and the Ivy."

Blinking to clear her vision, Therese noted that all eyes bar hers were fixed forward, with lips moving in synchrony with the words as they floated over the congregation's heads and twined, rising to the rafters in exquisite harmony.

Compelling and achingly beautiful sound continued to lift the congregation through a rousing "O Come, All Ye Faithful," which was followed by the ever-popular "Sir Christmas," sung by the choir in multiple parts to the transparent delight of every child and every child-at-heart.

The congregation returned with a joyous "Hark! The Herald Angels Sing," only to cede place to a wonderfully evocative rendering of "This Endris Night" delivered by the choir, again in all parts, but with the youthful sopranos leading the way, anchored by Faith yet with the three youngest voices soaring over all, pure and strong and with a quality of innocent joy that pierced the soul of all who heard them.

And then, although it seemed just a blink since the first note had sounded, the final hymn was upon them, and Reverend Colebatch, with a thoroughly delighted smile on his face, invited the congregation to rise and join with the choir in singing as the final carol "Joy to the World."

Therese reflected that not only the playing but also the choice of songs had been nothing less than a tour de force.

The sheer exuberance that infused the chorus was extraordinary; it reached each and every one present, wrapped about their hearts and swept them into the arms of the season. The choir sang at the tops of their voices, leading the way, and the flawless playing of organ and harp provided unwavering support.

The power of music to lift up the soul had never been so clearly demonstrated, at least not in Therese's lengthy experience.

At last, the final, triumphant note rang out, then choir and congregation abruptly fell silent.

For an instant, no one moved or spoke while the essence of what they'd created thrummed in the air.

The moment faded, the magic dissipated, and Reverend Colebatch stepped forward and thanked everyone for their attendance, then he raised his arms and intoned the benediction.

And an experience Therese felt certain would never come their way again, not in all its splendors, was over.

Therese glanced at Maude and wasn't surprised to see an expression of wonder on her face—much like the one Therese was sure wreathed her own features, as was the case with so many around them. Also notable were the unabashed tears of appreciative joy that glistened in many an eye—Maude's included. For her part, Therese had thought to bring a handkerchief, which, damp, was now crumpled in her hand.

The music might have faded, but joy and unalloyed delight yet remained, reflected in the faces of the congregation as they shuffled from the pews and made their way up the aisle in Reverend Colebatch's wake.

Tugging Maude down beside her, Therese sank onto the rear pew and remained seated as the congregation filed past.

She didn't think Maude had taken her eyes from Richard for the entire performance, even though, from their position, the best they could glimpse was a partial profile. His concentration on his role—playing, conducting, and singing—had been absolute from the first note. It had been an impressive performance—that concerted focus—almost as if he was submerged in the music...or as if he had become one with it, a willing conduit.

The only time they had been able to see anything of Richard's expression had been when Faith had played a short harp solo as an instrumental break during "Sir Christmas." Richard had turned to watch her play; even from the rear pew, Therese had seen the softening of his features, the emotion that had invested his expression and, doubtless, had been shining in his eyes.

Faith, her attention on her strings, hadn't looked up and hadn't seen—but many others had.

Therese had glanced at Maude and confirmed that she had seen that revealing look, too, and correctly interpreted it, but as Maude had no idea who Faith was, Maude had elected to reserve judgment. Satisfied, Therese had kept her lips shut.

Now, however, with the full measure of Richard's true worth—his true talent—laid before her, Maude had been knocked back on her heels and was no longer sure of her footing. Therese felt certain she'd accomplished her aim; regarding Richard, Maude's eyes had been opened, and with any luck, Maude finally understood her quiet nephew, at least far better than she had.

Mrs. Crimmins had already excused herself and slipped past, hurrying back to the manor to assist with the upcoming celebratory dinner. Others, like the Longfellows and Mrs. Colebatch, nodded to Therese as they made their way up the aisle, saying they would see her at the manor shortly.

She smiled and inclined her head to them and waited to see what Maude would do.

Finally, most of the congregation had streamed past and only the stragglers and Richard and his choir remained; in high good spirits, the latter group were gathered about the organ, talking and exclaiming. Maude, her gaze locked on an as-yet-unsuspecting Richard, drew in a long breath, then exhaled and said, "Thank you. You were quite right to do things this way—I needed to see, to experience...that."

Graciously, Therese inclined her head. "Richard might be the head of the junior branch of the Helmsleys, but his talent isn't something he can or should deny. And nor should his family. As you've just witnessed, his talent is important in its own right—through it, through the exercise of it, he reaches people, and in a way few others can, he brings great joy to others. Joy that wouldn't exist did he not employ his God-given talent."

Her gaze still fixed on her errant nephew, Maude nodded. "Whether with ecclesiastical or secular music, his playing was always moving."

"Powerfully so." Therese rose and stepped past Maude and into the aisle. "But he—his presence—has been a boon to others in multiple ways." Looking over her shoulder, Therese met Maude's eyes. "Come—it's time you faced him."

Therese walked forward, and Maude clutched her reticule, rose, and fell in behind her. As Maude was several inches shorter than Therese and still veiled, Richard didn't realize who was following Therese when, as she reached the railing, he turned to greet her.

He smiled and half bowed. "I hope we lived up to your expectations, Lady Osbaldestone."

"You did, indeed—in fact," she said, her smile sincere, "I do believe you exceeded them. Significantly." She swept her gaze over the choir's faintly flushed and still-excited faces. "It was a masterly performance, and you are all to be congratulated on serving up to Little Moseley such a tour de force."

With a graceful dip of her head to Richard, she stepped to the side to speak with her grandchildren—leaving Richard facing his aunt.

Richard blinked. For an instant, he tried to tell himself he was imagining the face behind the veil, but then the lady's hands rose, and even before she'd put back the heavy gauze, he knew.

He felt himself stiffen, and all joy fled; his expression, which had softened with ecstatic relief, set in stony lines.

But undeterred, Maude reached out a pleading hand and almost tremulously said, "No, no, dear boy. You misunderstand—or rather, I saw, I heard, and now, *I* understand." She touched his sleeve, lightly gripped as if to shake his arm. "After hearing that wonderful performance, I finally truly understand what music means to you—and what your music can mean to others."

Faced with his closed expression and his utter lack of response, Maude withdrew her hand and straightened. Her features firming with resolution, she nodded. "And if you wish to pursue music in whatever way or form, I will stand with you and work to make the rest of the family understand, too."

At the edge of his vision, Richard saw Lady Osbaldestone direct a rather severe, expectant look at him.

Having fallen silent, Maude shot a vague but interested smile at Faith, who was standing beside Richard; he'd been speaking with her—delightedly reviewing their performance—when Lady Osbaldestone had approached.

A moment before, he'd been so happy, so flown on success, but now Maude's arrival threatened to jerk him back into the smothering reality from which he'd fled...

Something inside him hardened to steel, and his mind simply said *No*. No, he wasn't going to let the happiness he'd found being simple Richard Mortimer, organist for St. Ignatius on the Hill, slip through his fingers.

The happiness Faith—her mere presence—anchored inside him.

In that moment, he realized that only Faith truly mattered. Only she was essential to the man he wished to be.

He turned to face her and saw her return Maude's tentative smile with one even more uncertain. Faith, of course, had no idea who the strange old lady was.

But it wasn't Maude's identity that was crucial at this juncture.

Richard reached out and took Faith's hands—first one, then, drawing her to face him, the other. He held on to her fingers, feeling her clever digits return the pressure of his clasp, and met her gaze as, mystified, she looked up at him. He drew in a huge breath and confessed, "My full name is Richard Harold Mortimer Helmsley. I'm the head of the junior branch of the Shropshire Helmsleys—my cousin a few times removed is the Earl of Montcargill."

He saw Faith's eyes widen, saw the frown that started forming behind the soft green, and hurried on, "I was my father's second son and not expected to inherit, not expected to have to manage the estate. So I went to university and fell in love with music, and I've spent my days since as a scholar of musical history. But then, a few months ago, my older brother died, and as my father is in declining health, I effectively became the head of the house. My relatives"—with a tip of his head, he indicated Maude—"got a bee in their bonnets over marrying me off. They were so persistent, pushing candidates at me and insisting I give up music and devote myself to living as lord of the manor and marrying and begetting an heir, that in order to have a chance to even think, I fled my home. I wanted time to myself, time to decide what I wanted from life and what I should do, not just about marriage but about my first love—music—too."

Maude leaned forward and said, "Him fleeing was entirely understandable, my dear—you shouldn't hold that against him. I freely admit that we—the family—did not treat him well. We thought only of ourselves and not at all of him. Worse, we acted as if he was still the boy we all remember him being, and..." Richard felt Maude's gaze touch his face, then she concluded, "Well, he's not."

He ignored the interruption and waited until Faith returned her green gaze to his eyes. As he had from the first, he looked past her gold-rimmed lenses and spoke directly to her—the lady he knew existed behind those spring-green eyes. "I saw the advertisement for an organist in Little Moseley. I settled matters with the estate's man-of-business, rode away from Helmsley Grange, came to Little Moseley, and took refuge here." He drew breath, then said, "What I found..."

Briefly, he looked out at the near-empty church, where the echoes of the recent jubilant celebration seemed to linger in the air, then he brought his gaze back to Faith's face, to her eyes. "What I found was so much more than just time and space in which to think and regain my equilibrium. I found support of a sort I hadn't imagined existed. I learned"—he glanced at the others, at Henry and his friends and Lady Osbaldestone and her grandchildren—"so much about family and community—all things I needed to understand and assimilate now that I'm the head of my house and responsible for so many more people than just me." Holding Faith's hands, never wanting to let go, he spoke what he now knew to be true. "Little Moseley challenged me to be the man I could be—the man I should be—and showed me what I need in my life in order to live it successfully from now on."

Standing beside Melissa, with Lottie, Jamie, and George before them,

Therese watched along with the others—with Henry, Dagenham, Kilburn, and George Wiley—as, with his heart in his eyes, Richard stood before Faith, and the silence was so complete, a pin striking the floor would have clanged.

Oblivious to all onlookers, Richard gently squeezed Faith's hands. "I found you." He drew a tight breath and went on, "And you are what I want and need in my life, and I fervently hope and, indeed, pray that you can see your way to looking past my cowardly act of fleeing. It wasn't my responsibilities I fled from—I fled an attempt to dictate my life that I just couldn't accept. I don't want you to look at me and see a man who runs away from commitment, because more than anything else in life, I want to commit myself to you."

Therese realized she was holding her breath. The silence was profound.

Faith didn't seem to know what to say, but then she'd never seemed the sort to speak before thinking.

Richard's attention remained wholly fixed on her, and she was focused unswervingly on him.

Richard swallowed, then, his tone lower, almost pleading, said, "I know we've only known each other for just over a week, yet from the moment I saw you, I knew—I simply knew. In that instant, I recognized that Fate had handed me more of a chance at happiness than I had ever thought to have. And I don't want to let that chance pass me by."

He paused, then, his tone now firm and true, went on, "My highest hope, the one that trumps all others, the one that is most important to me now, is, my dearest Faith, that you can find it in your heart to see me for the man I am and accept my heart as, with unwavering devotion, I offer it to you, and that you will agree to marry me."

His gaze locked with Faith's, he raised her hands, first one, then the other, to his lips, then fluidly, he went down on one knee and looked up at her. "Please marry me, Faith, so that, together, we can make music and work in harmony in all the spheres of our shared life."

Therese's palms itched with the urge to applaud, but she kept her hands folded on the head of her cane and, with all the others, looked at Faith—at the other half of love's equation.

Faith felt the gazes of those around them, but only distantly. Her wits were awhirl, her mind struggling to navigate the conflicting emotions Richard's words had unleashed. Yet through it all, his gaze anchored her. Like a beacon, he held her steady and drew her to him.

She had learned to distrust gentlemen who concealed their motives; she had vowed never to marry such a man.

Richard wasn't who he had said he was, wasn't the mild church organist he'd pretended to be, yet did that matter? It seemed he'd had good reason, and the lady from his family—from whom he'd apparently fled—seemed to think so, too.

He'd explained, but without knowing those involved, how could she judge...?

Yet she knew him.

They might only have become acquainted and worked and played together over the past week, yet she'd seen the man he truly was—his abilities, his caliber, his devotion to the welfare of others—and of that, the fundamental framework of his character, she had no doubts.

She could believe in him, couldn't she? He'd offered her his heart, had said he saw her as his chance for happiness. For what other reason would he—the man he truly was—wish to marry her? He didn't need her dowry, much less her father's diplomatic connections. He didn't need anything she would bring him except herself—her intrinsic abilities and her music, her love of music that matched his.

She was thinking too much, her inner self whispered, because the most important thing wasn't conveyed in words or even deeds. It was carried in the warm softness in his eyes when he looked at her.

Carried in the gentle and protective clasp of his hands about hers.

She had always dreamed of seeing just that look in a gentleman's eyes, had always hoped to react to a man's touch as she did to his.

It seemed she'd finally found her man, and he was Richard Harold Mortimer Helmsley.

At the last, she looked inward and found what she had always hoped to discover inside herself shining bright and true.

Faith smiled, softly, gently. She turned her hands in his and squeezed his fingers. "I didn't know—I wasn't sure. Not at first. But I know I can believe in you—and to my soul, I believe in what I feel for you." She drew a deeper breath and tightened her grip on his hands. Her gaze locked in the blue of his eyes, she said, "So yes—I don't care what name you go by, I believe in the man you are, and I would be honored beyond measure to be your wife."

Richard smiled and whispered, "Thank you, my love," and it seemed to Faith that the sun shone upon them.

Richard rose, and the release of the tension that had paralyzed the onlookers was so abrupt, most spontaneously cheered, then whoops, laughter, and congratulations rained down on Richard and Faith from all sides.

Maude was beaming fit to burst, and Henry clapped Richard on the shoulder with a hearty "Well done!" Then all the gentlemen present insisted on wringing Richard's hand before paying their grinning respects to a now-blushing Faith.

Melissa and Lottie had been first in line to joyously congratulate Faith; both were smiling as if their faces would crack and all but jigging with delight. Even Melissa.

Once the rowdier elements had had their moment, Therese stepped forward and, with regal graciousness, congratulated the newly engaged couple.

In truth, she felt for them. They should have had the chance to seal their troth with a kiss, but of course, they couldn't—not with so many others looking on.

Later, she vowed. Despite the fact they were all overdue to adjourn to the manor for a festive and now-likely-to-be-wildly-celebratory dinner, she would find Richard and Faith a moment alone.

The others closed about the somewhat dazed couple—drunk on the promise of impending happiness was Therese's experienced diagnosis—and prepared to chivvy them out of the church and down the path to the manor where, by now, the other guests, including the Swindons, would be waiting.

With Therese's three younger grandchildren leading and the older fellow-choristers bringing up the rear, Richard and Faith surrendered and walked hand in hand down the aisle toward the door.

Falling in behind Henry, Dagenham, and company, Therese arched a brow at Maude as the other lady joined her. "You will be very welcome at the manor, too."

Maude met Therese's eyes, then simply, yet with profound feeling, said, "Thank you."

Therese's lips curved. She inclined her head, then, with her gaze returning to the scrum before them, admitted, "This time, I had a significant degree of help." Her gaze found Melissa, happily chatting to Faith, then Lottie, who was skipping ahead. Therese's smile deepened. "Indeed, believe it or not, in this instance, one might say that I played second fiddle."

Two hours later, Therese sat in the carver at the foot of her dining table and, with profound satisfaction warming her heart, surveyed a company overflowing with joy.

Now that Maude had met the Swindons and any question of Faith's suitability as Richard's bride had been comprehensively laid to rest, Maude had relaxed and, relieved and grateful, was proving a delightful addition to the company.

Not being blind, the Swindons hadn't been surprised by Faith and Richard's news, but Richard's true identity had set the cherry on their cake and left both Swindons in high good spirits over having such a desirable outcome to report to Faith's parents.

The Longfellows and the Colebatches were delighted to observe that Little Moseley continued to foster love and marriage, while Henry, Dagenham, Kilburn, and George Wiley were buoyed by the all-embracing atmosphere of triumphant success, and also very pleased to have been included among Therese's dinner guests. Consequently being on their best behavior, the four talked and chatted and engaged the other guests and, despite the temptation of the season and the high spirits infecting the company, behaved in such an exemplary fashion that Eugenia directed an amazed glance up the table at Therese—a glance well-laced with wonder. In response, Therese, her lips curved in a smile she wouldn't have been able to contain even had she wished to, merely inclined her head. In her experience, young gentlemen did, indeed, eventually grow up. More, she rather felt that these four, all of whom seemed to appreciate the influence of Little Moseley, were maturing nicely; for them, she had rising hopes for what the future would bring.

Mrs. Woolsey, dressed for the season in spangled red and green draperies, was thoroughly delighted for the simple reason that everyone else was; nothing more was required to make her evening a success.

Jamie, George, and Lottie, all seated toward the middle of the table, were bouncing with happiness. Not only had they contributed in a meaningful way to a carol service that would live long in the collective memory of Little Moseley but they also had another matrimonial feather to stick in their caps.

As for Melissa…

Therese allowed her gaze to dwell on her older granddaughter. Melissa was quietly beaming. She was seated next to Dagenham, who continued to behave toward her with a circumspection that, more than anything else, fed Therese's suspicions that his might be an attraction beyond the fleeting. Regardless, not only was Melissa smiling again, there was an underlying warmth to her smiles—a gentle happiness that infused her whole expression—that signaled inner confidence and that she was now looking out upon the world with curiosity rather than wary resistance.

It was hard to reconcile the uncertain girl who had arrived at the manor's door not quite two weeks ago with the settled, apparently contented emerging young lady who, with an easy smile, replied to Dagenham's latest sally.

Little Moseley had, indeed, worked its magic. Melissa had come out of the "difficult" woods and was moving ahead with her life.

Having Dagenham hanging on her every word was a happy bonus.

Therese directed her gaze across the table—to Richard and Faith, seated side by side opposite Melissa and Dagenham. Toasts had been drunk to the pair, and congratulations bestowed in copious quantities.

When the party from the church had arrived and filed into the manor's front hall, Therese had taken charge, overseeing the gathering of coats, scarves, hats, and gloves by Crimmins, then directing her guests into the drawing room to join those already waiting. By exercising those talents that had seen her declared a grande dame at an early age, she'd ensured that Richard and Faith were the last of the group left in the hall. Of course, they'd been staring at each other; Therese had nudged Richard's arm, and when he'd looked her way, with her gaze, she'd directed his attention to the mistletoe hanging above the dining room door, berries and all...

Then she'd turned and gone into the drawing room, half closed the door behind her, and left Richard and Faith to take advantage as they would.

When they'd finally joined the company in the drawing room, Faith had been becomingly flushed, and her eyes had held an added sparkle, and Richard had looked faintly smug.

Viewing the pair now—the future of the junior branch of the Helmsley family tree—Therese counted the outcome another job well done on the part of Little Moseley.

She was still mentally congratulating all concerned—Fate included— when Christian Longfellow, doing duty at the opposite end of the table, lightly tapped his glass with a spoon and called for order.

The chatter died away, and everyone dutifully looked up the table. Christian smiled at them all. "I believe it's time for us to charge our glasses"—he paused as everyone readily reached for theirs—"and drink to the wonders of the season."

He held up a finger to stay the overenthusiastic. "Wonders such as Duggins behaving himself through the entire pageant"—everyone laughed—"a remarkable happening that I can only attribute to the enthralling spell cast by the indescribably beautiful a cappella performance delivered from the throats of certain of our company." Christian raised his glass and, accompanied by "hear, hear" from the Swindons, the Colebatches, Eugenia, Mrs. Woolsey, and Therese, he inclined his head to the choristers. "Clearly your performance soothed the savage breast—it certainly distracted Duggins from the nefarious acts that I'm quite sure he had planned."

Smiles abounded, and the children laughed, then George, seated beside Faith, gave her, Richard, and Maude a brief summary of Duggins's efforts at the previous year's re-enactment.

As the merriment quieted, Christian went on. "And of course"—he raised his glass to Richard and Faith, then continued around the board, including all the choristers—"we need to give due thanks for our stunningly wonderful carol service—an experience that will long be remembered in the annals of Little Moseley. And as part of that, we must direct especial thanks to those who tirelessly tracked down the missing book of carols without which said wonderful service would not have taken place."

Christian again raised his glass, this time to Melissa, then Jamie, George, and Lottie. "You have the village's deepest thanks."

Many thumped the table, and hear-hears reverberated through the room.

Melissa blushed prettily, which made Dagenham stare even more besottedly, while Jamie, George, and Lottie looked distinctly pleased.

"And lastly," Therese said, raising her glass and taking over the toast, "we should give thanks for Christmas itself—for the season of love and the wonder, magic, and mystery of that emotion that rises in so many different guises at this time of year."

She looked at her grandchildren and raised her glass to them. "I give you love in all its many forms and in all its splendor."

All around the table raised their glasses high and exuberantly declared "To love!" and drank.

EPILOGUE

*F*ive days later, Therese spent Christmas Day surrounded by her family. Wrapped in warmth and laughter, she acknowledged herself at peace and deeply content.

Snow had fallen from the morning of Christmas Eve, but despite the increasingly treacherous roads, all her family had managed to reach Winslow Abbey before a heavy dump had made travel impossible. Therese, Melissa, Jamie, George, and Lottie had left Little Moseley on the twenty-second and had arrived in good order at the abbey on the afternoon of the twenty-third.

There were reasons the family chose to gather at Winslow Abbey regardless of the bother of traveling to Northamptonshire in deepest winter. Chief amongst those reasons was the abbey's sheer size; it could easily accommodate all the children as well as their parents without any fuss. A corollary of the size was the number of staff, and as Celia's children were the youngest, her staff were most accustomed to dealing with rowdy, boisterous, rambunctious youngsters—and given the right circumstances, all Therese's grandchildren qualified. To Celia and her staff's credit, Therese had never seen any member of the abbey staff seriously discomposed or even thrown off balance by any of the children's sometimes outrageous antics.

Yet to Therese's mind, the principal quality that made the abbey so perfect a place for hosting Christmas for a large extended family was the multitude of reception rooms. Although there was a formal drawing room and dining room, the family never used them—not even for their Christmas feast. For that, they'd sat twenty-six about the table in the family dining room, and even then, they hadn't used every leaf in the table.

Now, as the ladies all rose from the festive board, strewn with the detritus of a delicious and successful Christmas luncheon and, comfortably or not-so-comfortably replete, headed for the family sitting room, Therese reflected that the relaxed comfort of Celia's home was an oft-appreciated yet rarely acknowledged blessing.

The sitting room was large. Celia led the ladies in, and Therese sank onto the well-stuffed chaise while others surrendered to the embrace of the equally well-padded armchairs.

They'd left the gentlemen at the table, passing a bottle of an excellent French brandy that Therese's son, Christopher, the only one of her children still unmarried and who worked in some secretive capacity attached to the Foreign Office, had somehow laid his hands on—much to the delight of his two brothers and two brothers-in-law.

Therese had heard the children making plans, and most had scattered to other rooms in search of games or had scampered up the stairs to the upper floors to play hide-and-seek. Only the two oldest girls, Henrietta's Amanda and Melissa, had trailed after the ladies. The pair followed them into the room and made for one of the window embrasures. There, they perched on the window seat and, heads together, whispered secrets.

Celia, ensconced in the armchair beside the corner of the chaise Therese occupied, sighed deeply, then she looked at Therese. "Once again, Mama, thank you for having Jamie, George, and Lottie to stay again. They were absolutely set on returning to Little Moseley, and I have to admit that having them away made preparations here much easier."

Therese smiled. "Strange though it may seem, it was, indeed, a pleasure. They've learned their way about and have proved entirely trustworthy." She met Celia's eyes, and her smile deepened. "You've raised them well, my dear. You would have been proud of the way they comported themselves." Therese paused, then added, "They are very quick learners, and through their time in Little Moseley, they're learning still more."

"I hope so," Celia said. "But what did they get up to this year? I haven't yet had time to sit down and listen to their adventures."

"Well, once again, they were in the thick of things, searching for a missing book of carols. For various reasons, it was essential to find the book—which had been misplaced within the village—in order to be able to hold the village carol service, which is a long-standing village tradition." Therese gave a brief summary of the efforts the children, this year led largely by Melissa, had expended and their eventual success in locating the book in time.

The other ladies—Therese's oldest son Monty's wife, Catherine, Therese's second son Lloyd's wife, Margaret, and Henrietta—relaxed in armchairs about the chaise and idly listened, amused and entertained by the tale.

"And out of all that," Therese concluded, "we had a romance bloom and blossom between the new church organist, who proved to be Richard Helmsley although he'd been calling himself Richard Mortimer, and Faith Collison, the daughter of a senior diplomat."

"Collison," Henrietta said. "I remember him and his wife—he's with the Foreign Office."

"Indeed." Therese nodded. "And I must tell you that Melissa as well as Lottie proved quite excellent at matchmaking. Not that Richard and Faith needed all that much help—just a gentle nudge here and there—but Melissa and Lottie accomplished the required assistance with aplomb." Therese smiled. "I was exceedingly proud of them."

Henrietta looked across the room at her daughters, still sharing confidences in the window embrasure. Although Melissa had arrived with Therese and her three cousins two days ago, Melissa's father, Reginald, Lord North, had been detained in London and, together with Henrietta and Amanda, had only just made it to the abbey before snow closed the roads.

"I haven't yet had time," Henrietta said, "to speak with Melissa privately at any length." Henrietta paused, then shook her head in amazement. "I don't know what you did, Mama, but whatever it was, you've performed a miracle. Since we've arrived, Melissa hasn't glowered once, not that I've seen."

Therese allowed her smile to turn self-deprecating. "It's not me you have to thank, my dear. Little Moseley at Christmastime is a place that seems to heal inner wounds, scrapes, and scratches, and even despite themselves, bring out the best in people, then nudge and steer them along their correct paths in life. Specifically, their path to future happiness."

She glanced across the room at Melissa and Amanda; the girls were fully absorbed in their discussion and too far away to hear if she spoke softly. Therese looked at Henrietta and lowered her voice. "As for her glowers, I rather suspect that a handsome young gentleman whispered in her ear that she's much prettier when she smiles." Therese had, indeed, heard Dagenham do just that when, early in his and Melissa's acquaintance, Melissa had attempted to send him to the right about with one of her blacker scowls.

Indeed, none of Melissa's discouragements had worked, leaving Therese inclined to consider Dagenham more than just a handsome face.

Henrietta, of course, fixed Therese with a suspicious and wary, distinctly maternal look. "*Which* handsome young gentleman?"

Her gaze on Henrietta's face, Therese arched her brows, then tipped her head slowly from side to side, patently debating. Eventually, however, in the face of Henrietta's and the others' mounting interest, after a quick glance at Melissa and Amanda confirmed both were still distracted, Therese offered, "I wasn't sure whether I should mention it—not when it's so early in the piece. The last thing I would wish is for you to overreact and attempt to push or even nudge—which, I warn you, might well be dramatically counterproductive—but even without that, given Melissa's age, who knows what might come of it?"

"Come of *what*, Mama?" Henrietta fixed Therese with a look she hadn't seen in decades. "Stop teasing—who was it? And what was he doing in Little Moseley, anyway? It's a quiet country backwater, as you've frequently assured us."

Therese smiled, amused to see her elder daughter reacting as if she was barely out of the schoolroom. "I believe I mentioned that, last year, young Henry Fitzgibbon had invited four of his Oxford friends to spend the weeks leading up to Christmas at Fulsom Hall in Little Moseley. Despite various adventures of an instructive nature, overall, the four had such a good time that, this year, three returned to spend the weeks before Christmas with Henry at Fulsom Hall. Henry and the three assisted in the search for the missing book of carols. They also joined the choir and helped make the village's Christmas pageant and the carol service the best in living and even ancient memory."

When Therese paused, Henrietta prompted, "And?"

"And," Therese replied, "one of Henry's three friends was Dagenham."

Henrietta blinked. From her expression, she was rapidly consulting her mental list of ton families—a list Therese knew to be nearly as complete as her own.

The other ladies were similarly occupied, but Henrietta got there first. *"No!"* Her eyes widened, and she turned them on Therese. "You can't mean to say that Melissa spent nearly two weeks in a tiny village being squired about and danced attendance on by *Viscount* Dagenham."

Therese arched her brows in an arrogantly superior way as if to say, *Can I not?*

Henrietta's face lit. Delighted and intrigued, she leaned closer and said, "Oh, Mama—do tell!"

∾

Dear Reader,

I hope you enjoyed revisiting the village of Little Moseley in company with Lady Osbaldestone and, this year, four of her grandchildren, and reading of their adventure in the run-up to this Christmas of long ago.

Of particular note in this year's tale are the carols that the choir and congregation perform during the village's Carol Service. The carols mentioned are all known to have been sung in Church of England churches during that period. Many of the more evocative carols of today were not written until the middle of the 19th century, and so were unknown to Lady Osbaldestone and her brood.

Over the coming years, I plan to bring you more annual Christmas adventures from Little Moseley, featuring Lady Osbaldestone, her grandchildren, and the other characters who inhabit the village. Of course, Lady Osbaldestone being who she is, romance is never far away.

Meanwhile, 2019 will see the release of a new Cynster Next Generation Novel, *A Conquest Impossible to Resist*, in which Prudence Cynster meets her match, scheduled for release on March 14, 2019.

That will be followed by the second in the Cavanaugh books, *The Pursuits of Lord Kit Cavanaugh*, scheduled for release on April 30, 2019.

That will be followed by a special release on June 20, 2019, details of which are currently under wraps. Then to round out the year, we'll have the third volume of Lady Osbaldestone's Christmas Chronicles for you to enjoy in the lead-up to Christmas.

In closing, from me and mine to you and yours: We wish you a happy and safe Festive Season and a productive and prosperous New Year.

Stephanie.

For alerts as new books are released, plus information on upcoming books, exclusive sweepstakes and sneak peeks into upcoming novels, sign up for Stephanie's Private Email Newsletter
http://www.stephanielaurens.com/newsletter-signup/

The ultimate source for detailed information on all Stephanie's published books, including covers, descriptions, and excerpts, is Stephanie's Website www.stephanielaurens.com

You can also follow Stephanie via her Amazon Author Page at
http://tinyurl.com/zc3e9mp

Goodreads members can follow Stephanie via her author page
https://www.goodreads.com/author/show/9241.Stephanie_Laurens

You can email Stephanie at stephanie@stephanielaurens.com

Or find her on Facebook
https://www.facebook.com/AuthorStephanieLaurens/

COMING NEXT:

The seventh volume in the Cynster Next Generation Novels
A CONQUEST IMPOSSIBLE TO RESIST
To be released on March 14, 2019

The tale of how Prudence Cynster, Demon and Felicity Cynster's eldest daughter and adamant spinster, meets her match.

Available for e-book pre-order in mid-December, 2018

AVAILABLE NOW:
The first volume in Lady Osbaldestone's Christmas Chronicles
LADY OSBALDESTONE'S CHRISTMAS GOOSE

#1 New York Times *bestselling author Stephanie Laurens brings you a lighthearted tale of Christmas long ago with a grandmother and three of*

her grandchildren, one lost soul, a lady driven to distraction, a recalcitrant donkey, and a flock of determined geese.

Three years after being widowed, Therese, Lady Osbaldestone finally settles into her dower property of Hartington Manor in the village of Little Moseley in Hampshire. She is in two minds as to whether life in the small village will generate sufficient interest to keep her amused over the months when she is not in London or visiting friends around the country. But she will see.

It's December, 1810, and Therese is looking forward to her usual Christmas with her family at Winslow Abbey, her youngest daughter, Celia's home. But then a carriage rolls up and disgorges Celia's three oldest children. Their father has contracted mumps, and their mother has sent the three—Jamie, George, and Lottie—to spend this Christmas with their grandmama in Little Moseley.

Therese has never had to manage small children, not even her own. She assumes the children will keep themselves amused, but quickly learns that what amuses three inquisitive, curious, and confident youngsters isn't compatible with village peace. Just when it seems she will have to set her mind to inventing something, she and the children learn that with only twelve days to go before Christmas, the village flock of geese has vanished.

Every household in the village is now missing the centerpiece of their Christmas feast. But how could an entire flock go missing without the slightest trace? The children are as mystified and as curious as Therese—and she seizes on the mystery as the perfect distraction for the three children as well as herself.

But while searching for the geese, she and her three helpers stumble on two locals who, it is clear, are in dire need of assistance in sorting out their lives. Never one to shy from a little matchmaking, Therese undertakes to guide Miss Eugenia Fitzgibbon into the arms of the determinedly reclusive Lord Longfellow. To her considerable surprise, she discovers that her grandchildren have inherited skills and talents from both her late husband as well as herself. And with all the customary village events held in the lead up to Christmas, she and her three helpers have opportunities galore in which to subtly nudge and steer.

Yet while their matchmaking appears to be succeeding, neither they nor anyone else have found so much as a feather from the village's geese. Larceny is ruled out; a flock of that size could not have been taken from the area without someone noticing. So where could the birds be? And with the days passing and Christmas inexorably approaching, will they find the blasted birds in time?

First in series. A novel of 60,000 words. A Christmas tale of romance and geese.

RECENTLY RELEASED IN THE CASEBOOK OF BARNABY ADAIR NOVELS:
THE CONFOUNDING CASE OF THE CARISBROOK EMERALDS
The sixth volume in
The Casebook of Barnaby Adair mystery-romances

#1 New York Times *bestselling author Stephanie Laurens brings you a tale of emerging and also established loves and the many facets of family, interwoven with mystery and murder.*

A young lady accused of theft and the gentleman who elects himself her champion enlist the aid of Stokes, Barnaby, Penelope, and friends in pursuing justice, only to find themselves tangled in a web of inter-family tensions and secrets.

When Miss Cara Di Abaccio is accused of stealing the Carisbrook emeralds by the infamously arrogant Lady Carisbrook and marched out of her guardian's house by Scotland Yard's finest, Hugo Adair, Barnaby Adair's cousin, takes umbrage and descends on Scotland Yard, breathing fire in Cara's defense.

Hugo discovers Inspector Stokes has been assigned to the case, and after surveying the evidence thus far, Stokes calls in his big guns when it comes to dealing with investigations in the ton—namely, the Honorable Barnaby Adair and his wife, Penelope.

Soon convinced of Cara's innocence and—given Hugo's apparent tendre for Cara—the need to clear her name, Penelope and Barnaby join Stokes and his team in pursuing the emeralds and, most importantly, who stole them.

But the deeper our intrepid investigators delve into the Carisbrook household, the more certain they become that all is not as it seems. Lady Carisbrook is a harpy, Franklin Carisbrook is secretive, Julia Carisbrook is overly timid, and Lord Carisbrook, otherwise a genial and honorable gentleman, holds himself distant from his family. More, his lordship attempts to shut down the investigation. And Stokes, Barnaby, and Penelope are convinced the Carisbrooks' staff are not sharing all they know.

Meanwhile, having been appointed Cara's watchdog until the mystery is resolved, Hugo, fascinated by Cara as he's been with no other young lady, seeks to entertain and amuse her...and, increasingly intently, to discover the way to her heart. Consequently, Penelope finds herself juggling the attractions of the investigation against the demands of the Adair family for her to actively encourage the budding romance.

What would her mentors advise? On that, Penelope is crystal clear.

Regardless, aided by Griselda, Violet, and Montague and calling on contacts in business, the underworld, and ton society, Penelope, Barnaby, and Stokes battle to peel back each layer of subterfuge and, step by step, eliminate the innocent and follow the emeralds' trail...

Yet instead of becoming clearer, the veils and shadows shrouding the Carisbrooks only grow murkier...until, abruptly, our investigators find themselves facing an inexplicable death, with a potential murderer whose conviction would shake society to its back teeth.

A historical novel of 78,000 words interweaving mystery, romance, and social intrigue.

The seventh volume in
The Casebook of Barnaby Adair mystery-romances
THE MURDER AT MANDEVILLE HALL

#1 NYT-bestselling author Stephanie Laurens brings you a tale of unexpected romance that blossoms against the backdrop of dastardly murder.

On discovering the lifeless body of an innocent ingénue, a peer attending a country house party joins forces with the lady-amazon sent to fetch the victim safely home in a race to expose the murderer before Stokes, assisted by Barnaby and Penelope, is forced to allow the guests, murderer included, to decamp.

Well-born rakehell and head of an ancient family, Alaric, Lord Carradale, has finally acknowledged reality and is preparing to find a bride. But loyalty to his childhood friend, Percy Mandeville, necessitates attending Percy's annual house party, held at neighboring Mandeville Hall. Yet despite deploying his legendary languid charm, by the second evening of the week-long event, Alaric is bored and restless.

Escaping from the soirée and the Hall, Alaric decides that as soon as he's free, he'll hie to London and find the mild-mannered, biddable lady he believes will ensure a peaceful life. But the following morning, on walking through the Mandeville Hall shrubbery on his way to join the other guests, he comes upon the corpse of a young lady-guest.

Constance Whittaker accepts that no gentleman will ever offer for her —she's too old, too tall, too buxom, too headstrong...too much in myriad ways. Now acting as her grandfather's agent, she arrives at Mandeville Hall to extricate her young cousin, Glynis, who unwisely accepted an invitation to the reputedly licentious house party.

But Glynis cannot be found.

A search is instituted. Venturing into the shrubbery, Constance discovers an outrageously handsome aristocrat crouched beside Glynis's lifeless form. Unsurprisingly, Constance leaps to the obvious conclusion.

Luckily, once the gentleman explains that he'd only just arrived, commonsense reasserts itself. More, as matters unfold and she and Carradale have to battle to get Glynis's death properly investigated, Constance discovers Alaric to be a worthy ally.

Yet even after Inspector Stokes of Scotland Yard arrives and takes charge of the case, along with his consultants, the Honorable Barnaby Adair and his wife, Penelope, the murderer's identity remains shrouded in mystery, and learning why Glynis was killed—all in the few days before the house party's guests will insist on leaving—tests the resolve of all concerned. Flung into each other's company, fiercely independent though Constance is, unsusceptible though Alaric is, neither can deny the connection that grows between them.

Then Constance vanishes.

Can Alaric unearth the one fact that will point to the murderer before the villain rips from the world the lady Alaric now craves for his own?

A historical novel of 75,000 words interweaving romance, mystery, and murder.

ALSO RECENTLY RELEASED:

The first volume in THE CAVANAUGHS
THE DESIGNS OF LORD RANDOLPH CAVANAGH

#1 New York Times *bestselling author Stephanie Laurens returns with a new series that captures the simmering desires and intrigues of early Victorians as only she can. Ryder Cavanaugh's step-siblings are determined to make their own marks in London society. Seeking fortune and passion, THE CAVANAUGHS will delight readers with their bold exploits.*

An independent nobleman
Lord Randolph Cavanaugh is loyal and devoted—but only to family. To the rest of the world he's aloof and untouchable, a respected and driven entrepreneur. But Rand yearns for more in life, and when he travels to Buckinghamshire to review a recent investment, he discovers a passionate woman who will challenge his rigid self-control...

A determined lady
Felicia Throgmorton intends to keep her family afloat. For decades, her father was consumed by his inventions and now, months after his death, with their finances in ruins, her brother insists on continuing their father's tinkering. Felicia is desperate to hold together what's left of the estate. Then she discovers she must help persuade their latest investor that her father's follies are a risk worth taking...

Together—the perfect team
Rand arrives at Throgmorton Hall to discover the invention on which he's staked his reputation has exploded, the inventor is not who he expected, and a fiercely intelligent woman now holds the key to his future success. But unflinching courage in the face of dismaying hurdles is a trait they share, and Rand and Felicia are forced to act together against ruthless foes to protect everything they hold dear.

ABOUT THE AUTHOR

#1 *New York Times* bestselling author Stephanie Laurens began writing romances as an escape from the dry world of professional science. Her hobby quickly became a career when her first novel was accepted for publication, and with entirely becoming alacrity, she gave up writing about facts in favor of writing fiction.

All Laurens's works to date are historical romances, ranging from medieval times to the mid-1800s, and her settings range from Scotland to India. The majority of her works are set in the period of the British Regency. Laurens has published more than 70 works of historical romance, including 39 *New York Times* bestsellers. Laurens has sold more than 20 million print, audio, and e-books globally. All her works are continuously available in print and e-book formats in English worldwide, and have been translated into many other languages. An international bestseller, among other accolades, Laurens has received the Romance Writers of America® prestigious RITA® Award for Best Romance Novella 2008 for *The Fall of Rogue Gerrard.*

Laurens's continuing novels featuring the Cynster family are widely regarded as classics of the historical romance genre. Other series include the *Bastion Club Novels*, the *Black Cobra Quartet*, and the *Casebook of Barnaby Adair Novels*. All her previous works remain available in print and all e-book formats.

For information on all published novels and on upcoming releases and updates on novels yet to come, visit Stephanie's website: www.stephanielaurens.com

To sign up for Stephanie's Email Newsletter (a private list) for heads-up alerts as new books are released, exclusive sneak peeks into upcoming books, and exclusive sweepstakes contests, follow the prompts at Stephanie's Email Newsletter Sign-up Page

Stephanie lives with her husband and a goofy black labradoodle in the hills outside Melbourne, Australia. When she isn't writing, she's reading, and if she isn't reading, she'll be tending her garden.

www.stephanielaurens.com
stephanie@stephanielaurens.com